THE SECRET ABOUT TIME

KATHRYN K. MURPHY

Caraway Press

ALSO BY KATHRYN K. MURPHY

The Firemark Series
Simply A Matter Of Time

The Sisters in Sirens Series
A Touch of Healing
A Touch of Fire

For my family

CHAPTER 1

Austin Brooks walked into the school's old library, still wiping the dust from his hands.

"You wanted to see me, sir?" His voice echoed up to the vaulted ceiling, surpassing the tall bookshelves.

Principal John Clarkson and Laurie Michaels, the librarian, sat at the circulation desk looking at the screen of the brand-new computer. Austin walked through patches of August sun, beaming through the floor-to-ceiling windows which overlooked the oaks on the front lawn of Brightrock Island's only school.

"You look like you've been busy," Laurie said, peering at Austin over her red-rimmed glasses.

"Yeah, I had to squeeze another bookcase in the office from my classroom. Stole the spare from under the stage. So what's up?" Austin eyed John. Following the chain of command was an old habit from his time in the navy that had never let him down.

"I hired someone to fill Lizzy's spot."

"Hey, that's great. Just in time with school starting next week. Who stepped up?"

The lines on John's face seemed to deepen as he stared at Austin.

"We had to go with someone from off the island."

Austin stopped dead. "You can't be serious."

John stared at him, his expression grave.

"I am."

Austin felt his jaw go slack.

"How? Why?"

"Didn't have a choice."

"I could've—"

John held up his hand, silencing Austin, who ground his teeth in response.

"I looked at it from every possible angle. The new federal law requires we have someone certified in the new trauma-informed care now. Can't just be anyone, and they have to be physically present. The council wasn't happy, but they approved the decision. The teacher we've hired—what's her name again, Laurie?"

Laurie and John looked about the same age, hovering somewhere near retirement, but that's what made hiring someone from the mainland a problem. At almost three hundred and seventy years old, John had been around longer than most of the buildings on their small, New England island. People who lived on Brightrock didn't age like they were supposed to, and hiring an outsider had never happened before.

Laurie jiggled the mouse and peered at the screen again. "Caitlyn Landry."

"Right. Caitlyn meets the requirements, has a great résumé, and no surviving family. Laurie researched her—"

"Googled, John."

"Thank you, Laurie. Googled her. Looks like the parents are both dead, no siblings."

Austin folded his arms and narrowed his eyes, even though he knew he shouldn't.

"So, how can this work? What if she…"—Austin waved one hand around in the air—"you know, finds out about us?"

"That's where you come in." John leveled a sharp gaze at Austin.

Austin was about to ask why him, when Laurie brought up exactly what he didn't want to remember.

"You're the one with the most experience with outsiders," Laurie said.

Austin swallowed and itched to pop a knuckle, but crossed his arms in front of him. "That was a long time ago." Not to mention how badly it had ended.

"None of us have been in close contact with outsiders as long as you were. Sailing around on a ship for four years to God knows where makes you the best bet."

Austin shifted his weight, but still couldn't get comfortable. "You can't expect me to cover for everyone."

"None of the students know until just before graduation," Laurie said, looking over the circulation desk while taking off her glasses. "We're pretty good at keeping secrets. You'll just be a little insurance."

"There's no way an adult can live on the island for an entire school year and not find out," Austin said, shaking his head.

"Well, I'm going to need you to make sure of that. Don't let her get too nosy." John pulled a Mont Blanc pen from his suit jacket and spun it on the lemon-waxed polished wood.

Austin propped his hands on his hips. "What about renewals? How am I supposed to explain when everyone disappears to a secret meeting?"

John didn't meet his eyes, still focused on the spinning pen. "It's done. I've already sent her a contract. She signed.

3

Besides, she's arriving on the next ferry. I need you to go pick her up and take her to her apartment."

"Wait, she has an apartment?"

"Lizzy agreed to rent her space out. Car too. Here're the keys." Laurie held her hand out, dangling the little cluster for him to take. Austin recognized his cousin's apartment, class-room, and car key on a keyring decorated with a scoop of pink ice cream on a cone. He could've throttled Lizzy for leaving, even though everyone knew she'd been asking for a chance to get away for years, but the sooner she got her certification, the sooner Caitlyn Landry could leave. With no choice, Austin took the keys and shoved them in his pocket.

"John, I don't like this. I don't see anything good coming of it."

John sucked in a breath and stood, pocketing the pen as he did.

"We're counting on you."

Austin felt like a trap had closed in on him. He never talked about what had happened in the navy, but of course FDR's fireside chats and NBC gave everyone a basic idea of America's fight against the Japanese. Maybe if they knew the details they would reconsider. Looking down at the keys in his palm, he felt like his plan to avoid everyone from off the island was slipping away. "I'm not sure I'm the right person for this."

"Austin, you look close to her age."

"I'm turning one hundred."

John nodded and spoke slowly, in a patronizing tone that made Austin want to run. He ground his molars instead.

"I know, but you look her age. She'll relate to you."

Austin shook his head. "I don't know about that."

CHAPTER 2

Caitlyn Landry gripped the weathered railing of the ferry and squinted at the dark churning waters beyond the bow. Her other hand clung to the handle of her only suitcase. Wind tangled her hair in a swirl around her head as the late August sun shone down hard on the deck. Gulls wafted overhead on the breeze and called down to where the sea slapped the hull, rocking everyone on the ferry left and right. An old white lighthouse on a rocky precipice, bathed in the golden afternoon sun, welcomed the ferry to the postcard-perfect New England bay of an almost forgotten island.

The crisp bite in the air brightened Caitlyn's soul. So accustomed to lazy, hazy, sweltering August heat, Caitlyn welcomed the change. Harsh New England accents and the broad blue Atlantic reminded her nothing of home, which was precisely what she wanted.

A dozen yachts coasted on each gentle swell, the sun glinting off their polish and chrome. Glimpses of mansions with gray cedar shingles poked out over the high, grass-covered dunes, their stellar windows no doubt drinking in the view. Underneath her feet, the roar of the engines died to a purr. The crew began scuttling about, throwing ropes to each other as the large ferry coasted toward the land where a long wooden dock led up to a row of preserved old shops and buildings, each with a unique sign hanging above the door.

"Excuse me, miss?" An older man carrying a walkie-talkie and wearing a faded ferry polo leaned over to get her attention. His weathered skin matched the ropes she had seen on deck. Gray hair escaped under the brim of a faded, sweat-stained baseball cap that matched the polo. On his chest, white letters spelled out the name *Mark*. "You the one heading to Brightrock?"

Caught off guard, she stumbled over her words.

"Ah...yes. Is there a problem?" She reached for her brown satchel to retrieve her ticket.

He held up his hand, which looked more like a baseball glove, to stop her.

"We don't get that many people who have a one-way ticket. Wanted to double check. Usually round-trip, same day." His brown eyes studied her, intent and waiting for her answer.

"That's right. It's, ah, just one way." The statement sounded strange to her ears, like an official declaration she was leaving her old life behind with no intention to return.

He massaged one hand with the other. Caitlyn opened her mouth to say something, but he nodded once and ambled away, slower than the younger crew members who were rushing about in preparation for their arrival.

Two new text messages popped up on her phone, hovering over the default background picture. Both were from Caleb. By now he'd figured out what she'd done. Guilt lapped at her gut, and she shoved the emotion aside along with all the other ones that had been haunting her. Caitlyn hit delete without even reading them and swiped to scan the information about where to find Austin Brooks, who was supposed to meet her. She hadn't needed to. Looking out, she could see only one man leaning against a truck, his arms folded in front of his chest, watching the ferry coast into port.

With a lurch, their forward movement ceased. Caitlyn released her death grip on the rail and made her way to the edge to disembark. She expected there to be a mass exodus of shuffling feet, but the remaining passengers all stayed on board. Leaning over the rail, they took in the views and snapped pictures of the quaint shops below, but no one followed her down the metal gangway.

She was barely on dry land when the engines from the ferry roared to life behind her, and Caitlyn glanced over her shoulder to see the large, white boat already coasting out of the small harbor. The sight made her feel utterly alone, but after the past few weeks she had become accustomed to the feeling and squashed the thought like a roach in an old house. Straightening her spine, she slapped on a smile to make a good first impression and walked over to the man.

"Austin Brooks, I presume?"

The tall blond studied her, his arms still folded in front of his broad chest, his chiseled face cold and unwelcoming.

"Yep."

Caitlyn stuck her hand out in greeting. "Caitlyn Landry. Nice to meet you."

Austin looked down with a small sneer on his face, reminding her of a schoolyard bully. A scar on his chin made him look like someone she didn't want to mess with. Caitlyn was about to take back her hand when he took it in his own.

The warm, strong hand swallowed hers. Up close he smelled clean like aftershave and something spicy, grounding her to the present. The firm, calloused handshake ended too soon, but the sensation of his skin touching hers lingered. Caitlyn shook her head to clear it and watched Austin to see if he had the same reaction.

Austin looked surprised, but with a slight frown, as if he hadn't expected—or appreciated—whatever had just happened.

"Well, thanks for meeting me here. Laurie Michaels said you're the new assistant principal. Congratulations."

His frown deepened. Caitlyn felt her smile falter before she reminded herself whoever had pissed in his cornflakes, it wasn't her. Still, it wasn't a great sign.

"Where's your stuff?" he asked, eyeing her bag with suspicion.

Caitlyn wanted to give him a smart remark but instead opted for a pleasant smile for her unpleasant new boss.

"This is everything. Laurie said the place was furnished."

"It is."

"Okay, great." Caitlyn smiled again, waiting for him to make the next move. According to Laurie's email, Austin was supposed to be her welcoming committee. So far, if this was it, she was pretty much screwed. Caitlyn would've considered getting back on the boat if she'd had anything worth going back to.

"Well, at least you know how to pack," Austin said, reaching down to take it for her.

Caitlyn pulled back.

"I'm good. Thanks, anyway." While it might not look like much, it was everything that was left from her life before.

Austin shrugged like he couldn't have brought himself to care even if she'd flung herself in the ocean.

"Is the apartment nearby?" she asked to break the awkward silence.

"Yep, sure is."

He led her down the brick sidewalk. Closer now, Caitlyn memorized all the shops as they walked past Kate's Diner and over to the Two Scoops Ice Cream Parlor. The small gray cedar-shingle building faced the harbor with a bright yellow door, flanked by two half barrels overflowing with flowers that swayed in the sea breeze.

Caitlyn followed Austin past the entrance and the large picture windows that looked in on a few tables and chairs in front of a counter that held an array of flavors behind glass.

At the corner of the building, the bricks continued straight, following the road toward a small gas station, but Austin turned down an alley where a red Ford Escape sat parked next to a staircase that led up to the second floor of the ice cream parlor.

He spun around. "Catch," Austin said, tossing the keys he had been twirling. Caitlyn reached out instinctively and felt the metal hit her palm before fumbling a few times with them. She looked down into her hands. A car key and fob sat next to two other keys, one brass colored and one silver. A key ring adorned with a scoop of pink ice cream held everything together.

"Classroom, apartment, and a car?" Caitlyn asked, looking up, unsure.

"Yep," Austin said, opening the door to the Escape. "The teacher you're replacing didn't want to take it with her."

"Laurie said I wouldn't need a car."

Austin sighed and looked like he was grinding his teeth instead of biting her head off.

"Look, on small islands, this isn't that weird. It's too much trouble to get cars on and off the mainland. Did you have a car?"

"I sold it."

"Great, so this works out. Let's head up to the apartment. Can I get your bag, or do you want to be stubborn?"

"I'm not—"

"Look, I'm going to feel weird if you're lugging this thing up there while I watch, so I'll ask again. May I please carry your bag for you?"

He looked irritated, like this whole welcoming committee thing was taking far too long.

Caitlyn bit her lip.

"Um, thanks. That'd be great, I guess."

Austin grabbed her luggage before bounding up the exterior stairs, taking them two at a time, to another yellow door. Caitlyn followed at a much slower pace and walked into the small living room that led to an eat-in kitchen with exquisite furnishings.

Austin set her bag down and held his hands out wide. "So what do you think?"

Caitlyn looked around at the small space adorned with plush tan chairs with blue and white pillows in front of a white coffee table. Behind them, two large windows framed with white sheers looked out over the picturesque harbor where white yachts dotted the blue of the water like clouds in the sky above. The kitchen was all white except for the stainless appliances. A small white table and chairs sat next to the kitchen in front of another window that looked out onto the same scene. All of it felt light, airy, and very expensive.

Caitlyn bit her lip and looked at the light wood floors covered by a rug she hadn't noticed. The money from the house and furniture had paid off some of the debt collectors, but there were still more she owed.

"This is…I mean, it's beautiful, but I can't afford this." She glanced up at Austin, sorry she had to disappoint him, but to her surprise, he grinned at her. His smile could've knocked her flat. Without the cold, calculating look, his face transformed from someone you didn't want to piss off to one of the most handsome men she'd ever seen.

"Oh, you can," he said with a quick nod as if that settled everything. "Besides you don't have a choice. This place is the only option."

CHAPTER 3

Caitlyn slapped down the papers and fidgeted with the pen in her hand as she had for the past twenty minutes. She wasn't a new teacher by any means, but excitement mixed with anxiety still spiked before the first class of the year. As usual, she'd barely slept the night before and had arrived far before dawn to triple-check everything.

She hadn't needed to. The room had practically been ready when she arrived. All the decorations had been left behind, extra supplies in the closet, and even a filing cabinet with carefully labeled activities for later units. All of it suggested whoever had left the position had loved their job, but Caitlyn felt out of place. Having everything saved a ton of time, but it also felt like she was living someone else's life. Rather than a vacant space where she could leave her mark, Caitlyn felt like she was living in someone else's perfect house, always wondering if she was putting things back where they belonged.

Even the furniture was different. Caitlyn ran her hands over the unmarred top of the new desk. Her old green metal desk had been army surplus from after Vietnam that had somehow found its way into the Louisiana public school system.

The top of it had been partially torn off, and one drawer squeaked every time it opened, no matter how much WD-40 or graphite she dumped on it. The right side looked like someone had kicked it in so that one leg buckled at almost a right angle. If one thing in education didn't keep well, it was furniture. Although maybe that wasn't fair. The chunk of old metal had made it, but it was a world away from Caitlyn's room now.

Four chimes of a sterile digital bell rang in the ceiling above her. On instinct, she moved to the hall. In her old school, security had been paramount. Standing at the door in between classes had been less about greeting the students and more about liability.

Ready for the onslaught, Caitlyn was met with silence. No trampling feet, no din rising up through the stairwells. She looked down the long hallway of the second floor. Glossy, painted lockers without dents lined the walls. The polished linoleum gleamed in the morning light that was coming in from the windows on either side. The high, ornate ceilings, which had exposed beams polished to a shine, made her think of the cathedrals back home.

Caitlyn looked at the wall across from her. Unlike the schools she knew, manufactured from cinder block and metal, this was crafted. There was a baseboard, chair rail, and up high, crown molding like at the plantations she and her mom had visited a long time ago. The walls between were painted a light cream color. But teachers still weren't coming out of the rooms.

Caitlyn searched out the window in the hall to see what the grounds looked like from up here and to maybe catch a glimpse of the incoming kids. Perfectly mowed green grass and oak trees created a landscape in front of her, obscuring the view of the sea that she knew was just beyond. Hoping to get a good view from a bad angle, she strained her neck to try to see the front.

"Hey, you good?" a voice from behind asked, making her jump.

"Yeah, just trying to see where the kids are."

"Oh, don't worry. They're coming," said the teacher.

The halls remained silent. "You sure about that?" Caitlyn asked with a frown.

The tall, elegant lady let out a laugh. "Oh, yeah. They'll be here. I'm Connie Farrell. Secondary English." She stuck out a thin, manicured hand, a wood bangle dancing around her wrist. Caitlyn took it, surprised at the strength.

"It's just so...quiet," Caitlyn said, staring back at the window.

The teacher grinned. "Yeah, we're kind of different around here. Small population and all that."

Mrs. Farrell wore tan slacks that were loose, in a high fashion sort of way, with a white blouse tucked in and cinched with a small, expensive-looking belt. Her chestnut hair curled into a frenzy of tangles as if trying to escape from the knot she had pulled it up into. Despite her relaxed posture, her eyes were keen and sharp like a general. The whole effect was that of a teacher who had been in the game for a while and knew what was up.

"I can see that," Caitlyn said.

"Where did you say you were from again? I know you said in the faculty meeting, but I'm afraid I was working on my Romeo and Juliet unit." She winked.

"Louisiana."

"Public or private?"

"Public."

"Wow."

Caitlyn wasn't sure how to take that, so she just said, "Yeah." The hallway was still quiet and empty. A few voices of children had started to drift up the staircase from down below.

"You couldn't have found a more different public school —or place for that matter."

"I wanted different. Needed a change." No need to get into why. Caitlyn shook off the unpleasant memories clawing to the forefront of her mind and focused on Connie.

"Well, you got it. Let me guess. Your old school was over-crowded? Yeah," she said when Caitlyn nodded, "that's not going to be a problem here."

Connie had that same grin on her face, one of those smiles people had when they had a secret and found it amusing. Caitlyn liked her immediately.

A door opened down the hall.

"Here's one now," Connie said, turning her attention to a skinny boy wearing Chuck Taylor sneakers and a blue hoodie. "Hey, Jimmy."

Jimmy smiled back before looking at Caitlyn as he walked into the classroom a few doors down from Connie.

"I've taught him and all of his brothers," Connie said. "He's one of my favorites from that family."

"I like collecting siblings too. Feels like I'm completing the set," Caitlyn said. "How long have you taught?"

Connie turned back to her and gave her an enigmatic smile. "Since God was a boy."

The door to the stairs opened again. A small boy who looked to be middle school age walked through, leaning forward to counterbalance the weight of the enormous black backpack he was toting. He started toward them, then stopped when he noticed her. Caitlyn smiled back at him.

The student looked from her to Connie and back, before

turning around and searching the other side of the hallway. His shoulders fell as he shifted from his left to right foot.

"Good morning, Charles," Connie called out to him. The boy turned back to her, his face full of hopeful determination.

Despite the weight of his massive bag, he walked right over. "Good morning, Mrs. Farrell. Do you know where Ms. Brooks is now?"

Caitlyn frowned at hearing the name and made a mental note to ask Austin if they had been related.

"Nope, because she's taking the year off to go to the mainland."

"I'm taking her place for the year," Caitlyn said with a bright smile of encouragement. "Good morning, Charles. I'm Ms. Landry."

It was clear this was not the news the boy had been hoping for. His shoulders sunk even lower than before, and his look of despair rivaled utter devastation.

"Say hello, Charles," Connie prompted in a patient teacher voice.

"Hi," he said before turning back to Connie. "Do you know when she'll be back? She is coming back, right? I've been waiting to be in her class for so long."

"Ms. Brooks will be back next year." Before Charles could speak, Connie kept going. "We're going over our summer reading in second period today. You do have it, don't you?"

"Yeah, but—"

"Go to class, Charles. Have a great day," Connie said with an amused smile, looking past him down the hall to where more students were coming up from below. "Good morning, everyone." The bangle danced around her thin wrist as she waved to kids and teachers that had finally emerged.

It was more than clear Charles wanted to press, but the

veteran move had worked, and with great reluctance, he turned toward Caitlyn and headed into the room.

"Good morning. Please find your seat, and follow the instructions on the board," Caitlyn said in her most enthusiastic teacher voice. If Charles's reaction was any indication of how all the students felt, that didn't bode well for her first day.

The child had almost sunk into the floor—and not because of the weight on his back. "Okay," he said, trudging past, all of the wind knocked out of his sails.

"Don't take it personally," Connie said, leaning over. "All the kids liked Lizzy. I'm sure they'll love you once they get to know you.

Caitlyn stood taller with a bright smile as the next student approached, wondering in the back of her mind if anyone missed her at her old school like Charles clearly missed Ms. Brooks.

CHAPTER 4

Austin marched through the halls, high-fiving and fist-bumping as he went. It felt good to be back. The sound of lockers slamming, constant chatter, and shouts of "Hey Mr. Brooks" filled the halls as packs of students meandered through the hallways of Brightrock, filling it with nervous energy. All of it keyed Austin up.

The walkie-talkie at the small of his back sounded off, and he pulled it up to his ear.

"Office to Brooks."

Austin pivoted and headed for a staircase to get to the library. "Go ahead."

"The server's down again."

"On my way," he said, heading toward an old staircase.

Through the window, he could see a few cars dropping off students as well as the two buses that drove around the island. Next to the flag, the elementary teachers collected their new and old students to make sure the little ones didn't get lost in the shuffle. Older students in hoodies and polos stood around in packs, not bothering to head toward the building.

The school's student population had leveled off around one hundred. Thanks to Brightrock's water, no one bought anti-aging cream until they were about to hit the one hundred mark, and it wasn't just skin cells that were affected. As far as everyone on the island could tell, the change was on the cellular level, and as a result, reproductive cycles slowed to a crawl. Not that Austin needed to worry about that. All marriages had to be approved by the council to prevent any inbreeding, and while his parents and grandparents had married for convenience and then fallen in love, the old model didn't sit quite right with the younger generation. He had tried to date a few girls while in the navy but never pursued anything serious. The council would've freaked out, and while the girls were all nice enough, no one had been special enough to risk facing exile.

A nervous chatter rose from the stairs below him before a pack of middle school girls appeared in the hall. Judging by the urgency, he guessed it was their first time on the second floor where the upper grades were located.

"Good morning," he said in passing.

The girls murmured a reply, but none of them were smiling. Their backpacks were almost larger than them, and they moved faster than all of the other grades, in a strange mix of knowing where they were going but still being self-conscious about it. Austin smiled as he passed them in the hall. Middle school still terrified students even at a small school like Brightrock. Having more than one teacher, a locker, and access to hall passes changed everything. Not to mention they got their school-issued computer in the sixth grade.

Thinking of sixth grade, he headed toward Caitlyn's room. He hadn't seen her since showing her the apartment and dropping her at the main office to talk to John and Laurie. Still pissed over being involved, Austin wished he could just wash his hands and be done with Caitlyn Landry, but he couldn't. After everything he had already done for this community, Austin wouldn't let one person screw up almost four hundred years of secrecy. Besides, Austin knew John would ask, and this way he wouldn't have to lie.

He frowned when she wasn't at her door. Across the hall, Connie grinned at him, waving a few fingers. He waved back, turned into Caitlyn's classroom, and slammed right into her. Hot liquid splashed onto his chest, soaking his shirt and searing into his skin.

"Hey, watch it!" Caitlyn looked down and swore under her breath.

"Oh my God, I'm so sorry," Austin said, looking around for something to do, not having a clue what.

"This is what I get for trying to dress up," she said, still looking down with her hands splayed out in disbelief. A few sixth graders gaped openmouthed from inside the room. One girl put her hand in front of her mouth in a mix of horrified laughter.

Connie made a low sound from across the hall. "That's going to stain. I think I have something for that in my purse. I'll be right back."

Caitlyn's once light gray dress now had a wet brown splotch down the front, though her yellow cardigan had been spared. She set her coffee tumbler down on a nearby desk and grabbed a few tissues in an attempt to blot the damage.

Austin hadn't fared much better. His white shirt now looked like it had been used to clean the locker room.

"What can I do for you, Mr. Brooks?" Caitlyn glared up at him, even though she was in heels. She wore lipstick, and her hair had been swept up into a bun, though Austin was surprised he'd even noticed.

He stammered. "I wanted to check on you." No one

looked at him like that. The annoyance and frustration in her eyes could've burned a hole through his head.

"I'm fine, thank you." Her tone was clipped and deliberate.

"Right. Okay, then. I'll just head back downstairs. Can I get you anything—maybe a washcloth or something?"

"I'm fine." She propped her hands on her hips and leveled her gaze at him.

"I am really sorry."

Caitlyn blew out a breath. "Don't worry about it. Accidents happen. Thanks, Connie," she said, accepting the little towelette. "I'll try to get this out in between classes. Do you need one?" Caitlyn asked, eyeing Austin's soiled shirt.

He waved his hand. "I'll be fine. Have a jacket in my office."

The radio squawked at the small of his back, calling him away again. Austin answered and clipped it back on his belt.

"Do you want me to bring you more coffee?" he asked, turning to go.

"No, I've had enough for now. Actually, I do have a quick question," Caitlyn said, throwing the tissues in the can under the pencil sharpener.

"Fire away."

"How long had Lizzy taught here?"

Austin froze. He slid on his best mask of nonchalance and tried to ignore the prickling on the back of his neck and the heat rushing toward his face.

"A while I think, not sure," he lied. "Why do you ask?"

"Just curious," Caitlyn said. "Room is really settled in, and some of her files go way back."

Austin nodded, not sure what he should say. His senses were on high alert, but he tried to give away nothing.

Caitlyn checked the kids. "All right. Showtime. I'll see you around." She gave him a thumbs-up as she turned to go back into her room in her ruined dress, her head held high. The kids who had still been staring spun around to keep working on whatever warm-up was in front of them.

"Yeah, good luck today," Austin said, but the secretary's voice boomed over the intercom, drowning him out.

"Good morning, Brightrock, and welcome back, students! Please stand for the Pledge of Allegiance."

CHAPTER 5

On Friday afternoon, Austin pulled on the old brass handle to Kate's Diner, and the sound of laughter ricocheted toward him. The faculty happy hour was well under way, which was good, because he needed a drink.

After what had happened a few days ago on the first day of school, Austin had marched straight into John's office and told him about Caitlyn's question.

"She's not dumb, that's obvious," Austin had said. "She's going to figure this out."

"I don't think her question is unreasonable. Just check in with her. She trusts you enough to come to you with questions, and that's what we need. Build a relationship with her, like you would with any new teacher. Get her to trust you, so she believes you."

Austin ground his teeth at the memory. He was trapped and could feel the noose sliding tighter every time he saw Caitlyn. It's not that he had anything against her personally. His opinion of her had actually improved dramatically after the coffee incident, but she was an outsider, a threat, and his problem to manage.

One of the teachers called, waving him over to the corner booth of the old diner, which was decorated like the hull of an old whaler. Across the table, Connie lounged in the corner under a large brass diving helmet mounted on the wall. Caitlyn, who stood out as the only one without a school polo, sat on the edge. In the absence of spirit wear, she had chosen a white collared shirt and navy-blue cardigan, which matched Brightrock's school colors.

Austin plopped down in the booth across from Caitlyn, where he could keep an eye on her and an ear out for trouble. The waitress put his go-to order, a boilermaker, in front of him. On autopilot, he dropped the shot in the beer and took a drink. In his younger days, he used to like a double but now considered one probably for the best. The navy had taught Austin many things, one being how a man should drink.

"Caitlyn was telling us about kids at her old school," Connie said, holding a glass of wine.

"Oh yeah?" he asked, turning his attention to Caitlyn.

"Nothing big," she said, tossing it off with a shrug. "Just the usual stuff."

Austin waited for her to continue and was disappointed when she didn't. He had to admit he did like the sound of her voice. Having her talk about her own life meant less talking about them, and Austin was all about keeping the conversation on her. He eyed the others, wondering if anything had slipped before he'd arrived.

"Sounds like I missed a story. Got any more?" Austin asked, trying to change the focus.

Caitlyn thought for a bit, reaching up to play with her necklace, a gold chain that held a single diamond, while she looked up at the light as if searching her memory. "I once found an egg in the corner of my room."

"Wait. Hold on—did you say an egg?" Connie asked. Other people frowned and looked puzzled.

"An egg. Apparently, it had rolled into the corner while I had a sub for a bit, and no one noticed. Needless to say, there was a lot of cleaning afterward."

"Okay…" Austin prompted, amused by the setup.

"So I'm cleaning where it was, right? And I see that one of the tiles is loose."

"Custodian never noticed it?" Erin asked.

Caitlyn pulled her lips into a thin line and shook her head. "Bigger fish to fry. A tile popping up was the least of their worries."

"Let's not forget there was an egg in a corner," Austin pointed out. "We've established where the bar was set." Everyone laughed.

"Right. So, I go to pull up the tile to see if I can get a new one from surplus. Underneath, I find a folded piece of paper. It was like buried treasure, really, only much more disturbing."

"Boobs?" Erin asked.

Caitlyn took another sip of her beer and shook her head. "Poorly drawn male genitalia this time."

"Learning starts at home," Connie said without missing a beat.

"You know, that reminds me. One of the kids said something weird the other day," Caitlyn said.

"Weirder than usual?" Connie asked with a grin.

"Yeah, it's probably nothing, but I wanted to ask you guys about it. I had the kids do a little About Me assignment that they then presented so we could all get to know each other before we got going, you know?"

The teachers around the table all nodded.

"Yeah, well, on his, he talked about how he doesn't talk to his parents that much, but he really likes his cook."

"Is this Charles?" Connie asked.

"Yeah, he also mentioned that his parents collect guns, like a lot of them, which was a little concerning."

"I think they're antiques," Austin said, shutting down any speculation. His own father had told him the stories of a failed attempt to go West that had ended in disaster during the nineteenth century. Charles's family had been the ones to organize the doomed journey.

Caitlyn frowned. "I don't know. It just feels like he doesn't have a great relationship with his parents. Like he wants them to notice him or something like that."

"Did he say anything else?"

"Not really, but I got the feeling something wasn't right when I had him stay after class. Tried to get him to open up, but he didn't say much."

"He did seem anxious that first day back," Connie said, a line forming between her brows as she went deep into thought.

"Yeah, maybe have Laurie talk to him. I wouldn't worry about the guns. We have a lot of antique collectors on the island," Austin said, hoping Caitlyn would accept his explanation.

"Oh, okay, I didn't realize that. Guess I have a lot to learn," Caitlyn said.

"You could keep an eye on him. See if he warms up through the next few weeks."

Austin shifted in his seat. The kids on Brightrock didn't know their secret until they graduated and had turned eighteen. Austin hoped Charles hadn't seen too much and wouldn't have too much more to tell Caitlyn.

Austin relaxed when the conversation shifted back toward what school events would be coming up soon, including field trips, football games with schools on the mainland, and the Halloween dance, Austin's personal favorite. They kept trading stories around the table and ordered two plates of loaded chili cheese fries, which led to everyone ordering entrees for dinner.

Throughout the meal, Austin's eyes kept going back to Caitlyn. She held her fork with approachable etiquette and picked away at her salad with grilled chicken, stopping on occasion to wipe her delicate mouth with the napkin she kept folded in her lap. She wasn't skinny, and even from a lousy vantage point with the table in the way, Austin knew she had enough of the good stuff in the right places from when he had first met her.

"Well folks, that about does it for me," Connie said. "I've seen far too much of you people already." Everyone laughed as they too started reaching for purses and keys after their bills were paid.

As they meandered out, each thanking the staff like family as they left, Austin made sure to fall in step with Caitlyn.

"So overall, how's your first week been?" he asked.

"Not too bad," she said with an easy smile, flicking her hair out of her face. "In fact, it was pretty great. The kids miss Ms. Brooks though, so it'll take some time for them to warm up to me."

"If that was your only problem, I'd say you're doing fine. I mean, aside from the coffee thing."

"Oh, don't get me wrong, compared to my last school, this has been very different. Really relaxing, but then again, we do cover more content faster."

"Yeah, we're pretty different around here."

"Funny enough," she said, turning to look at him, "that's what Connie said too."

Austin made a note to talk to Connie. The English

teacher had a way with words, and while he didn't consider her a risk for sharing their secret, he wouldn't put it past her to have a little fun getting close to the line.

They walked out onto the brick sidewalk that lined the waterfront on Easterly Bay. The sea breeze swelled in the faded light, bringing with it a chill that held the promise of autumn. A few stars twinkled above them, the first of many to come. Water lapped against the boats tied in for the night, while gulls floated on the breeze above.

"I can understand why no one leaves," Caitlyn said at his elbow. "It's beautiful here."

"I left for a little bit," Austin said, shoving his hands in his pockets. Caitlyn tugged her sweater around her, before tucking her hands under each arm.

"Oh yeah?"

"Navy. They ended up paying for my college, so it was a pretty good deal. GI Bill and all that. So how do you like Brightrock? You said it's different from what you're used to."

"I guess it's just smaller, but in some ways, it's the same."

"Oh yeah? How's that?" he asked, surprised at how interested he was in the answer.

"Everyone knows everyone. Louisiana can be a lot like that too. Well, here's my stop," she said, stopping in front of Two Scoops, the ice cream parlor. Austin felt a bit blindsided, not quite ready for the conversation to end. He'd figured by now he'd want to be rid of Caitlyn, but apparently not.

"Have you warmed up to the place yet?" he asked, studying her features.

Caitlyn glanced back up at the apartment windows on the second floor. "It's still too much, but yeah, I totally love it."

He smiled and before he knew what he was doing, said, "If you're not doing anything this weekend, I could take you around Brightrock and show you the sights."

"I was planning to catch up on some lesson plans."

Austin raised his eyebrows. "On the weekend?"

She smiled, making her eyes crinkle with silent laughter. "Yeah, I know. I like to get ahead. It helps me when I run out of steam and fall into a Netflix binge habit later in the year."

Austin grinned. "It'll be a good little orientation. Besides, we're an island. It won't take too long. Think about it and let me know."

CHAPTER 6

The following afternoon, Austin hadn't slept a wink and had a headache the size of Montana. He jerked his old Ford Ranger around on the road as he drove toward the marina, swearing at everyone and everything in his way. He didn't know what he'd been thinking when he'd offered Caitlyn a tour of the island. Her very presence endangered everything he had sworn to protect. One slipup and the whole island's secret could be out forever. And yet, as if the invitation itself hadn't been enough, Austin had answered her text this morning with a frigging exclamation point.

Austin felt like banging his head against the steering wheel. John had said to get closer to her, but he shouldn't, couldn't—and yet a thrum of excitement ran through him as he whipped the truck into a space in front of the Two Scoops Ice Cream Parlor.

The morning sun sat in a crisp blue sky with billowy, white clouds. For most people, the temp would be almost chilly when the wind blew, but Austin lived for these days and had opted for a simple T-shirt. Caitlyn was sitting outside of the old eighteenth-century building on a metal bench, feeding the gulls.

She wore a darker pair of jeans that were cuffed below her calf, showing off slim ankles down to the same brown shoes as yesterday. A camel sweater that came to her elbows hugged her curves before it dipped down into a V-neck that framed the gold chain with the solitaire diamond. On instinct, Austin needed to know who gave it to her and why she wore it. The thought made him want to squeeze his head in his palms until the damn thing popped off his neck.

The breeze from the water tossed her hair around her face, even though most of it was tied back into a high pony-tail. She smiled while throwing out bits of seed for the ravenous birds.

"You're only encouraging them," he said as he walked up.

"I know, but I can't help it. I love birds," Caitlyn said, emptying out the contents of the plastic bag before balling it up and shoving it into her purse. As they had the previous night, the pair of them fell into a natural rhythm as they walked back to the Ford.

Thankfully, she didn't say anything, which gave Austin a chance to calm down.

"So where in Louisiana are you from?" he asked to fill the silence, figuring that was a safe enough topic.

"Just outside Baton Rouge. The swamps, basically."

"Tabasco, alligators, and all of that?"

"Yep, that's the place. I was in town, but I knew people who had gators come after their pets and chickens."

"Well, you're probably going to find this tour of Brightrock a little dull. We don't have anything like that here."

"You have sharks. Jaws, lobster, and all of that," she said, making sure to leave out the r in lobster so that it sounded like lobstah. They clambered into the truck, and he fired up the engine.

"At least our sharks are tagged, so we know when they're coming," he pointed out. "So seeing as how you're from the bayou, what's the weirdest thing you've ever eaten?" he asked her.

"Like seafood or—?"

"Weirdest ever."

Caitlyn bit her lower lip and squinted through the windshield at the winding road ahead of them.

"Um, see, I'm not sure how weird this is, but I've had alligator if that's what you're asking, but I think tongue would probably be the top of the list."

"Did you like it?" Maybe this whole conversation thing was going to be easier than he thought.

Caitlyn turned to him and tucked one corner of her lip under her teeth while she shrugged. "The person who cooked it knew what they were doing, but I wouldn't seek it out. How about you?"

"Tons of stuff."

"Really? I didn't think Brightrock—"

Austin shook his head. "Navy. Most of our time was in Southeast Asia. Wild stuff over there."

"That's right. Did you learn to use chopsticks? I can never get it right."

"Uh, not really." Austin thought back to his time on and off the boat. Considering that for most of it he had been either drunk or hungover, there wasn't a whole lot of time left for soaking up the local culture, unless the culture involved alcohol or girls. Those days felt like a lifetime ago. Thinking about it now, Austin wasn't even sure if he was the same person. The training and sailing had felt like a grand adventure until all of it had gone to hell. He shook his head, refusing to let unwelcome memories surface now.

They drove past the diner, ferry booth, and charter fishing shacks before turning past Captain Newbury's House and Museum. The horizon was stretched out between the dunes in front of them so that the water met the sky in a picturesque seascape that would have made for a high property value had it been on better soil. They passed cottages with their signature cedar shingles and a multitude of hydrangea bushes, which Caitlyn commented on every time they passed one.

Austin drove along the island's airstrip, swooping around the hairpin turn at the northeast tip of the island before coasting down to the parking lots of Crescent Beach. Shoals of exposed sand peaked out of the water as they stretched into the North Bay, mimicking the moon and leaving only a thin opening through which boats could pass. Calm water inside the bay lapped on one side of the shoals, while the Atlantic beckoned surfers on the other side. The effect was that of a long two-sided beach. That combined with shallow waters and soft sand made Crescent Beach in North Bay the go-to spot for everyone on the island.

"This is beautiful," Caitlyn said.

"You should see it on the Fourth of July," he said cutting the engine and letting his arm rest on the window.

"Oh yeah?"

"Everyone is out here, wicked clam bakes, and once the sun goes down, we set off the fireworks. Then after that, the fires start."

"Fires?"

"Yeah, we light fires with driftwood and all stay out having picnics and dancing until the stars come out."

"Sounds perfect. In Louisiana, the mosquitos will carry you off after dark."

"What do they do down there on the Fourth?"

"Same thing, but not on the beach. At least, in my experience," Caitlyn added. "We would grill steaks, hamburgers, hot dogs, make potato salad, that kind of thing, but it was all during the day and usually indoors. It's just too hot."

"Yeah, but you guys have Mardi Gras," Austin pointed out.

"Oh yeah." Caitlyn's eyes took on a glow, and she smiled to herself while watching the bathers dart in and out of the water.

"I've never been to Mardi Gras," he said.

"There's nothing like it. It's a season, really," Caitlyn said, looking at him before turning back to watch the water. "Schools are out for a week."

"Seriously?"

"Seriously. There's a parade every night leading up and several on the day. Marching bands, krewe floats, king cake, and food. All of it is just so…" She shook her head. "I don't know how to describe it other than it makes you feel alive and a part of something and happy. All of it is so happy."

"I bet all that alcohol helps."

"Yeah, that's part of it," she said, tilting her head to the side. "Last year, someone died falling off of a float. They were drunk and hadn't strapped in."

"Jesus."

"Yeah, that's the ugly part, but the people I hung out with didn't drink that much. We were more excited about the beads and doubloons. One time we caught enough cups that when they were all stacked inside each other, it reached the roof of the house." Caitlyn laughed at the memory, and Austin couldn't help but smile along with her. "I think that was the time I got hit in the teeth with some big beads. Let me tell you something, those suckers hurt something fierce." She laughed again. "It's my fault though. Took my eyes off the prize."

"That'll get you every time," he said. Austin could see

Caitlyn light up when she talked about her home. He had been that way in the navy.

In his younger days, he hadn't appreciated Brightrock. Everything had changed once he joined the navy. All of a sudden, Austin came from the most stable, typical family and the most idyllic, beautiful place. Hearing the experiences of others and leaving home for four years was enough to make anyone grateful. What really sealed the deal, though, had been the sounds of enemy planes overhead. Gunfire had a way of making every man homesick and religious.

"Are you going back for Mardi Gras this year?"

The effect was immediate. A shadow crossed over Caitlyn's face, and the corners of her soft smile dropped.

"Ah no, probably not this year." She looked down.

Caitlyn had said she had wanted different, but what she hadn't mentioned was how. John and Laurie had mentioned she didn't have any family, but for some reason, Austin needed to know why.

"Want to walk out on the shoals? We've been sitting for a bit."

They walked side by side along the grassy dunes, each slipping in the sand. As much as he hated to admit it, it was easy being with her. Austin didn't feel the need to fill the void and neither, it seemed, did Caitlyn. Most of the time he either felt like he was doing all the talking or a woman was, but for the first time, he felt a click with someone from the opposite sex that had nothing to do with sex at all.

"What is king cake anyway?" he asked as they approached the beginning of the shoals, which stretched out in front of them, a sandy peninsula wrapping around the Bay.

"You mean besides delicious?" Caitlyn said, laughing.

"Okay, yeah, besides that."

"Um, I'm not sure how to describe it. Every bakery really

takes their own approach, but it has a cinnamon flavor and icing."

"Like a cinnamon roll?"

"Basically. Some are more yeasted, so like a huge dough-nut, and others are more rolled with almond, cream cheese, or jam filling."

"Oh man, I could get behind that."

"It's great. People order them weeks in advance, and some even order them from around the country, but that's an expensive piece of cake. Even if it is king cake."

"We do pancakes here and call it Shrove Tuesday."

"Oh, that's nice," Caitlyn said, but it sounded like she was just being polite. There wasn't a pancake on earth that could compete with what she'd been describing.

"I guess it's the Episcopalian equivalent." Austin had a thought and looked at her before asking. "So, I'm guessing that means you're Catholic then?"

"Yep, but don't hold it against me. I'm pretty chill," she said with an easy smile.

Austin laughed. "Why do I get the feeling you've said that before?"

She shrugged. "I'm guessing I'm in the minority here on Brightrock."

"Yeah, kind of." You have no idea how true that is, he added to himself. "But don't worry, we're pretty chill too." At least most of them were, Austin thought.

"I didn't know what to expect. I knew the Kennedys were Catholic and that Boston has a lot of Catholics—or at least, so I've heard."

"Yeah, we were settled by separatists, like way back." Boy, did that not sound convincing at all.

"Louisiana was settled by Catholics. Isn't it funny how those ties to the past run deep? I think that's part of the reason I wanted to teach history."

"What part of history do you like the most?" he asked, trying to steer the conversation to something more manageable.

"Everything."

"No, really."

"No, really. I love it all. I mean, my focus is American—" Caitlyn must have seen a tell because she smiled in his direction. "I take it that was the answer you were hoping for."

"Best damn country in the world," he said. "What part of American history?"

"Oh, I don't know," Caitlyn said with a smile even though she had made it sound like she was exasperated.

"Oh, come on. Are you more American Revolution, or Civil War, or twentieth century?"

"I guess if I had to pick, it'd be World War II."

Austin couldn't resist and did a fist pump into the air.

"I guess that was the right answer again," Caitlyn said, laughing.

A huge smile lit his face, though telling her why was out of the question. Just knowing it was her favorite made him happy for a reason he couldn't put his finger on.

"Have you studied it a lot?" she asked as they reached the end of the shoals. "You seem to be really excited about it."

"Greatest generation and all that, hell yeah." He grinned at her. "You could say I've studied it, yeah."

"There's a lot to study." They turned around and headed back, each watching the water recede little by little with the tide as they walked. "Are you more interested in Europe or the Pacific?"

"Pacific," Austin answered with ease. "You?"

"I go back and forth."

Walking alongside him with her shoes in her hands and her feet in the sand, it was clear she didn't feel the need to agree with him or disagree with him. She accepted his answer and replied with one of her own, not concerned with how he might respond.

Maybe because of her attitude, Austin felt himself crave her approval. He didn't think of himself as a handsome guy, and never before had he felt the need to chase after a woman for conversation, but now, a little of the urge was there. They both reached the truck, and Austin made sure he opened her door while telling himself that the action was out of habit and good manners and nothing more.

Once Austin recognized the feeling, he shut it down in his mind. There was absolutely nothing between them. Couldn't be.

CHAPTER 7

A ustin almost missed that she had asked him a question. Not because he wasn't listening, but because he had been listening to the sound of her voice instead of the words. Her accent reminded him of some of the older residents of Brightrock. Their voices drawled out words in a smooth cadence that made him think of the ocean. Just like waves when they crashed, each word rose and fell at its own pace, unrushed and deliberate. Listening to Caitlyn talk relaxed his shoulders, which were always tight as rocks. It wasn't a southern accent, as he had heard on TV and in movies. Caitlyn said something else, and he realized then it was her vowels. They were different and somehow stretched with almost a different pronunciation.

"Earth to Austin," she said for what must have been the second time judging by the look on her face.

"Sorry about that," he said. "Sometimes I get all up in my head."

"I can tell."

Her "I" sounded almost Australian, but not as harsh. He wondered if she could speak French. Austin shook his head to snap out of it. "What were we talking about? Seafood, right?"

"Yeah, but it doesn't matter. Tell me about this place. What's with all the fences?"

Sure enough, on the right-hand side of the Ford, outside Caitlyn's window, chain-link fences separated them from what looked like untouched woods. Austin had passed by it so many times that he didn't think much of it anymore.

"Oh, it's just a nature preserve. We're isolated out here, so the wildlife developed differently." All of that was true, but there was much more to the story. Behind that fence was the first meetinghouse built when the founders arrived in the seventeenth century. Next to it was a spring house with seven iron locks, protecting the water Caitlyn would never know about.

"That's interesting," Caitlyn said, watching the trees go by. Keeping secrets was part of living on Brightrock and had never bothered him before. Watching her now, sitting in the passenger seat, looking out the window, he felt guilt set up shop in his chest. Which was ridiculous. He knew he couldn't tell her, so thinking about it was a complete waste of headspace.

Still, he glanced at her again. She sat, arms folded over her thighs with one leg crossed over the other. Her hands were relaxed, nails trimmed but unpainted. The ring intrigued him, along with her necklace. Austin had driven this road longer than he cared to admit, so he shot a few more glances in her direction.

"So, all of this security is just for the wildlife? It seems like an awful lot," Caitlyn commented, still looking out the window.

Austin shifted in his seat. "Yeah, you know how the government is. Once we got it approved, it became one of those things. Regulation after regulation came down from on high."

"No hunting then?" Caitlyn turned to him with a grin.

"Nope. No way."

The trees and fence gave way when they reached a small intersection. Going straight would bring them back to the waterfront. Not wanting to end the ride—for reasons he would sort through later—Austin turned right and kept driving.

"So, on your left is Cedar Inn, our only bed and breakfast." Austin gestured as he slowed the car. A tan stone driveway turned into the property sculpted by a landscape architect on Nantucket. Made of cedar shingles with white trim and a wraparound porch, the seven bedroom, seven and a half bathroom, two kitchen property hosted people from all over the world, five couples at a time.

All of the appliances, plumbing, HVAC, fixtures and just about everything else were as up to date as any guest could want. Austin knew because he had helped renovate almost every square inch of the property. The owners took care of the rest, and though Austin had never stayed there, he heard the reviews were almost perfect, something which unheard of in their business.

"It's beautiful."

"Yeah, and they have the best banana bread."

"Oh really?" Caitlyn said to herself, the challenge evident in her voice.

"You know banana bread then?"

"Yes sir, I do," Caitlyn said, jutting her chin out. "Why are they the only place to stay? I would've thought tourism was quite the major industry here."

Austin continued on the drive. "Well, for one, we're too small to support something like that, but I think if we started to have more beds, more people would move in. We like to keep the washashores out."

"I figured you guys liked to keep to yourselves. That interview was one of the toughest I've had. Didn't think I had a chance of getting the job."

"Yeah, we don't like people."

Caitlyn laughed. "Well, geez, sounds like I'm in for a rough year."

"I wouldn't worry about it," he said, but his hands tightened on the wheel.

Austin had been honest with her at least about that situation. Sal and Alex had to fight tooth and nail to pass their idea for an inn with the town. Bringing outsiders in overnight hadn't set well with everyone. Months of debate had taken place until everyone agreed the move would be good for the town. After all, having a bed and breakfast, ice cream parlor, and postcard stands in the general store made Brightrock look a little more normal. That didn't mean people welcomed the newcomers though.

Austin hadn't relaxed his grip on the wheel. Why did he care so much? He shook his head with a small frown. Keeping her close was just business, a necessary evil, so she didn't figure out they were all damn near ancient. Once Lizzy came back, Caitlyn was as good as gone. The less she knew, the better.

"Oh, hey, we're back at school," Caitlyn said, bringing him back to present.

"Yep, can't get away from this place around here." Though for a moment, Austin wished he could, another impulse that puzzled him.

As they approached the center of the island, Austin pointed out the sights that he was sure she'd already seen. All of the government buildings were near each other and nestled around a rotary with three large oak trees and a flag-pole in the center.

"So, there's the library next to the sheriff's office, which is next to the fire department." As the Ford circled the round-about, Austin continued, "And there's the Town Hall, post office, and we don't need to discuss that building," he said to her laughter as they passed the school again.

"It is a beautiful building. Hard to believe it's public."

"Has its challenges, but then I'm sure every school does."

They headed back to the waterfront, talking about various buildings they had seen. Caitlyn seemed surprised to learn that Austin had never worked in another building, as was the case for most of the staff.

"That's rare in education. Y'all must like it here."

"We were all born and raised on Brightrock." Austin knew he was getting dangerously close to the line, so he added, "Just draws you back and begs you to stay."

"Thanks for taking me around," Caitlyn said as they pulled back into the marina's parking lot.

"Sure thing. I love showing people this place," he lied. He'd never shown anyone Brightrock before. No one had ever been invited before.

"I can tell." Caitlyn pushed her door open, and Austin hopped out to meet her by the tailgate.

"Most of the boats are out now," he said, looking at the marina. "Normally, I'd point out the good ones, but they're not here."

The wind from the water rushed by them both. Caitlyn pulled the hair out of her face and tucked it behind one ear before folding her hands under her arms. "There's still a lot."

"Mine is right over there."

Caitlyn looked to where he had pointed, then back at him. A frown crossed her features, and her brows knitted together. "No way. That one?"

"Yep. That's her."

Caitlyn followed him over to where a boat rocked in the slow swells, tugging on her ropes. Black script spelled out *Bombshell* painted like a credit in a golden age of Hollywood movie on the aft hull. Next to her name, a painting of a blonde pin-up girl straddling an anchor winked at them. Forty-two feet of white fiberglass inlaid with gleaming teak shone like the diamond around Caitlyn's neck in the sun.

"Want the tour?" Austin reached into his pocket and pulled out his keys and tossed them once in the air before catching them with ease.

"It's gorgeous."

"She," he said. It was a knee-jerk reaction he couldn't help.

"Oh, okay, geez," Caitlyn said with a laugh. "Should I let you two get a room?"

"Nah, we're good. I come by at least twice a week. In fact, I'm due to take her out. We could see the island from the sea if you're interested. It's a whole new vantage point from which to appreciate things."

Caitlyn's eyes roamed the boat, but she looked hesitant. Austin smiled.

"Just see her today and consider it an open offer. You've been on boats before, right?"

"Oh yeah, tons of times, but they weren't like this."

"No one's like her," he said.

He hadn't planned on offering to take the boat out, curious about where the invitation had come from. All of it felt so natural, like this was the next logical step.

Austin watched her stare at the *Bombshell* with excitement in her eyes and a small smile on her pink lips. It felt good seeing she seemed to genuinely want to go.

He really wanted to take her out and show off some more, another desire he didn't understand, but driving around with someone was one thing, and boarding a boat and taking off into the Atlantic was something else. He needed to take it slow. John wouldn't approve—no one would—but if anyone asked, he could easily defend the offer.

He hopped on board and slid the key into the lock, opening the cabin before going back and extending a hand. Caitlyn took it and climbed on board, her skin warm and soft against his own. His chest swelled when he took the weight of her as she stepped down, unsteady and unsure of her footing.

Austin ran his hand along the trim covering the entrance to the interior. "I bought her when I got back from the navy."

Caitlyn walked around on the deck, looking at every detail. "You must take good care of her. I've never seen a boat this clean."

"Yeah, other guys bought cars and motorcycles, but not a kid from New England."

"I guess not, so tell me about her."

Those were the magic words, and Austin's chest expanded when he heard them.

"Oh God, where do I begin?" he said with a smile before launching into the specs like a proud papa.

CHAPTER 8

F our weeks had gone by in a flash from that Saturday tour Austin had given Caitlyn. She still hadn't taken him up on the offer to go for a boat ride, not because she didn't want to, but her to-do list had exploded in September, and she needed the weekends to keep up. He'd been on her mind a lot though. Before she went to bed each night, Caitlyn replayed everything Austin had told her during their drive around the island. She liked that she'd made him laugh a couple of times and had revisited those moments more than she wanted to admit. At least he had warmed up to her after that first encounter when she'd arrived. Every morning, he had been at her classroom door without fail for a quick check-in. Everyone else at the school had been distant, even the students, but Austin was a constant presence she could count on.

Caitlyn watched the copy machine churn out yet another copy for the project on Jamestown and early American settlements she was handing out. Production stopped, and the machine let out a series of shrill beeps.

"Don't you dare."

Caitlyn pulled the doors open and started tinkering through all of the usual sticking points. It didn't take long to realize the jams were predictable and in the same place every time. At least three different handwritten notes adorned different sides of the machine, each with a unique warning about the evils of putting paper in drawer one, the location of the elusive hole punch tray, and who to call for toner.

"Alright, we're done here," she said, pulling out a crumpled piece of paper which looked like an accordion. "Rubric's online anyway."

Caitlyn went to the counter to get paper towels in a futile attempt to wipe away the toner on her hands. She didn't know why she bothered, because they were streaked with dry erase marker from earlier anyway. Grabbing what was left of her stack of copies, she headed back to her room in the dark hallway, the lone emergency light guiding her way.

It was past eight, and this was not the first time she had stayed until dark. Caitlyn knew which lights were the emergency ones that remained on all the time, which was knowledge she really hadn't wanted but always managed to acquire at every school she'd worked at.

"Hey, James," she called down the hallway with the electives classrooms.

James waved back as he drove the floor polisher he had affectionately named the Green Machine. Caitlyn hit the stairs quickly and shuffled down to the end of the hallway and her room.

Sitting down at the computer, she jiggled the wireless mouse to wake it up and crossed off extra copies of rubrics on her to-do list. Though she knew what she needed to do, Caitlyn put her head in her hands to rest her eyes and took a mental health moment.

Caitlyn drew in a breath and tried to relax her body, starting with her toes and working her way up. She had thought that moving here would be different and that her to-do list would relax with a smaller class. While some things had improved, like the number of projects she had to grade, they covered content quicker than students at her old school, always keeping her on her toes. At least the money was good. She had paid off one credit card but still had too many to go. All of the bills served as a constant reminder of the hell she had left behind.

The memories she didn't want drifted up like always. The voices of her parents, visions of an empty house, and a quiet blonde teen looking somewhat hopeful in Caitlyn's old classroom before getting up and waving goodbye.

"Hey."

She jumped and spun around to see Austin in the doorway.

"Sorry, thought you left your light on." He held up both hands. As usual, his sleeves were rolled up and his tie slack. Peeking out from under the cuff of one sleeve was the edge of what looked to be a dark red birthmark. He always managed to make disheveled look great. He came closer.

"You okay?"

"Yeah," she said, but she was sure she gave the complete opposite impression.

"I'm so convinced."

Austin sat on a table in front of her, tossing a water bottle in the air, trying to flip it and land it right side up just like the kids.

"How's it going?"

She scrubbed her face with her hands before leaning on her elbows on her desk and propping up her head.

"Fine."

Austin didn't say anything and instead just kept tossing his water bottle in the air.

"How are you?" she asked when he said nothing.

"I'm good. Busy, but good."

"Why are you here so late?"

"I could ask you the same question."

"I'm working on my to-do list. You?"

"I like being here when no one else is." Austin caught the water bottle and set it down before looking at her. "It helps me think. Sometimes I get so wired, I can't throttle down until I have time like this. And before you ask, the answer is yes."

Caitlyn frowned. "What do you mean?"

"I do have ADHD. All of the teachers ask, and the ones that don't know, assume."

"That's okay. This place is lucky to have you. I've never been in admin, but being outside looking in, it seems you have more than enough on your plate. They need high energy."

Austin shrugged off her compliment. "So, what's on your to-do list?"

"Conferences, grades, emails, the usual."

"All easy."

"None of it is hard. It's just piling up right now and stressing me out." Caitlyn didn't want to get into the real reasons.

"You need to give the kids some self-directed work."

"I do, but—"

"No, no buts. It's not like you're showing a movie."

"No, it's not that. I do a lot of research and projects, but I like to get involved and really be there to work with them."

"Give them some space and let them come to you with questions, just for one day," he added when she looked at him. "Maybe two."

"I'll think about it."

"Conferences are coming up, and you're here past eight."

"I just like to come in with everything ready."

"Is everything ready for the kids to work on their own tomorrow?"

Caitlyn paused before looking at her desk. "I mean, they're working on a project. I just made the rubric—"

"Sounds like a good time to have a workday."

"So…what? Explain it, then just let them work on it?"

"Yep."

Caitlyn took a quick glance at her calendar on the wall. "I can do that, but—"

"Great, I'll be right back."

Before she could stop him, Austin jumped down on the floor and ran out of the room. Caitlyn sat alone in silence before she heard footsteps running back down the hall toward her room.

Austin slid back through her door, his black dress shoes letting him ski on the linoleum. One hand held his water bottle, and the other hand clutched a green pencil bag and what looked to be like a rolled poster.

"Boom!"

Caitlyn stared at him, stifling a laugh. "Um, what just happened?"

With a flick of his wrist, he unfurled the poster, which Caitlyn now recognized as a chessboard. Austin grabbed two chairs and brought them together before he dumped out the contents of the bag, spilling chess pieces everywhere.

"Seriously?"

"White or black?"

"You didn't even ask if I play."

"Come on." Austin was already setting up the game with a single-minded focus.

Caitlyn sighed and went to sit down in the student chair across from him, claiming ownership of the white pieces.

Austin looked up at her when they were all set up and said, "Your move."

Caitlyn looked back at him and sighed. "I'm going to lose. I'm a horrible player."

"We'll see about that." He sent her a devilish grin that made her breath freeze in her lungs. His blue eyes glowed in the light from her desk lamp and sent a shiver up her spine.

"Okay, prepare for a swift victory."

"Oh, don't worry. I can't end a game."

Caitlyn moved her knight on the king's side. "What do you mean?" she asked.

Austin shook his head and gave her a lopsided grin. "Can't close the deal. I end up just chasing pieces around the board forever." He selected his pawn and took advantage of the two-space hop.

Caitlyn reached forward to move as he pulled back, but their hands met over the board. Freezing, they hung suspended in midair, connected. Her breath caught in her lungs, and she felt her lips part. Seconds stretched as they stayed, her hand touching his.

Caitlyn drew in a breath and pulled her hand back, still feeling Austin's warmth, tingling on her skin. His blue eyes glowed in the dark as he watched her across the board. All his earlier distractions had melted away. He stared at her, fixated.

"It's still your move," he said. One corner of his mouth lifted.

CHAPTER 9

Caitlyn sat at her desk and waited for the sound of the familiar footsteps coming down the hall. The room was dark except for the pool of light from her desk lamp, and she listened to soft piano music as she graded and entered scores into the grade book. Austin had been stopping by every night now for a few days.

Thinking about how different he now seemed from the cold person who'd met her at the ferry, Caitlyn's lips turned upwards. She knew she could win him over with enough time and smiled a satisfied grin now that she'd done it.

Turns out they actually had a lot in common. While they played games, they chatted about big stuff like religion and politics, and little stuff, like songs, food, and travel. There were a few differences, like how he hadn't read much fiction since college, but other than that blemish, Caitlyn found that their preferences fit like a glove.

They hadn't talked about everything though. Austin had asked her about family and Louisiana, but Caitlyn couldn't get into that mess. While it didn't feel right to shut him out,

Caitlyn didn't have a choice. She couldn't go there herself. Couldn't relive the pain she'd left behind.

As it was, the bill collectors had finally stopped calling. With Caitlyn's first paycheck, she had managed to pay off the remaining amount owed on cancer treatments that hadn't worked. With her increased salary, Caitlyn had finished up the payments earlier than expected. Now she finally felt a sense of freedom, like some invisible shackles had been cut away, leaving her to heal in peace. How the hell was someone supposed to grieve a loss when debt collectors called day and night? Their monotone voices barely registered the emotion of a normal human as they stayed on the script, even after Caitlyn had sold everything and set up the payment plan. People could talk all day long about personal space and self-care, but the real world didn't give a shit about any of that. Caitlyn had learned the hard way she was all on her own. Including Austin in all her personal drama wasn't happening anytime soon. As far as she was concerned, the less she thought about it, the better. There were still more to pay, but she had managed to consolidate the rest and could see the light at the end of the tunnel, even if it was just a distant glimmering speck. One day she'd be debt-free again. Maybe by then she'd feel like a whole person again too.

The sound of his familiar clip-clop echoed down the hall, snapping her out of her dark thoughts. Caitlyn saved her work and closed her email before swiveling her chair toward the door, right on cue.

"Helllllloooooo," he said as he pulled a chair up and set up the board. One thing they had found was a mutual love of *Seinfeld*.

Caitlyn settled in, and they exchanged updates on their various projects at work, while they started their game in the usual fashion. Austin liked to try the same strategy a student had shown him a few years ago.

"So, how'd the early American projects go?" Austin asked, taking her rook out in a move she hadn't seen coming. "The colonies, right?"

"Freaking awesome," Caitlyn said, studying the board of dwindling options.

"That's great!"

"Yeah, Charles brought in a bunch of stuff." Caitlyn pointed to the back table where a variety of artifacts were laid out.

Austin turned and stared at the pile.

"Oh," he said, sounding surprised. "That's cool."

"I'm pretty sure a bunch of that stuff should be in a museum. If it's real, that is. Charles swore up and down that it was."

Caitlyn plucked up a pawn and moved toward Austin's queen.

"Your move."

"Oh, yeah, um, there." Austin moved a piece on the other side of the board and furrowed his brow.

"You should check out the stuff he brought. It's really neat. Said a lot of it is just from his home."

Austin nodded, but a cloud had settled over his features.

"You okay?" she asked when he didn't say anything.

"Yeah, fine. Great. Sorry, guess I'm just tired. What did Charles say during the presentation?"

"He was kind of nervous but got a lot of the facts right. Talked about the clothes and hardships, but then he got a few details wrong. Wrong generations and such. I thought about taking off points, but then I figured it was just nerves."

Austin looked like he might throw up.

"You sure you're okay? You really don't look good."

He waved away her concern. "Maybe that old Hot Pocket didn't sit right. What family members did he mention?"

Caitlyn attacked with her pawn, knocking down the

queen with a flick. "Boom! I love doing that. Yeah, he said it was his great-grandfather's stuff." She laughed. "Can you imagine? Poor kid's math is way wrong."

Austin didn't flinch.

"I asked him about that, you know, like a clarifying question, and he was adamant he got it right. I was like, no. That's not possible. But he was red as a beet and breathing weird, so I didn't want to make it a big deal in front of everyone. Seriously, are you okay? You're getting pale."

"Yeah, rock steady." He gave her a weak smile, along with a bobbing nod that did little to convince her. "How were the other presentations?"

Caitlyn shrugged and moved another piece to counter Austin's blatant attack on her bishop. "Good. Really good. Top-notch research. Really blew my expectations away, but Charles definitely set the bar high."

"Right, right. That's good though! I'm glad it went great." Austin's knee sprang up and down. He popped a few knuckles.

"Yeah, me too." She let out a laugh, and when he glanced up at her said, "I still can't get over it. Great-grandfather. Apparently, these kids have little concept of time. I mean, Jesus."

Austin jumped up, scattering pieces all over the table.

"Woah, what the hell?"

"I've got to go," he said, grabbing his water bottle and rushing out the door.

"Okay, I'll pick up! Feel better!" she called after him, but he didn't answer.

Caitlyn dropped the discarded pieces into the bag and turned off the light before getting her purse. On the way out, she meandered through the halls looking for Austin. The small window to his office was pitch black, deserted.

Caitlyn pulled out her phone and fired off a text with

some well wishes for whatever that Hot Pocket was doing now. She watched to see if he would respond and was disappointed when the phone was silent. He was so easy to talk to, and Caitlyn had started to look forward to their talks, staying far later than she ever had before just for the chance to see him. The realization hit with a wave of shame.

Crushing on her boss was not okay. Shaken, Caitlyn silenced her phone and dropped it into her purse, headed to the parking lot. Walking toward the cars, Caitlyn purposely tried to avoid looking for Austin's truck, but out of habit she noticed his vacant spot. She mentally shook herself. She was not this type of person. Not the type who had affairs or flings or one-night stands with men at work. She had always prided herself on staying away from the drama. Above it all and focusing on the kids.

She had come here in part for the money, which she really did need, but also to get away from what had been the worst year of her life. Focusing on the kids had been the plan to ground her again after everything that happened. It hadn't just been her parents, but the other death that had come right on the heels of her parents' funerals. Her colleagues had said it hadn't been her fault, but—

No, she was not going to go down that road again. She needed to learn to stop the negative cycle before it took hold.

Hoping Austin was okay, Caitlyn avoided looking at the empty spot where Austin's truck belonged and climbed into the car. Plugging in her phone to play the same piano solo, Caitlyn drove back to the apartment alone in the dark.

CHAPTER 10

A ustin sat at his desk in front of a computer screen filled with data reports on discipline. He had taken off his shoes and propped his feet up in his office in a blissful time of silence. The dress shoes hurt his feet more than when he had just been in the classroom every day, but like a belt, he felt some things were just essential.

Austin's small office was dark now with the overhead lights off, illuminated by a small lamp on the desk. Reports, grades, and a bunch of files he hadn't had the time to go through yet covered the desk and obscured part of the keyboard. His walkie-talkie and keys lay on top of the mess. Since he still didn't feel like cleaning it today, he looked at his watch to see if it was time to go up to Caitlyn's classroom yet.

Playing chess with Caitlyn had become a habit for Austin and something he looked forward to more with each passing night. They talked about everything. At least, as much of everything as they could without Austin revealing any truths about the island or himself. Throughout their chats, Austin found that he had to keep reminding himself of the rules so that he didn't let too much out. With Caitlyn, he felt he could relax, and around an outsider, that was dangerous—for both of them. And even though they talked every night, after a few times, Austin found he kept hitting a wall. He wasn't the only one holding things back.

As much as he tried to find out more about Caitlyn's background and life in Louisiana, she always evaded or changed the subject. She loved to talk about the place but shut down whenever he asked about people. Even though he was doing the same thing, Austin hated feeling shut out. It only made him try harder.

Still, their chats had been an excellent way to build trust and figure out if she had started to suspect anything weird. That incident with Charles had just about given Austin a heart attack, for more than one reason. Austin had called Charles into his office the next morning, almost making the poor kid cry. Adults on Brightrock weren't supposed to tell children about the secret, letting them learn at their first renewal when they signed their freedom away in exchange for hundreds of more years. Every now and then a kid figured something out, but even then, most of the time the others just ignored them, writing them off as weird. In Charles's case, the poor kid had the right information, but Austin carefully spoke to him about how what he was suggesting was impossible. After sending him back to class, Austin had called Charles's parents to discuss how to handle their slipup.

Austin glanced at the clock. The building closed at nine, and the custodians cleaned the top floor first, so he waited until they were done to head up. It was almost six, which meant it was almost time to go. He reached in his bag and pulled out a tattered history book on John Paul Jones he had promised to loan Caitlyn.

A knock at the door made him jump.

Austin yanked his feet down and hopped up to open the door. John still wore his yellow traffic vest from dismissal and stood in a rumpled suit jacket, looking exhausted.

"Got a minute?"

"Yeah, here, have a seat. I was just looking at the incident report data." Austin tilted the computer screen so John could see it before reaching over to flick on the overhead lights.

The small office barely had enough office for three adults with the desk, filing cabinet, and bookcase. He squeezed around where John was sitting and made it back behind his desk to sit. The man looked more shabby than usual. Discipline calls were wearing him out too.

"Let me guess," John said, leaning on the arm of the chair, sarcasm evident in his voice. "They're up."

"Well, yes and no," Austin said, prepared to launch into his analysis. Part of the reason he got the admin job was that he loved data.

John nodded, listening as he sat slouched in the visitor's chair across from the desk. Austin kept pointing out highlights that he had noticed, such as the rise in infractions after lunch.

Austin looked over when the principal didn't say anything. "What?"

John sighed, sinking even lower into the uncomfortable, old chair.

"We need to talk, Austin."

Though a weird feeling set up shop in his stomach, Austin didn't let it show.

"Sure. What's up?" he said putting on a solid poker face.

"What are you still doing here?"

Austin frowned. "What do you mean? I'm looking at the data and trying to find my desk under all of this," he said, gesturing at the mess in front of him.

"You know what I mean," John said without flinching.

"I could ask you the same question."

"Austin—"

"I'm salaried, aren't I? So what does it matter?"

John pulled a hand over his face, before pausing as if gathering his thoughts. "It's after five."

"Yeah."

"There are four people in this building."

"Okay."

"You."

"Uh-huh."

"Me."

"Right." Austin could see where this was going and didn't like it one bit.

"James."

"He works until nine."

"Right, and one more."

Austin knew he could feign innocence by asking who but instead remained quiet. He wanted to pelt his water bottle against the wall.

"You know the rules."

So he had been right about where this was going. "I'm not sure I follow," Austin said, poker face still in place.

John looked at him without blinking. "You're getting too close."

"I'm keeping an eye on her. Wasn't that your idea?"

"She isn't one of us."

"I'm aware," Austin said before he could bite back the response.

"I'm concerned you're spending too much time with her. Getting too close. That sort of thing."

"All I'm doing is following orders. Your orders. Besides, how else would we know if Caitlyn hears something from one of the kids or a teacher slips up? I have to be close to her. The question we should be asking is why is she still here at night? As you said, it's getting close to six. Clearly, she needs help."

"Are you sure she isn't staying because of you?"

"I'm not asking her to stay."

"No, but would she stay if you didn't go see her?"

"Go see her?" Austin knew it was a shot in the dark, but he had learned not to fall into a self-incriminating trap after being arrested the first time. He had learned that lesson the hard way.

"It's come to my attention that you've been spending a lot of time with Caitlyn."

"No more than I would with any other person here," Austin said. It was a true enough statement.

John blew out another breath. "I'm not saying you wouldn't, but Austin, this isn't just about work. She isn't one of us."

"Yeah, you said that already." He knew his temper was starting to show, but he didn't seem to care as much at that moment.

"Listen, I don't want to have to turn you in."

Austin raised his eyebrows. He hadn't thought it could escalate that quickly. "Turn me in? For what? We're talking about classes and school. Besides, this was your idea, remember?"

"Yeah, I know. I didn't expect you to take it this far. I just meant check in every once in a while. Like I said, you're getting too close. It would be for your own good. I like you. Hell, everyone likes you, so I'd hate to see you do something stupid."

"Thanks for looking out for me, but I got it."

"Don't be like that."

"No, really." Pissed, Austin stood up. John hustled to do the same. "Appreciate it, but I'm trying to focus on my job." He dropped the worn book back into the old leather bag and grabbed it off the hook he'd mounted when he had moved into the cramped office just a few weeks prior. Didn't make sense to wave their chess games in front of John's face. Better just to leave and catch up with Caitlyn at a less obvious time. He went to move past the principal, who stood in his way.

John spoke with a calm tone that made no attempt to hide his meaning. "Austin, you need to knock this off."

"Still don't know what you're talking about, but I do know you're in my way." He also knew he was out of line and he didn't care.

The principal's mouth thinned. John had played linebacker before all the safety regulations and it showed, his nose crooked in several places. When he spoke, it was in a calm voice. "Austin, I'm telling you to keep an eye on her from a distance. She isn't one of us."

"You know you keep saying that, right?"

"Then it shouldn't be a problem."

"I don't see a problem."

The principal stared at him with narrowed eyes, as if trying to figure out if Austin would listen. At last, he stepped back out of his way. "See you at the refuge. Don't forget, they changed the time to midnight."

Austin ground his teeth all the way to the parking lot. When he got behind the wheel, he glanced up at Caitlyn's classroom window. He could still see the glow from the lamp on her desk.

CHAPTER 11

Austin pulled through the gate and into the refuge along with a row of cars all heading in the same direction. Before, he had always felt a sense of pride and community, but now they were like mice trapped in a maze. Austin tried to ease his grip on the wheel, but he couldn't. All of it was bullshit, but what choice did he have? Right now Austin wanted to forget all of his vows and honor, and really wanted to tell the council where they could shove their terms and conditions before giving the finger to the whole damn rock and leaving for good. Only a few had done the same and presumably died at the average rate without the island's water. Once you burned a bridge like that, the damage was done, and you could never communicate with anyone on the island again. The council wasn't quick to forgive or forget.

He drove the old truck into an open space and watched as family and friends ambled toward the old clapboard meetinghouse in the middle of a small clearing. The skies overhead looked like rain as fat, dark gray clouds swirled above, stirring the wind and rustling the trees. He recognized his parents' car as they pulled in a few rows over. His dad got out first and went around to get the door for his mom, even though she didn't need it. The pair of them smiled and waved to other couples as they all headed inside for the Renewal.

Austin smiled a little as he watched them. During his time in the Pacific, Austin wanted nothing more than to come back and see them. He had left to protect America but also to send money back home to his family, who had desperately needed it. Most of the wealth on Brightrock had been tied to the stock market, and when that had gone tits up, things had gotten desperate. After all, they couldn't exactly apply for all the programs like everyone else or just go and get a job.

He loved them all even though he hadn't been the same when he had come back. Instead of moving back into the house, he had elected to buy a small garden shed on the other side of the island. There he could try to forget what had happened.

Austin checked the clock on the dash and wondered if Ethan would come back today. Most of the time, he would make the official meetings, but depending on whatever work shit he had going on, sometimes he couldn't make it and would arrange something different with the council. The lucky bastard had become a pro at straddling the line. The thought had tempted Austin more than once, but the problem was he didn't have a distinctive enough job to warrant such approval from the council. Back when he had served in the navy, special dispensations had been no problem, but once that ended, so did the special treatment. Ethan managed money, so naturally, they let him do whatever he wanted.

In his worn-out gray suit and an old coat, John ambled toward the doors at the end of the old meetinghouse. The last few stragglers followed him. The ceremony would start soon, and if Austin didn't make an appearance, the number of questions he'd have to answer from concerned family and friends would make him want to bash his head into a wall, especially after what John had said.

With no other option and no excuse good enough, he slammed the truck door shut and stalked toward the building, his shoulders hunched against the dropping temperature. The meetinghouse, built soon after the founders arrived, stood on the highest point of the island. Sharp granite rocks jutted out of the earth, giving the hill an almost violent look as if the terrain itself guarded against the sacred waters below. The large building sat next to a smaller matching one, which held seven locks on an iron gate that barred entry into the sacred interior. Only members of the council held keys, and no one person could access the well without the others.

Austin headed for the double doors and pushed through into the ample open space. Above him, the hammerbeam construction resembled an inverted ship's hull. When he had first been allowed in after he had graduated from high school, Austin had stared up and wondered why anyone would build a ceiling that looked like a capsized ship. Now, casting a glance upward, he still thought it was depressing, but at least it was warm inside.

Candles flickered around the open space, scented with lemon wax. Most of the murmuring members of the community were seated in the square box pews looking toward the raised platform at the front. A sole, wooden pulpit stood flanked by a dozen of the town council members seated on either side. Timothy Chappell and Aunt Mary each sat next to the pulpit with a few papers in their hands. Chappell had his reading glasses on. Austin groaned as he sat down. He reached for his phone to pass the time, but his empty pocket reminded him it was in the truck as protocol demanded. No technology was allowed in the sacred space. Chappell was a stickler for tradition, and it was probably for the best. The last thing any of them needed was this shit on YouTube. Talk about going viral.

Chappell stood and a hush went over the crowd as he approached the pulpit.

"Thank you for arriving on time. Let us open in prayer."

Austin bowed his head and recited the rote words from memory. The general prayer of thanks had echoed in these walls too many times to count. Whether or not any of them actually believed in God, Austin didn't know. None of this not-aging crap was in the Bible. Listening to the way Aunt Tee and Aunt Mary told it, once most of the founders, reformers fleeing England, realized they weren't aging anymore, they had a big-ass existential crisis that had fizzled out over time. Many still worshiped and had only expanded their beliefs a little to include this little immortality detour before picking up the pieces and moving on with life as usual.

The town council ran through matters to be put to a public vote. Chappell stood up there in a full three-piece tweed suit, enjoying the formality the occasion brought. His British accent echoed up to the rafters while he talked about the annual budget. To entertain himself, Austin imagined the know-it-all when he found out he hadn't aged in years and cracked a smirk at the thought of the tight-ass confronting something he couldn't explain. He almost wished he could've been there.

Austin leaned forward and then back again, aching to get out of the box he was sitting inside. He just wanted to get on with things. If Austin had his way, the damn ceremony would be a drive-thru. He crossed his arms again and fought off a yawn. The meeting time change had been made a few summers back to avoid the interest of tourists. Studying the dark floorboards beneath him, Austin wondered if Caitlyn had missed him this evening at school, whether she was asleep yet, and what she would think of all this cult shit. He pictured her back in her apartment over the ice cream parlor watching TV or lying in bed, reading. To pass the time, he tried to guess what she might be doing based on their past conversations.

Austin smiled to himself and lifted his head when Chappell's droning finally ended. After what seemed like the better part of an hour, the most painstaking matters to be addressed had finished.

"Will there be any other business brought before the council?"

Austin prayed for silence and thanked the good God above when everyone kept their damn mouth shut.

Chappell nodded. "We will now conduct the oath. Please stand and raise your right hand."

The shuffling of feet and creaking floorboards would've drowned him out, so, always willing to stretch a ceremony, Chappell waited for silence.

"Please repeat after me," he said with a weighty pause. Austin rolled his eyes and sighed. It was a good thing he always sat in the back. He hadn't seen Ethan yet and once again vowed to see if there was any way he could get out of these meetings like his brother often did.

Chappell opened a red, leather-bound book to the front page and inhaled. "I do solemnly swear."

"I do solemnly swear," Austin said, his voice getting lost in the cult-like choral response echoing around him.

"That I will keep confidential all proceedings of this meeting."

"That I will keep confidential all proceedings of this meeting."

Chappell paused as if quoting God himself. "That I will bear true faith and allegiance to the same."

Austin shoved his hands in his pockets and looked around the room at the other people. He had taken this oath for years and watched with boredom as those around him repeated the words.

Chappell was warmed up now. His voice boomed with authority like a Puritan preacher. "That I take this obligation freely, without any mental reservation or purpose of evasion."

The voices swam around Austin, making his skin tight and itchy. Close quarters didn't bother him so much after being on the boat in the Pacific, but damn if brainwashing didn't creep him out. Maybe he had spent too much time away, as no one else ever seemed concerned.

"And that I will well and faithfully uphold the duties of the contract into which I am about to enter." Chappell was almost yelling now. He paused, no doubt for words to sink into the flock before him, and in a reverent voice that Austin didn't buy said, "So help me God."

Austin leaned back and folded his arms in front of his chest, ready to get out of this place already. He watched as Chappell, breathing hard, scanned the crowd through his tortoiseshell glasses.

Aunt Mary stepped up next to him and waited until he reclaimed his original chair next to the pulpit. Dressed in a simple red sweater and black slacks, she looked almost casual next to Chappell, but Austin knew from personal experience that those shrewd eyes missed virtually nothing. Even though he was against the back wall, he sat a little straighter when she put on the glasses that hung around her neck by a plain chain. She didn't need dramatics to be taken seriously.

"Thank you. The non-disclosure agreement has been updated again. If you would like a copy to take home for your review, you may find them on the tables at the front and at the end of the aisles.

"The changes the council approved focus on section two, under which you find an updated list of media platforms that would be considered a violation. All other sections remain as they were previously. For any questions regarding these updates, please contact any member of the council directly. We will be happy to speak with you on these matters.

"Additionally, many people are now aware we have a new teacher hired to stay in compliance with federal law." Austin sat up and glanced toward John, who didn't flinch at the news. "The council of elders voted to approve this measure and give Lizzy Brooks approval to return to school on a special dispensation. The council would remind everyone that friendly conversation is welcome with Ms. Caitlyn Landry, but interactions are to be treated with caution."

As Aunt Mary continued to more mundane matters, Austin schooled his features to remain stoic. It wasn't about him unless he made it about him. Surely, this was just a general warning to everyone. Still, he didn't like it.

"As always, your signature on this register will not only act as a means of keeping attendance but will also signify your agreement to the terms and conditions of the updated NDA. At this time, please come forward in an orderly fashion to sign the register."

Aunt Mary watched the crowd, eyeing all of them as one by one, they stood in line and approached the red leather book Chappell had held. It sat displayed on a wide oak table at the center aisle in front of the raised platform.

Austin counted the minutes of his extended life that ticked by while in line. Some people took far too long, creating a John Hancock that didn't change the price of tea in China. Austin appreciated those who did a quick scribble and moved the hell on with things. It wasn't like they all wouldn't be back in three months' time. When it was his turn, Austin snatched up the standard Bic pen and chicken-scratched his name on the parchment before returning to his seat.

Looking satisfied when everyone had finished and was sitting back down, Aunt Mary nodded once and motioned for the ushers to come forward. Austin's father stood and walked to the front, along with a few other men and women. Heading toward the eaves of the meetinghouse, they returned, each carrying a sleeve of Dixie cups and a pewter pitcher, filled with the water from the well, no doubt gathered by the council before anyone had arrived.

The ushers positioned themselves at key points along the aisles, where community members lined up to get their portion of the water. Long ago, the question of hygiene had been answered by members of the community bringing their goblets from the house. Everyone received one as a gift when they came to their first ceremony after their high school graduation. Austin never brought his, instead opting for the disposable cups provided by the ushers.

As with signing the register, Austin was one of the last people to return to his original seat, Dixie cup in hand.

Aunt Mary stood at the pulpit, her thick, pale hand wrapped around a delicate green wine glass she brought from home every time.

"To your health, and may all of us live long in prosperity." She brought the old glass to her lips, the signal for everyone else to do the same. Austin drank his water like a shot and promptly crumpled the Dixie cup in his hand. The warmth in his gut that followed felt similar to that caused by alcohol, but much lighter, dissipating after a few seconds.

His aunt raised her empty glass again. "Thank you, everyone, and on your way out, please make sure to thank the volunteers who so kindly brought the refreshments at the back. Have a good evening and as always, drive safe."

CHAPTER 12

When her planning period came, Caitlyn walked out of her room and through the halls to the sound of music coming from the electives hall. The sounds of a choir lifted through the stairwells serenading the halls with tunes accented by the occasional off-note.

Being a teacher meant she didn't often get to see what other people were doing in their classrooms. In fact, she felt more alone here than she had expected. The whole effect was isolating. When Austin hadn't shown up last night, Caitlyn had felt that same sinking feeling.

What made it odd was that Austin had always been consistent, and he had been the one to reach out to her about their chess meets. He was the one who had looked forward to them. He was the one who had pestered her to play. He was the one who had let her undo moves to keep the game going longer. He was the one who had made her start to like chess.

And he was the one who had bailed last night.

It's not like they'd had an agreement, but Caitlyn still

wondered if something had happened and wanted to check on him. She clicked along in her boots in the hallway toward his office, which was located in the Auditorium, under the stage, next to the boiler room.

A mix of teachers stood in the hallway, each holding coffee cups, chatting about something. One short teacher wearing a big scarf said something that ignited a burst of laughter from the group.

"Morning, guys," Caitlyn said as she walked closer.

The laughter ceased. A few teachers took a sip of coffee while others offered a small smile, before saying a weak, "Hey."

As Caitlyn neared, a few shuffled their feet and started to turn away, mumbling excuses about what they needed to do.

Caitlyn's skin felt tight all over. "I'm just going to see Austin. Didn't mean to interrupt," Caitlyn added with a smile.

A chorus of half-hearted excuses that Caitlyn didn't believe for a second erupted. She gave them a smile and nodded, walking past them. As she made her way down the hall, she could feel their eyes on her and heard the faint sound of whispering in her wake.

Caitlyn tried to let the feeling roll off her back. It was just being new. She didn't need to be in on every inside joke. She hadn't planned on talking to them anyway, so why would it bother her that they didn't include her? She pushed the thought to the back of her brain as she rounded the corner to Austin's office.

The little room was cramped and smelled of strong coffee. What must have been an old supply closet now had a desk, two chairs, and an old bookcase with shelves that bowed in the middle. Austin sat behind his desk, squinting at the computer screen in front of him, his glasses lying on a stack of papers at his elbow next to a walkie-talkie. He looked up when she walked in and smiled wide. Dark circles hung beneath his eyes.

"Late night last night?" Caitlyn asked, sitting down in the old visitor chair. "I came to check on you. Surprised I didn't see you."

A dark expression crossed Austin's face, the happy smile faltering so quickly Caitlyn almost didn't notice it.

"Yeah, sorry about that. I had to run and take care of some family stuff. Got time for a game now?" he asked, standing to reach behind him and grab the pack of chess pieces off a filing cabinet.

"Sure, why not?" Caitlyn said, setting papers aside to clear some room on his desk.

They started their game in the usual way. "I think I'm getting addicted," Caitlyn noted.

Austin glanced up and smiled a wry grin. "Chess has a way of doing that. Especially when you have a great partner."

Caitlyn laughed. "I don't know about that, but it's relaxing. Check."

She slid her piece forward, trapping his king with her queen and bishop. Austin moved a pawn to protect the king. They played on, chatting about different things, falling back into the steady conversations that always happened between them.

Looking at him, Caitlyn felt a smile spread across her face. With his blond hair and blue eyes, Austin looked like the poster-perfect boy scout, minus the scar on his chin. He probably looked like the all-American sailor in his uniform.

"You never told me why you joined the navy," Caitlyn said, watching him attack her bishop and move it aside.

"Wanted to serve but didn't want to kill anyone. Good way to make some money. Family needed it."

"That's really admirable. No pun intended."

Austin let out a laugh and shrugged, but his ears turned

pink. Caitlyn knew he avoided praise but couldn't see why. Austin was a great admin with the kids. He knew all of them and took the time to reach out to them and their parents. He wasn't afraid to get real with them and share what his own life had looked like.

That authenticity got him more of a following than most admins had. Kids wanted to know about the admin, and once they understood that someone knew where they were and had been through it themselves, they were more apt to listen. Relationships were key.

"Mr. Brooks?" a voice called from the door, making them both jump.

Erin, the art and Spanish teacher, stood at the door, her eyes wide and darting between Austin and Caitlyn before focusing on the chess board between them.

"What's up?" Austin asked. His voice was light, but there was a defensive edge in his eyes.

"I can come back later. I didn't realize I was interrupting," the teacher said, still stunned.

Caitlyn stood and smoothed her skirt. "You know, that's okay. I was just heading out. I need to get some stuff done. I'll catch up with you guys later."

As Caitlyn left Austin's office, she felt her skin get tight all over again. Though she tried to shake it, she couldn't ignore the sense that she had done something wrong, but what it was, Caitlyn couldn't figure out.

CHAPTER 13

The following Friday night, Austin jogged to the gym with a multi-tool in his hand, ducking under a drooping, half-hung banner of paper spiders. A few kids milled around in the main hallway of the school, opening packages of fake spider web cotton they would no doubt string everywhere. Pumpkins, fake tombstones, and a skeleton that shrieked when you walked by all lined the corridor toward the gym doors where the DJ was setting up.

"Alright! This looks great," Austin said to a few of the student helpers who had set up a backdrop where kids could take selfies in their costumes.

"Thanks, Mr. Brooks," they answered in chorus as he jogged over to the DJ. He loved the Halloween dance. Something about fall spiked his blood with pumpkin-spice whatever and made him feel festive. He was also looking forward to seeing Caitlyn for more than a passing minute. They hadn't had another chance to sit down together since Erin had walked in on them. Thank God he had been able to explain he was under orders from John to maintain contact and act as liaison. The move had convinced her enough to not tell John or anyone else. After all, it wasn't like he had been lying.

Austin checked his phone and swore under his breath. With ten minutes to go, he needed to fix the strobe light quickly before things got started. He hustled over to where the DJ had set up just inside the gym and crouched down over the piece of rented equipment.

The bass started pumping as he worked on the light, unscrewing the little panel. Two tiny, frayed wires had come apart during the ferry ride, breaking the circuit. Austin bobbed his head to the music while he reached in his pocket and dug out the electrical tape. As he grooved to the beat, he set to work reconnecting the wires and securing them with the tape.

Work like this reminded him of his time in the navy and gave him a pang in his gut. He missed working with his hands. When he had been in the Pacific, the high pressure played to his strength, giving him an outlet for the energy he was never able to shake. The constant threat of the Japanese had given everything he did more purpose. Raised the stakes. There had always been something mission-critical to do and someone new to do it with. Unlike Brightrock, the navy brought together people from all walks of life. There were a few assholes everyone hated, but several of the guys who had scarred his arms in bar fights had become lifelong friends. Some he'd still spoken with on the phone up until a few years ago when they died and he didn't. Right until the end, a few had always asked to see him in person, but of course, he still looked the same, so that was never going to happen. His appearance was liable to give some of his old buddies their last heart attack.

A burst of dark laughter came from the other side of the gym, followed by cheers and giggling as the students lit up a Dracula decoration which would jeer at anyone who came too close. Austin jiggled the little panel back into place and checked a few more connections, trying to figure out the problem. He liked teaching, mostly because of the kids, but crawling around on all fours on the gym floor with a tool in his hand just felt right.

A blinding light reflected up from the floor. Austin popped up and flashed a thumbs-up at the DJ who already had his headphones on while he stood hunched over his laptop, queuing up the music for the dance. The young, skinny college kid they hired from the Cape threw him an upward nod with a smile and mouthed thanks. Austin set the strobe light into its mount and jogged back over to where Laurie, dressed as Professor McGonagall, helped some student government kids set up the snack table.

"Ready for me to kill the lights?" Austin said. He was itching to get the party started.

She tilted her witch hat back on her head, looking up at him from under the brim. "Yeah, we're about ready. Could you bring in the other cases of water too?"

"Sure thing," Austin said, ready to bolt.

"Where's your costume?" she added.

"Yeah, Mr. Brooks, you gotta wear a costume."

He flashed a smile and tilted his head, revealing fangs he ordered online as well as the two bite marks he'd applied on his neck in his office before coming to set up.

"Ooooh nice," said Maggie, who had gone vampire too. Her costume matched her daily outfit so well that the only thing she had to add was fangs before trading her signature black hoodie for a cape. Otherwise, she looked like the same moody seventh grader with black eyeliner who waved to him in the hallways.

"Business casual vampire. I like it," Laurie said with a smile. "I'm surprised you left the tie on."

Austin smoothed down the black satin tie over his now

crumpled white dress shirt. "Same reason I never wear jeans. Like to look professional in front of the kids."

"Good for you. I'm wearing jeans under this costume," Laurie said with a laugh. While she went back to laying out drinks, Austin made a beeline for the box in the equipment storage room. In a flash, he popped the keyring off his belt loop and let himself into the cramped little room. He dug past the gymnastics equipment, basketballs, and tennis rackets before reaching his goal and plunged the gym into darkness. Cries of delight from behind him planted a broad smile on his face.

He strode out of the room, locking it behind him, and marveled at how cool the gym looked. The DJ they rented had outdone himself. The lighting effects were stellar, mimicking a dance club in a severe lightning storm. The bass thumped through the floor and up into his chest as the kids who'd helped decorate started to get in the mood and dance around.

Not that they hadn't done an excellent job too. The decorations looked spectacular. Every kind of Halloween item a teenager would love stood on display in the gym. Green, glowing pumpkins against the walls, floating ghosts from the raised basketball hoops, and carved jack-o'-lanterns from the art classes had all turned the space into a proper Halloween dance club. Austin spun on his heel and headed for the hallway light switch.

Sure enough, the hallway rivaled an abandoned mansion in the number of spider webs clinging to every surface.

"Mr. Brooks!" A ninth grader dressed as a cat ran over to him and fell into step. "Are you going to turn off the hall lights yet?"

"Sure am."

"YESSSS!" said the girl, as she pumped her fist in the air and peeled off to circle back to her cluster of decorator friends. "Hey guys, Mr. Brooks is going to turn off the lights."

"Make sure you guys get the trash, okay?" Austin headed for the lightbox and gave an encore performance. More squeals of delight echoed down through the hall.

Walking back to chaperone, Austin pulled out his radio and let James and the other custodians know the kids would be cleaning up Monday in study hall. He didn't want them to have to go out of their way, fighting the spider web cavern that was now the main hall.

Brightrock's annual Halloween dance hosted all of the secondary students. Sixth grade and up attended in exchange for hosting the Fall festival for the younger grades. Since it had become a rite of passage, most of the middle school students arrived early and stood at the doors, leaving the older students to arrive fashionably late so that they gave the impression they had to really think about whether they wanted to come.

As if that was even a thought. This was the only thing happening on the whole island.

Within five minutes, ghosts, zombies, and God knew what else had filled the gym and were all laughing and dancing around with their friends. Since Laurie ran the yearbook, she helped take pictures in front of the backdrop the kids had made, adding to the collection of memories the students would see at the end of the year. John greeted the kids at the door dressed in overalls, a plaid shirt stuffed with straw, and a ridiculous, brown hat.

Other teachers milled around, talking to each other on the perimeter with half an eye on the vibrating pack of kids. Glen always came as Frankenstein. He had bought that costume in the seventies, and what had started as recycling had turned into an anticipated tradition. Connie stood next to him. Half of her blonde hair had been sprayed black, and the massive fur coat over ice pick heels made her the perfect Cruella de Vil. Of course, to make sure the kids got it, she had a small stuffed dalmatian sticking out of her evening bag.

Austin scanned the growing crowd, looking for Caitlyn. Like the kids, every teacher, officially chaperoning or not, came to the dance for some entertainment. He made a loop and then did another, waving to kids as he went. He itched to see her and pulled his mouth into a grim line when he didn't.

After John had slapped him on the wrist, a move that still stung, Austin hadn't come around after hours for a few days. He kept meaning to stop by during the day when it would have been less conspicuous, but his schedule had exploded with meetings. In the past, that wouldn't have been a problem. Now though, his day job was really starting to get in the way of things. Disappointed Caitlyn wasn't there, Austin went to stand across the gym with his back against the wall and a perfect view of the door. He crossed his arms and settled in to watch the kids have fun and keep an eye out in case she showed.

In a matter of minutes, the older students started to arrive, coming in packs of no less than five, and the DJ took the cue and cranked the music up so even the most sullen of zombies had no choice but to dance on the fringe of the crowd.

Austin rested his head against the wall and watched the dancing get underway. As much as he loved dances, he never danced himself. Just being around the energy gave him a kick and freed up the tension that seemed to live in his shoulders daily now. Tomorrow was Halloween, which meant he still had time to run by the general store and pick up a pumpkin brought in from the mainland and a big bag of candy. The stash he kept in his office for the kids had been pretty much depleted by visitors. He never ate candy himself since the sugar keyed him up too much.

Something caught his eye in the doorway. Austin had to blink twice to make sure he hadn't totally lost it. Once he realized what he was seeing, a lick of desire punched into his gut. Before he knew what he was doing, Austin had left the wall behind and like a ship following a beacon, headed straight toward his goal. Screw whoever saw him.

CHAPTER 14

Caitlyn stepped in the doorway to the Halloween dance club that had been the gym just that morning. The crowd of kids in costumes jumped to a fast beat, fueled by a communal sugar high from the large bowls of candy placed at strategic points around the dark gym.

Light effects cast an eerie glow over the walls while throwing flickering shadows over everything. The floor pounded with the beat, and the kids screamed when the song changed to the latest hit.

"Hey, great costume!" a voice yelled above the deafening noise to her left. Laurie was dressed in a green cape and witch hat, with square brass spectacles. As always, she looked bright and happy, even though the temperature in the room was rapidly rising and her costume looked sweltering.

"Thanks!" Caitlyn yelled back. "I figured I'd go with the history vibe, you know?"

"Looks perfect! I could tell exactly who you were when you walked in!"

"I like the library reference!" Caitlyn said, admiring

Laurie's costume. Laurie beamed at the compliment from under her witch hat.

"Who else is here?" Caitlyn asked. She leaned in to hear Laurie better as she ran through everyone who'd arrived and what they were wearing.

Caitlyn hadn't seen Austin in days and missed their nightly chess games. Every time she had tried to meet up with him, a crisis had pulled him in the other direction like the school or universe was working against them. Still, she wondered why the after-hours visits had stopped. To add insult to injury, every time she approached him during the day, Austin found an excuse to cut her off and leave.

Caitlyn nodded to Laurie who was now chatting away about the yearbook photos they had gotten so far. A few of the kids who were dating had come wearing couples' costumes. Laurie pointed out the dancing butterfly and bug catcher who were so close together you would have thought they were conjoined.

"Should we break them apart?" Caitlyn asked before someone tapped her on the shoulder.

Austin stood behind her, looking like he always did except for the addition of some alarmingly realistic bite marks on his neck.

"Hey, you look like you could use a Band-Aid," she said, laughing.

"Can I talk to you?" His jaw had a firm set to it, and he wasn't smiling.

She turned to excuse herself from Laurie only to realize she was already wrapped up in taking pictures of a bunch of Disney princesses who'd just walked in together.

"Don't they need us to chaperone?" she asked, looking at the perimeter where all the other teachers were.

"No. Come on," Austin said, leading her out a side door.

His eyes had a weird, determined set to them like he needed to talk and needed to do it now.

Caitlyn followed in his wake as they walked alongside the wall leading to the entrance to the locker rooms. Austin pushed through a set of doors, holding them for her as always. The pattern continued until they were outside, behind the school, heading for the fields and the track.

The night air hit her like a wave of oxygen after being underwater. The gym, while awesome, had quickly become an oven that reeked of teen spirit—and not in a good way.

Caitlyn spun around to see Austin, but he kept walking past her. "Let's keep going."

"Where are we going?"

"Away from everyone."

Caitlyn frowned. She had only just arrived, and while she wanted to catch up, she figured she and Austin would just chat while watching the kids wear themselves out.

"Austin. What's going on?" she asked as they rounded the corner past the dumpster and walked to the outer fields where an old oak tree watched the stars come out.

"Nothing. Just need some air," Austin said, not facing her.

They stopped just under the canopy of the leaves, which rattled in the breeze, their fallen comrades crunching under Caitlyn's boots. In the dark, she realized how big he was and how alone they were. His sleeves were rolled up so Caitlyn could see his birthmark, carelessly exposing powerful, tan arms that had been built by hauling ropes instead of some overpriced gym. His jaw held the stubble of five o'clock shadow, confirming he had been at work all day, making the scar on his chin look more menacing.

Austin's bright blue eyes gleamed, and a slow smile grew across his face, revealing fangs to go with the bite.

"Nice costume," she said, aware that she felt all sorts of feelings she had no business feeling. If she was honest with herself, the hours she had spent online to find a costume that would get Austin's attention could've qualified for a part-time job.

"I like yours way better."

Caitlyn looked down. She smiled to the ground, pleased that he approved. "Thanks. I was going for the history vibe," she said, not meeting his eye. "You know I was thinking of coming as Cleo—"

When she looked up, Austin stood inches away from her. She froze.

"I like this a lot," he said in a low voice that sounded more like a purr from a large cat.

"Oh." Her brain dumped the English language right when she tried to come up with something to say. "That's cool."

He smiled again in the night as if he could sense her pulse. Caitlyn wondered what one of those fangs might feel like grazing on her neck, a thought she immediately regretted because of the shot of heat that spiked her temperature. Any second now, she'd start sweating through her shirt despite the fresh, night air.

Sexy, Caitlyn, real sexy, she thought.

"I love your hair," Austin said while admiring it. The smell of his aftershave seemed stronger out here, which made no sense at all. She studied the column of his neck, now inches from her face. His tie lay slack, exposing the hint of his collarbone under his unbuttoned collar. Caitlyn wanted to put her hand there and peel it away, revealing more skin.

"Thanks," she said. "It took forever. That's why I was late." She didn't mention why she had taken so long with her hair and makeup. Getting the scarf over the victory roll hairstyle had taken several tries before she got the hang of it.

"It's just like it was," Austin said in such a low voice, Caitlyn almost couldn't hear him.

Caitlyn drew in a shaky breath. The autumn air had a

chill, and the stars sparkled overhead. The bass from the school floated over the air and reached their ears. "I'm glad you like it," she said, looking up at him.

Austin met her eyes, inches from her face. Caitlyn knew she should be ashamed. Her mother and family would've disapproved of everything that was happening, yet she stayed, rooted to the spot.

"I may have to start calling you Rosie," Austin said, giving her another long look. Caitlyn could almost feel her blood sizzle as his eyes passed over her.

She had tried to match Rosie the Riveter as close as possible. Her cuffed denim shirt and red headscarf did most of the talking, but Caitlyn had gone the extra mile and ordered the baggy, blue work pants, which were cuffed to reveal bright red socks and work boots.

"I knew you liked World War II—" she started to say.

Caitlyn shut up immediately when she realized what she had just revealed. The shift in the air told her Austin had realized it too. He had frozen solid in front of her. She wasn't even sure he was breathing, not that she was all that interested at the moment. Having the earth suddenly swallow her whole seemed so much more appealing.

"Well, I better head back," she said, mortified.

Austin put a hand out to stop her. His steady fingers touched the outside of her shoulder.

"Caitlyn?" he asked.

"Yeah?" she said, not wanting to look up at him. Caitlyn looked down at the red socks, feeling her face warm despite the dropping temperature. She hadn't known exactly what she wanted when she had bought them online to complete the look.

Caitlyn ran her tongue over her teeth. After the fifth try at home, she finally managed to avoid any red lipstick on her teeth, but the fear of a streak sealed her lips just in case.

Warmth radiated across the cold void between them. Caitlyn could feel him watching her face.

"Look at me," Austin said, his low voice soft but firm. He didn't move, waiting on her. The darkness obscured the forties-style work boots she was ashamed to admit she'd special ordered based on how much he seemed to know about the decade.

Caitlyn could feel his gaze on her face. She held her breath. Now they were alone outside, and if she didn't do something soon, they'd freeze. Reluctantly, Caitlyn raised her eyes.

Tropical blue pools almost glowed back at her in the dark. Intensity thrummed out of Austin. His tight jaw reminded her of the muscles she couldn't see under his shirt. One corner of his mouth pulled back, revealing a smirk that Caitlyn thought about more than she cared to admit. He raised an eyebrow, sending a shockwave over her already frigid arms.

"I love it."

Caitlyn's heart bloomed in her chest. "Really?" she asked.

Austin nodded, sending her into orbit. Tension flowed out of her shoulders. A breathy giggle of relief mixed with embarrassment escaped her.

"I kind of hoped you would," she said, beaming. No need to mention the hours that had gone into this. At least she could keep some dignity.

Austin's smirk grew into a full smile, showing off his fake fangs that looked real. "Come here," he said.

Austin stood inches from her now, and as she drew in air, the whispers of his aftershave tempted her nose to bury into him and smell more. The fang marks, oozing with fake blood, looked even more real up close. So close. He stood about a head taller than her, his chest in front of her, and she tilted her chin up to meet the heavy blue gaze blazing down over her. Blond stubble on his jaw glinted in the dim light.

The bass from inside thumped through the brick walls of the school gym, over the tennis courts, and out to the back fields where they stood alone under the old oak tree. A leaf broke away and fell with clumsy grace behind Austin, catching the light of the full moon as it fluttered on the chilled October breeze, raising bumps on Caitlyn's exposed arms and neck. The flimsy costume held little warmth, and the chill began to creep through the fabric, sending a shiver down her spine.

Warm, rough hands cupped her face, and his eyes, burning like blue flames, drew her in closer as he tilted his head to one side. Caitlyn's eyes widened at the contact. He halted, waiting, his touch light and calm. When he didn't move, she searched his eyes. She ran her tongue over her lower lip and didn't pull away, but pressed forward the barest inch, granting him permission, hoping for more. Austin pulled her toward him before lowering his lips to meet hers, accepting her invitation. The contact sent sparks from the crown of her head through every part of her skin like she had been struck by lightning.

Soft and warm, his mouth melded to hers. He tasted like the coffee he loved, and Caitlyn craved to know more of him. Caitlyn leaned into his chest and opened her lips in welcome, beckoning. His hands left her face, their warmth lingering on her cheeks, and wrapped around her shoulders, enveloping her in strength and heat. Austin took a moment to pull out the plastic fangs. His mouth yielded, and they explored each other, thirsty for more. Heat rose in her chest in spite of the cool breeze. Caitlyn raised her arms and wrapped them around his broad shoulders, pulling him close and holding him against her to bring her body into full contact with his. Austin backed them both against the truck and ran his hands along the length of her back as they tasted each other for the first time, alone in the dark.

A voice came from the walkie-talkie at the small of his back. Its sound broke them apart like a frigid ax. Breathing heavy, Austin slid his arms from her as he pulled back and swore under his breath before reaching behind him to yank the walkie-talkie off his belt. His parted lips, swollen from the pressure of her own, drew in a hard breath as he watched her with hungry, bright eyes, looking like a real version of the vampire he impersonated for the dance.

Caitlyn's heart raced in her chest, and she licked her humming lips, now cold in his absence. The heat that radiated from him faded to dying embers, too weak to fight off the cold. Caitlyn felt her heart sink as she watched his calm mask of professionalism drop back into place, shielding his wants and needs from even her.

"Austin, what's your location?" Laurie's voice crackled over the walkie-talkie again with more urgency.

He swore under his breath.

"Checking something outside. What do you need?"

He looked pissed as hell and ready to throw the godforsaken thing across the fifty-yard line.

"Can you please come to the auditorium? We need you to take a look at something."

"10-4," he said before reaching out to take her hand. Caitlyn gave it to him, knowing instinctively they'd have to let go when they reached the lights of the parking lot.

CHAPTER 15

Austin wanted to punch something as he stomped into the gym to find Laurie. The DJ had moved into a deafening, crazed techno beat and had the lights flashing right along. Standing there could give almost anyone a migraine.

Whatever Laurie wanted had better be damn good. Austin hadn't been that excited since VJ-Day, which had been the best party of his life. He looked around at the gyrating crowd of teens, unimpressed. These kids thought they were having fun, but they had no idea what fun even looked like.

Seeing Caitlyn across the gym had sent Austin's pulse into orbit. The Rosie the Riveter costume could've put him on a crash cart, between her whiskey-colored hair up in a victory roll with the scarf that matched her plump red lips, and the work pants that showed off her tiny waist and ample curves, all without being too revealing.

The crowd in the gym let out a shrill scream of excitement when the music changed again, and they started jumping in unison, stressing the already abused hardwood floor. Austin could feel a headache setting up in his temple already, and he hadn't even found Laurie. Having his arms around Caitlyn had lit his spine on fire. He hadn't known precisely what he'd planned to do when he'd headed out to the fields, but he knew he'd wanted her to himself. When his dream woman walked into a room, he didn't feel like sharing the view.

The kiss had only tempted him more. What he'd intended to be a sweet thank you had shocked him with its heat and desire. He hadn't been a shrinking violet, but he had never had a kiss like that. That Caitlyn also hinted she had worn that costume for him made him want to pick her up and rush home to partake in all sorts of fun explorations in the dark. Even the work boots matched what he remembered from the mechanics on the boat back in the forties.

So yeah, the building had better be on fire or collapsing, and so far, he didn't see any damage, which made him want to throw a chair.

Caitlyn had taken up a position on the perimeter when they walked in separately. Austin had waited a full minute in the locker room before coming out into the open. In that time, he had watched her make easy conversation. Her red lips looked so perfect and inviting. The gym may have been absolute mayhem, but all he could see was Caitlyn, and she was perfect.

Austin's eyes locked on Laurie, still over by the now empty photo backdrop.

Seeing no immediate emergency, Austin wanted to just avoid her, but she saw him first and waved him over. Austin shoved his fists in his pockets and tried to drum up his normal easygoing nature, but the set to his jaw was hard to control.

"Hey, we couldn't find you," Laurie said with a smile.

"Stepped outside for a bit. What's going on?" Austin said. Better to cut to the chase and deal with whatever bullshit had happened so he could get back to more important matters. Like spending time with the hottest woman he'd seen in seven decades.

"We handled it," Laurie said with a wave of her hand, but her eyes looked concerned. "Why don't we go into the library for a bit?"

Austin had two choices. He could tell her to fuck off, but that would only upset the person who helped him numerous times during his day. Laurie ran the school and managed to keep all the teachers and admin from going crazy. She deserved respect, and it wasn't entirely her fault that her timing was shit. So Austin went with option number two, forcing a curt nod before following along through the throng of kids in costumes bouncing all over the place.

Once they were inside the library, the quiet seemed awe-inspiring and put the volume in the gym into perspective.

"What's up?" Austin said, pulling a chair up to the desk and turning it around backward before he straddled it.

"God, it's so hot in there. I just needed a break."

Austin nodded and waited for her to continue. She wouldn't have asked him here without reason.

"Did you see Caitlyn's costume?"

Oh yeah, he saw it alright. The best thing he'd laid eyes on in about forever. "Yeah, I noticed it. She did a great job with the history vibe," Austin said, trying to act cool.

Laurie took off her hat and set it on the circulation desk before giving him a look. "Noticed she was gone too," she said in a quiet voice.

"Huh? That's weird. Didn't see her." He knew what she could prove and what she couldn't. There were perks to being the person who fixed the cameras around the property.

"I get that you would be attracted to her—"

"Never said that," said Austin.

"You don't have to," Laurie said, looking down at him. "I taught you, remember?"

Laurie had been one of the few teachers Austin had liked as a student. Before Lizzy took over as the history teacher, Laurie had the subject. She hadn't put up with any crap but had a subtle way of going about things. It helped tremendously that she had seen his intelligence and recognized his behavior problems were caused by mind-numbing boredom.

Austin didn't say anything. Couldn't incriminate someone who didn't confirm or deny, though in her usual way, Laurie was looking for tells of confirmation.

She came around the front of the desk and leaned into it before sighing and looking at him. "You know the rules. She's a nice girl, but she's not one of us."

"Never said she was," Austin countered. He fought to keep his jaw relaxed but had a feeling he might be losing the battle. He wanted to point out that she'd been sitting there when John had hoisted this little assignment on him, but then that would confirm everything Laurie was thinking.

"I just want you to be careful," Laurie said, looking concerned. "At some point, she's going to leave. I don't want to see her get hurt. Or you."

Austin eyed Laurie and sized up her words. She seemed sincere enough. One of the many things he liked about her was that she didn't sugarcoat shit.

Laurie looked at him. The lines on her face had deepened since he had last taken the time to study her. "Just be careful," she said when he didn't speak. "This is only temporary, and you know it."

CHAPTER 16

Caitlyn hadn't seen Austin since the dance, and she was kinda okay with that. Kinda.

She missed their chess games and conversations, but she had all sorts of feelings after what had been a really stellar kiss. Sure, she had dressed that way on purpose, hoping to impress him for reasons she didn't want to think about, but once it had reached the point where their lips met, Caitlyn knew she was in over her head, especially when he brought his finger to his lips, asking for her silence.

The last relationship she had been in ended poorly. She was too much up in her head for this and she was pretty sure that somewhere in her contract, or the general rules of life, was the idea that getting with the boss was a big no-no.

She wasn't that type of person, and after all, it was only November. She needed to cool it before things got out of hand. Given where her emotions were, it was no wonder she was all over the place. For all she knew, inappropriate feelings for superiors could be part of the grieving process, but getting fired for sleeping with the boss was the last thing she needed. She needed this job and the great pay it had. All things considered, Caitlyn needed to get a handle on things and fast.

This close to Thanksgiving, all of the kids were getting antsy. Incidents were popping up left and right, everything from boys fighting over the girls in the halls to girls melting down in the bathroom over boys. The teachers were cranky, the kids were cranky, and the data showed it.

There wasn't a salon or anything like a spa on Brightrock, so Caitlyn had taken the weekend to recharge with a trip to Nantucket. Getting distance from Austin seemed like the best idea possible.

Since she had never been before, Caitlyn booked herself a room and treated herself to a haircut and spa day, followed by shopping. The eating alone didn't bother her so much anymore, as long as she had a book or her phone.

Caitlyn sat on a bench waiting on the ferry to go back to Brightrock with a few shopping bags of clothes she had treated herself to sitting next to the new moccasins she had splurged on at Murray's Toggery Shop.

The visit had been a success, and she was already looking forward to her trip back. Nantucket in November hung on during the winds that ripped through the old whaling town. Old brick buildings stood against the onslaught, having seen far worse, while a few remaining tourists and locals ducked in for cover.

A few leaves skittered over the brick sidewalk by Caitlyn, and she pulled her coat closer while the bags shook with the wind. She checked her watch to see how much longer until the ferry arrived, before going back to the historical fiction she had gotten from the Nantucket Bookworks.

The story sucked her in until she got the sense that someone was watching her.

Caitlyn looked up and noticed a man wearing an old gray raincoat watching her from across the wharf. He sat on the bench, one knee over the other, facing her. The wind swept his white hair around his face, but he was too far away to make out much more detail other than he was wearing a red, Nantucket baseball cap. Something about him was familiar, but she couldn't put her finger on it.

She glanced around and saw that indeed she was alone, yet the man sat facing her and made no attempt to look anywhere else.

Caitlyn shifted on the bench and took a quick peek at her watch to check the time. The ferry would be there in ten minutes, which wasn't long enough to get up and go back into a store. Many of them had already closed. Caitlyn pulled out her cell phone even though there wasn't anyone she could call anymore.

Caitlyn tilted her head and tried to get a look at the man without being too obvious. He looked right back at her. She fought the urge to jump. So it wouldn't look like she had watched him, she craned her head as if she was stretching while reading her book.

Out of the corner of her eye, the man stood but kept his eyes on her. Caitlyn sucked in a breath and gripped the book tighter in an effort not to squirm under his gaze. The wind blew again and through her hair she could see him taking steps in her direction. She reached up and tucked her hair behind her ear so she could see better. Another quick check of her surroundings told her no one was around.

She knew she had options. Her phone was in her hand, though with no one to call it might as well have been useless. Still, she could act like she was talking to someone as a deterrent. The keys to her apartment back on Brightrock were deep in the bowels of her purse. Trusting her vibes, she stilled and watched for his next move. It was possible that he, too, was waiting on the ferry to Brightrock and just needed the time.

When he kept coming closer, Caitlyn looked up and met his stare head-on. In a rush, the face clicked into place in her memory. The man from the ferry studied her, his eyes narrowing as if he was trying to place her as well.

"Hello," she said in a pleasant, but firm and clear voice.

"Are you going on the ferry to Brightrock?" he asked in a gravelly voice that one would expect from an old sailor. Tan, weathered, and lined, this man looked as though he had spent more than a few winters on Nantucket and most of the summers on the water. Something told her that if she saw his hands, they would be the size of baseball gloves, calloused and hard, but at the present moment he had them shoved in his pockets.

"Yes, it'll be here in a few minutes."

He nodded at her, not taking his eyes off of her, which was unsettling. Caitlyn kept glaring right back at him, giving off what she hoped was her best I'm-reading-don't-fuck-with-me attitude. Women who had experienced assault talked about the power of showing strength.

"I work for the ferry. Have all my life." The stare continued as he studied her face to an extent which was making her more than a little uncomfortable as his eyes raked over her features.

"That's nice. Is there something I can help you with?" she asked in a clipped tone. She really hoped he wasn't going to be working on her ferry but had a feeling she was about to be disappointed.

He kept staring at her with a frown on his face.

"I've seen you before."

"Can I help you?" There was a challenge in her voice along with a question. Caitlyn considered the possibility the man in front of her had a delay and weighed it against the potential that he was just a rude lech who needed to be reported. Regardless of what it was, he continued to loom over her.

The man stared hard at her in an unkind way. "We don't see many people from Brightrock and never a new face. I remember everyone that has come through here."

"I'm sorry, what did you say your name was?" She was starting to get pissed off now. Caitlyn hadn't done a damn thing to him, and she felt like she was getting the third degree.

"Schmidty. Mark Schmidt. I've been here my whole life."

"That's nice." A horn announced the arrival of the ferry. Caitlyn all but crumpled with relief but somehow managed to keep her spine ramrod straight in her show of strength. "Have a good day." She marched off, and though she didn't look back once, Caitlyn was sure Mark Schmidt watched her the whole way down the wharf and onto the ferry.

It wasn't until she was boarded and seated inside the warmth of the small cabin that she glanced back, only to meet his eerie stare from behind a door.

Mark Schmidt's eyes bored into her. Caitlyn frowned and moved to get up to report him, but he turned and walked away.

A shiver went over her, and though Caitlyn sat back down, there was something in her gut that told her Mark Schmidt had memorized her face and would be thinking about it all night.

But why he would care, she didn't know.

CHAPTER 17

Austin let himself into his cramped office and flopped into the chair, scrubbing his face. He hadn't slept well again. It had been a long time since he couldn't get someone off his mind, and he wasn't used to it.

Over the weekend, Austin had also come to the conclusion he didn't give two shits what John Clarkson thought about Caitlyn, but he wasn't stupid. Running to her when he'd been told to back off wouldn't get him any points with anyone, but he hadn't been able to stop thinking about her since their too-brief kiss.

Watching her from afar for the remainder of the Halloween dance had been an exercise in restraint. Austin had been ready to meet up later, when Laurie had intercepted Caitlyn and talked her ear off all the way to her car and then some.

The problem continued for the next two weeks. The following Friday he made a point to go straight to her classroom after the bell only to find the door locked and her talking with Laurie inside. Over the weekend, Austin took a couple of passes by the ice cream parlor, only to miss Caitlyn every time.

Finally, after two weeks of nothing more than quick waves in the halls, Austin broke down and texted her, only to learn Caitlyn was off the island on a trip to Nantucket. Austin had been about to lose control and text that he missed her, something he never thought he would've done, when she said she'd stop by his office as soon as possible for them to catch up. Austin wished she would've told him about her trip. He would've loved to have her alone, away from prying eyes, to learn more about her and maybe sneak in another kiss. He frowned to himself when he thought of what people would say at work if that ever got out.

All of it was asinine. John had ordered him to keep an eye on her, but now, Austin was the bad guy for getting too close. None of it made a bit of sense. Caitlyn had been on Brightrock for two months now and didn't have the slightest suspicion about anything. John should've started to relax.

In fact, Caitlyn was a great addition to the school, and sharing another kiss wouldn't hurt. It wasn't like he was telling her about the island. They were both adults who worked together. That was it, nothing more.

An uneasy feeling popped up in his gut when he remembered Laurie's voice saying "temporary." Not wanting to think about it, Austin crumpled the paper in front of him and threw it in the trash can, only to watch it bounce off the rim.

It was the Monday before the long Thanksgiving break. He wondered if Caitlyn had plans for the holiday and committed himself to finding out before the day ended.

Austin popped his Navy coffee tumbler under the single cup coffee maker and sat down to check his email, listening to the little machine percolate. Soon, the aroma of coffee filled the small office, and he'd read most of what had been sent over the weekend.

As a rule, Austin didn't check email on the weekends. Instead, he preferred to get to work earlier than anyone else and savor the quiet, which helped ramp him up. For him, the school day was usually a whirlwind of energy. Running from problem to problem both fed his hunger for action and exhausted him daily, but he loved the work.

The only issue had been that planning for his lessons had become a day-by-day affair, and after a sip of black coffee, Austin dug around in his filing cabinet for something he could assign the students that had to do with their current unit on mitosis.

Two knocks turned him around.

Caitlyn stood in a pair of gray pants and a white shirt with a blue sweater over it. Her honey-colored hair was shorter and shaped around her face.

"Hey," Austin said with genuine excitement. He slid the drawer home, figuring he had plenty of time to pull something together. He had taught the class for thirty-five years now, so he wasn't worried. It was part of the reason he still agreed to teach a few classes even though he had taken on the role of admin. "What's going on? I've been meaning to catch up with you. How was your trip?"

"It was nice." Caitlyn's smile didn't match her eyes.

"Yeah?" he asked. "I want to hear all about it." God, it felt good to see her, like a puzzle piece had just clicked into place.

Caitlyn turned and stared at his bookcase, which held a series of old science textbooks, gifts from students, wrestling mementos, and trinkets he had picked up in his travels. "Nothing much. Did the tourist thing. Got my hair cut. Did some thinking. People talked to me, at least. Listen, I've been meaning to talk to you. About what happened at the dance…"

Austin set his cup down and leaned forward into his chair. "Wait, back up. What is that supposed to mean?"

"The, um, kiss?"

Austin waved a hand. "No, not that. People don't talk to you?" From where he was sitting, Laurie and John wouldn't leave her alone. Sure, the others had been warned, but that didn't mean they shouldn't say anything to her.

Caitlyn puffed out a breath from her lower lip, which took Austin back to the kiss at the dance. It was pink and didn't have any of the slick, glossy shit many women put on, making it perfectly kissable. Her bangs flew up in her face with the sigh.

"You and Laurie are the only ones who talk to me around here."

"That's not true," he started to say, even though he knew in his heart she spoke the truth. And worse, he knew the reason for it.

"Okay, Connie too, but I walk around here and doors close as I pass. Conversations end. Whatever the joke is, I seem to always just miss it." She spun around on her heel and sat down in the guest chair in front of him, staring at his coffee tumbler. "It's isolating, and it sucks."

Austin leaned in so they were only a few feet apart even with the desk between them. "Hey, don't say that. You're great here. I'm sure people will warm up after you've been here awhile."

"It's already Thanksgiving."

Perfect opening.

Austin leaned back in his chair and pumped his fist. "Yeah, it is! I'm about to get me some stuffinnnng. What are your plans?"

Caitlyn shrugged and looked at him. "I don't know. I guess I'll get a turkey."

He flopped down, so the chair hit hard. "Wait, you're not

going home?" He had been sure she was going to go back to Louisiana.

Her eyes dropped down and away from his, finding keen interest in the pencils and pens he had shoved into the coffee mug on his desk, which hadn't held a beverage since he could remember. "Ah, no. I'll be here."

"Want to come to my family's house? No one should be alone on Turkey day." He could do damage control later. Besides, it was always easier to ask for forgiveness than permission, wasn't it?

Caitlyn looked at Austin, unsure. "Are you sure? I don't want to impose."

"Of course I'm sure!"

"Well, I'll think about it. I really don't want to be a burden. I didn't come here looking for an invite. I really didn't."

"Well, you have one. I can't believe I didn't know you didn't have plans. Your family isn't coming?" he asked, probing for more information.

Caitlyn looked down and fidgeted with her hands, twisting her ring around her finger. She shook her head before looking back at him. "Thanks for the invite. Are you sure?"

"I'm sure."

"Sure, sure?"

"Sure, sure."

"Can I bring something?"

"Yeah, bring something Louisiana-inspired. I've been eating the same stuff for years, and a little spice wouldn't hurt anything." The same could be said for the whole island.

"Okay, well, I'll think about it." She stood. "I'd better head back to my room. Thanks again for inviting me."

"Sure thing. It was the least I could do. Hey, wait a

second," Austin said when she turned to the door, ready to open it, one hand on the knob.

"Yeah?"

"What else happened on your trip? You don't seem that relaxed."

Caitlyn shrugged. "It's probably nothing."

"Okay?"

"There was this weird guy on the ferry. Kinda spoiled the end."

Austin's chest tightened. Caitlyn didn't know anything about them, so there was no reason she needed to take the same precautions as the rest of them, but still. He wanted to say all sorts of things, but everything that came to mind revealed too much.

"Don't go off the island again without telling me, okay?" That felt weird to say and probably sounded strange to hear.

"Okay…"

"It's just…people get weird and jealous of us, you know? And besides, I can take you there in my boat. Save you a trip on the ferry and all that."

She smiled again. "Okay, thanks."

"You bet."

After she left, Austin stood in his office, staring at the closed door. Her loneliness made his chest ache, and the fact no one else was talking to her pissed him off even more.

CHAPTER 18

Caitlyn pulled the casserole dish out of the oven. The rice dressing smelled like home and brought up a series of memories that touched her heart and made her long for something with such desperation she had to look away from the dish.

She glanced at the clock on the stove, knowing Austin would arrive soon to pick her up. Caitlyn kept picking at the hem of her skirt. She didn't know anything about Austin's family, let alone dress code, so she had opted for a tan turtleneck sweater and mostly black plaid pencil skirt with tan and burgundy highlights. Good manners made her dig out the black tights and heels.

She crept down the stairs in the heels she hadn't worn since the beginning of the school year, clutching the casserole dish, when she ran into Austin halfway.

"Hey...woah, let me get that for you," Austin said, reaching out to take the carrier from her hands, freeing her up to grip the handrail.

"Thanks."

"You look great."

"So do you." He did. Forgoing his regular black suit pants and necktie, Austin was dressed in a rust-colored sweater that looked to be super soft over a collared shirt. He wore dark jeans with brown leather shoes that shone despite the gloomy and damp November morning.

"I clean up pretty good. At least, when I want to," he added with a wink.

They hustled to the truck, which he'd left idling in the lot. Austin pulled the door open for her and once she was seated, handed her the casserole dish which she held in her lap.

"What'd ya make?"

Caitlyn squirmed in the seat, wishing she hadn't agreed to come. "Rice dressing."

"What's that?"

Oh boy, she thought.

"Um, it's a rice dish, with meat and spices."

"Isn't dressing the word for stuffing?"

"Yeah, I think so."

"Does it taste like stuffing?"

"You mean like Stove Top?" she asked, hoping not, as her mother would have taken strong offense at the comparison.

"Yeah."

"Not really."

"Oh, okay. That's cool."

Caitlyn swallowed as they turned off the main road, which had been their tour route at the beginning of the school year. "Thanks again for inviting me."

"You're welcome. No one should be alone on a holiday."

"Mhmm," was all she could manage. Nerves started to flutter in her chest. This had seemed like a good idea at the time, but now that they were actually going, she wasn't so sure. Lounging at home in her robe, watching the parades from the couch until it was time for her to pop a small turkey breast for one into the oven sounded like a much better idea.

"I'm surprised you didn't go home for the break," Austin said.

She looked out the window, pretending to watch the scenery. "You know the cost of flying these days."

"What about Christmas?"

"What do you mean?" she asked, still looking out the window, hoping he would drop it.

"Uh…are you going back home for the break? It's longer."

"No, probably not." Definitely not. Caitlyn couldn't even bear to think about it. "So, tell me about your parents? What should I expect?"

Now it was Austin's turn to clam up, apparently. "I mean, they're parents. I don't know how else to describe them. Anyway, you'll see for yourself. Here we are."

He pulled into a driveway which was flanked by two brick pillars, each topped with a wrought iron light and decorated with a wreath and red bow. On either side of the driveway, dense, tall pine trees obscured any view of the surrounding properties. The only thing that lay before them was a pristine paved driveway, lined on one side with expensive cars all parallel parked on the right. Caitlyn squeezed her toes in her heels, already dreading the walk, the standing, and then the walk back.

"Don't worry, it's not as long as it looks," Austin said, opening his side, taking the casserole dish from her, and hopping out. They started walking down the driveway past a few BMWs, Mercedes, and other cars she didn't recognize but still looked expensive. By comparison, the Ford looked lost, like a landscaper who had parked in the wrong part of the country club.

"So anything I should know about your family? Crazy uncles, weird cousins, that sort of thing?" she asked, hoping to break the tension.

Austin shot her a small grin. "All of the above."

"Wow, this should be fun."

"It'll be entertaining at least."

"Families usually are," she said, trying not to think of her own.

"Yeah, well, we're about to get one heck of a show," he said, sucking in a breath.

"Were your parents okay with me crashing?"

"I didn't tell them."

Caitlyn stopped cold while her heart sank into a pit in her stomach.

"What?"

"I didn't tell them. Come on, let's go." Austin stopped and waited for her to walk again.

"Did you just say that you didn't tell them I was coming? What are they going to think when I just show up?" Panic gripped her, almost as hard as she was clutching her small handbag.

"It'll be fine. Come on."

Caitlyn stood frozen to the spot and watched him walk away. This was her chance. She could go back to her apartment and avoid certain embarrassment. With a quick glance behind her, she knew the walk back to her place was doable, but it would take at least an hour if not longer.

On cue, her big toe throbbed like it always did in these shoes. Every time she wore the damn things, she swore it would be the last time, but inevitably she would forget, put them on, and her toes would be numb by lunch.

Austin glanced back at her. "Seriously, it'll be fine. Besides, it's better to ask for forgiveness anyway. Don't worry, if anything they'll be annoyed with me, not you."

"That doesn't make me feel any better."

"Look, if it gets weird, we can go, but I don't think it's going to get too weird. Besides, since you'll be there, everyone will have to play nice." His features softened into the warm, almost goofy grin that Caitlyn knew too well. Guilt swamped her.

They shouldn't have kissed at the Halloween dance, and she shouldn't be here right now, but despite the fact that he was her boss and this was definitely not the right time, everything felt right.

Austin held his grin in place and raised one eyebrow in question. God help her, but that did it. Caitlyn stepped forward, and they walked together in silence until, at the top of the hill, the woods opened up to reveal a stunning sight.

"My God," Caitlyn said, trying not to gawk. The panty-hose had been a good bet.

A straight-up mansion stood in front of her, the kind she had only seen as a visitor with a map in her hand after she'd paid admission.

The Victorian house had a widow's walk, turrets, and spires that soared upwards into the sky. New, blonde cedar shingles adorned with white trim made the house look like a costly gingerbread project with extra-large windows. A wrap-around covered porch held a kaleidoscope of pump-kins, gourds, and hay bales arranged as if on the cover of a magazine which, now that Caitlyn thought about it, was a genuine possibility.

Perfect green grass swelled up and around stone walls that guarded slate patios, adorned with wrought iron furni-ture. As they approached, Caitlyn could hear water trickling and noticed a pond nestled in the garden bed where a small fountain beckoned her to sit and relax.

"Austin, this is unreal," Caitlyn said, almost breathless.

"You know, I don't really pay that much attention to be honest. It's always just been my family's house."

"Did you grow up here?"

"Yeah, though personally, I always thought it looked like the home of a vampire sea captain." He set the casserole carrier down and put his hands on his hips. Austin smiled as he stared up at the structure with her.

"Man, if you saw where I grew up. Pah!" Caitlyn said without thinking.

Austin's gaze swiveled and zeroed in on her. Immediately she wished she could take that statement back. She did not need anyone to talk about her home. If they did, she'd probably start crying on the spot.

"I'd love to see it," he said, low and serious.

There was no way. Even considering Austin had been in the navy, his background couldn't have looked more opposite to everything Caitlyn had ever known. She had to hold in a snort.

"Are you ready?" she asked.

"Caitlyn."

"Yeah?"

His eyes hadn't left her face, and the effect was unnerving. She looked back at the house, noting that the rocking chairs had several pillows and throws that were just begging to be snuggled around someone. Caitlyn smelled smoke and wondered if they had a fire pit around back, or if it was just the fire in the hearth.

"Look at me."

"What?" She turned to face him, just as he caught her chin in his hands and held her with the lightest touch, before raising her face to look him in the eye.

Caitlyn held her breath.

Austin's hands were warm, his fingers delicate. His blue eyes were shining despite the gloomy November day, and this close, she could see the stubble on his cheek and jawline where a thin scar hooked around his chin.

"Don't treat me any different."

It was as if he had read her mind. "I'm not."

His hand didn't move away. Instead, one finger crept up

Caitlyn's jaw the barest distance, sending goosebumps scattering up her arms.

Caitlyn knew that doing this right here was a bad idea, but so help her God, she didn't pull away. There was something about him that drew her in. Something more. A tug inside her that pushed away all of the boundaries and cast off the rules. There could be consequences, and nothing changed who they both were, but none of that mattered in that moment. All Caitlyn wanted was to lean into him.

Austin's eyes pleaded into hers, flicking from one to the other, searching for proof that she wouldn't see him differently. Caitlyn wanted to tell him that it didn't matter, but the air in her lungs had vanished, and she felt her chest tighten, almost crushing her when the rogue finger grazed her hair behind her ear.

Her lids lowered in bliss and then his lips met hers. A wave of excitement crashed into her, almost sending her knees out from under her. She slid both palms up his cloud-soft sweater and kissed him back.

Austin's hand cupped the back of her neck, while his other hand pulled her in closer, so their bodies pressed against each other. Austin was warm and stable. Caitlyn melted into him. Austin's hand swept up into her hair at the base of her neck and knotted his fingers deep against her scalp.

The heat rose between them. Caitlyn wanted more and parted her lips, inviting him in. Austin parted his own and flicked his tongue out the moment she did. They darted and explored each other's mouths. Austin's hand glided down to the small of her back and splayed open, pressing her even harder against his body, while Caitlyn wrapped herself around the back of his broad shoulders.

They both gasped for breath without breaking away. Starved, they held on fast to one another, pushing each other further, fueling the flames that had erupted between them. The first shot of heat flared inside her, making her want more, much more than was possible here. It clawed at her, urging her on. For relief, Caitlyn shifted her legs apart, only to have Austin's thigh fill the space and press hard against her core, igniting her even further.

A throat cleared from a few feet away.

Caitlyn's heart stopped. She sprang away from Austin. Panicked, she tried to straighten her skirt while moving as little as possible. She looked in the direction of the house and shrunk with horror.

A crowd of people stood at the windows and in the doorway, all staring out at them. A woman who looked to be in her late forties stood in the door. Her short hair was a blonde color, styled with artistic perfection like her home. The dark jeans looked almost as expensive as her crisp white shirt and leopard print sweater.

"Austin?" the woman said. "Perhaps you and your guest would like to come inside?"

Austin whisked up the stairs two at a time to hug her with one arm while kissing her on the cheek. "Hey, Mom. Happy Thanksgiving."

His mom hugged him back and beamed with a warm, knowing smile.

"Are you going to introduce me to your friend?"

"Oh no, no, no. We're not together."

An icy cold chill blasted away any lingering warmth from their kiss.

"This is just the new teacher," Austin continued. "She didn't have anywhere to go, and I figured we could squeeze in one more."

CHAPTER 19

Austin knew he had fucked up.

He stood on the porch before following in Caitlyn's wake as his mom gave her the tour.

It was a good thing he didn't have a problem with apologies. God knew he had made plenty, but something about Caitlyn threw him off.

True, she was the first to meet his parents, but she didn't know that. Hell, his mom would be thrilled that he'd finally brought someone around. Granted, it wasn't the person she wanted him to marry, but she'd get over that.

Caitlyn's face, when she looked at the house, made him see it in a whole new light. As much as he hated to admit it, he cared about what she thought of him. For years, he had prided himself on not caring about the opinions of others, but somehow she'd managed to blow her way right through his wall. The scariest part was that she did it without even trying. Shit, she probably didn't even know the effect she had on him.

He shouldn't have kissed her. Certainly not right in front

of the house in plain sight of everyone, but he couldn't help it.

Austin had only intended to reassure her he was the same goofball she knew, regardless of the number of commas in his family's portfolio. But his mind had switched off the moment they were close. He'd been drawn to her without conscious thought of what he was doing or where he was doing it. Then once it had happened, instead of backing off like a gentleman, he had gone totally haywire. Circuits fried. Off the deep end and with no way to come back up for air.

He'd kissed plenty of girls, but nothing came close to that.

Especially not while sober.

He wondered what would've happened if his mom hadn't intervened.

A warm flush rose up in him at the thought. Austin needed to get her away and explain himself as soon as possible. But given that she was surrounded by people, that wasn't going to happen anytime soon. He could almost feel the knots forming in his shoulders as he gritted his teeth, already annoyed with his family who, for the first time in history, managed to all be in the same room, focused on the same subject.

He had wanted to stick close to Caitlyn, but wouldn't you know she was being whisked away down the hall and out of earshot.

Not like she would listen to him anyway. He had been halfway up that tight black skirt before he blew it with his lame-ass introduction. He didn't know what they were, but given what had gone down, more than coworkers was probably a safe bet. He needed to make sure no one in his family told John.

"Hey, man, happy Thanksgiving," Ethan said at his elbow before a thick hand clapped him on the shoulder.

"Happy Thanksgiving," Austin said with far less joy in his

voice, giving Ethan a quick glance before turning back to see where his mom was taking Caitlyn.

"Well?"

"Well, what?"

When he didn't say anything else, Austin turned to face his brother. All beard now, Ethan managed to look the same age despite being younger, while still having Austin beat in size and height. Football turned finance, he was poured into a dark green sweater that made him look like an outdoorsman in Bangor, rather than the broker he was.

"Who is she?"

The usually spacious foyer now felt cramped and hot. "We work together."

"Oh, come on. You expect me to believe that after your little display?"

Austin ground his teeth, hoping they could just get on with the meal already, so he could get the hell out of here.

Ethan didn't budge.

"She's the new history teacher," he said in what he hoped was a matter-of-fact tone that would stem off further questions. Pointedly, he shut the front door behind him.

Ethan's eyebrows rose. "How is that possible?"

"New federal law and we needed a long-term substitute for Lizzy. She was the best one."

Austin's eyes tracked down the hall to where his mom had swept Caitlyn, hoping to catch a glimpse of her. Hopefully, his family wasn't peppering her with questions. When he had first thought about inviting her, Austin had been so preoccupied about the glaring problems, he had failed to consider how his family might react if they liked her. Or worse, he thought, if they all assumed he brought her to meet everyone.

"Dude, you're screwed." Ethan shook his head before taking another pull from his beer with a smug grin.

Austin thought about knocking the Sam Adams while Ethan was drinking so it would spill down his shirt and someone else could be miserable too.

Instead, with great composure and a passive expression, Austin turned to face his brother and said, "Oh yeah? How do you figure that?"

Ethan had the gall to chuckle. Austin tucked his hands in his pockets so he wouldn't be tempted to ruin Thanksgiving any more than he had. "Mom freaked out when she saw you guys." He paused to take another pull on his beer. "I don't want to alarm you, but there was hand-wringing."

"What the hell is that supposed to mean?"

"You're screwed."

"Yeah, you covered that already."

A burst of laughter followed by chatter came from the other room. Ethan threw an arm that felt like a log around Austin's shoulders. "You can call her whatever you want, but mom mentioned the word girlfriend." He laughed. "So that about settles it."

Oh, shit. "That's not how it is, and they all know it. All of them were warned about her by the council at the last renewal, which you missed by the way."

Ethan shrugged. "Work's a bitch. Yeah, mom was all flustered."

Austin's jaw clenched while he resumed grinding his molars down. He shrugged off his brother's arm. "Whatever. Doesn't matter what they think."

"Suit yourself, buddy."

Pissed now, he raised one eyebrow in Ethan's direction. "Want me to let them know about your little secret?"

All of the humor spilled right out of Ethan as his brows lowered. His voice dropped to a whisper and had an eerie calm to it. "That's a low blow."

"Then back the fuck off, okay?"

Ethan eyed him a few seconds, sizing him up. "Well, this is unexpected. You sure she's just a coworker? You're not acting like this is another hit it and quit it."

"I don't get in your business, do I?" asked Austin, the not-so-subtle threat still in his voice.

Ethan held up his hands. "Dude, don't bite me, but you're being weird."

"Why is everyone all up in my shit all of a sudden?"

"Gee, I don't know. You brought a girl to a holiday dinner for the first time and started sucking her face off in front of the fam. Must just be that we're a nosy bunch."

"Whatever." Austin glared into the library to their right. A warm fire crackled pleasantly for no one. For the first time he could remember, the leather chairs were all unoccupied.

"Hey, chill the fuck out, man. You're the only one making this weird."

Austin bit back the retort that he had already fired up. Feeling like a wolf cornered, he leaned back against the wall and took in the sounds around him.

CHAPTER 20

Caitlyn sat under a massive chandelier on a tiny folding chair wedged between Austin and his brother at the far corner of a table bigger than her kitchen. The room was painted a golden yellow, offset with bright white wainscoting and columns of all things. An oil painting of a ship caught in the turmoil of a storm dominated one side of the room, while the other had huge windows flanked by heavy sage drapes that stretched at least twenty feet up. Oak logs crackled in a large stone fireplace on the wall nearest to her. Squashed between two large men who weren't enjoying themselves, the flames made the room feel hot and smothering.

Dishes filled with food sat on the buffet table along the wall with the oil painting, showing offa picture-perfect meal. Tiffany candlesticks holding hand-dipped candles flanked an actual cornucopia bursting with autumnal flowers set on a thick tablecloth that draped over the edge of the table past her knees. Caitlyn wasn't sure if she should pull it up onto her lap or let the fabric rest around her calves where it tickled and made her skin itch. She squirmed in the tiny seat

118

and studied the crystal wine glasses, trying to determine why there were three and what she would do with each one.

Across the table sat a carousel of family members Caitlyn had met in a whirlwind. She didn't remember anyone's name and had managed to just smile and nod in the kitchen after Austin's mom had scooped her up. After a brief nice-to-meet-you, thank-you-for-coming, Caitlyn had shared her pitiful dish. A silver dome shaded the turkey from view. Mashed potatoes were piped—piped like a swirl with rosettes for God's sake—into a silver chafing dish seated over a warm flame. Sweet potatoes rested on an oval platter next to a set of matching tongs. Compared with the other dishes, Caitlyn knew for sure she would be taking most of the rice dressing in the little glass casserole dish home. Much like herself, it sat on the side between two larger dishes, awkward and out of place.

This had been a mistake. It didn't help that one of Austin's great aunts hadn't stopped giving her the eye since Austin tossed her aside like an ugly fish on the front step. The old woman's expression reminded Caitlyn of a nun at her elementary school who obviously hated children and never smiled. Instead of a habit, Mrs. Brooks sat wrapped in Hermès as if the chair were a throne, looking down with disdain and disapproval.

From the kitchen, another great aunt, or some such relation, eased into the room, burdened with age but smiling a warm glow. Caitlyn remembered her as Mrs. Taylor, who looked elegant and huggable at the same time while wearing a cream and brown suit. Something about her reminded Caitlyn of her Maw Maw back in Louisiana when she was a little girl.

"Come here and let me take a look at my boys." A knobby branch of an arm extended out with a diamond that rivaled the ice in her water glass and a Cartier watch dangled on the thin wrist where the jacket cuff ended. "Well, come on. I can't remember the last time I've seen you together." The woman's hair was a chestnut brown and cut short so that it framed her smiling face. As she walked, she braced herself on the backs of chairs, passing the nun look-alike who sat like a frog with her blue-black hair cropped tight.

Aunt Tee peppered them both with questions, as relatives do, then when satisfied, called back to Austin's mom in the kitchen. "Katie, what do you need help with? The boys are ready to pass the drinks."

"Can I help with anything?" Caitlyn stood.

"Thank you, dear. I'm sure we could use another person to bring out the bread and set it on the table. I think it's in the kitchen. Boys, go ahead." Aunt Tee waved them away so that the two large men lumbered off into the chaos of the kitchen.

Caitlyn knew when she heard an order. She entered the kitchen and saw some of Austin's family talking down at the other end of the enormous room. A marble island stretched almost as long as the dining room table on gleaming white cabinets. Austin's mom reached into a fridge that Caitlyn had first thought was a cabinet and began pulling out pitchers of water and shoving them in Austin's direction, while Ethan pulled a white wine from a wine fridge that was the size of Caitlyn's actual refrigerator back at the apartment.

"You okay?" Austin whispered in her ear.

The warmth of his breath rekindled the fire in her chest from the front lawn. Caitlyn tamped it down. He couldn't just abandon her and then swoop back around like everything was hunky-dory. This needed to end, and if it weren't for his whole family being around, she'd tell him so right now. Once this was all over, she was going to thank him with a firm handshake and walk away from Austin Brooks for good.

"I'm fine. Thank you," Caitlyn said, moving right along. It sounded bitchier than she wanted, but Austin deserved it. Thanksgiving be damned. He was the one who'd invited her here, after all. On top of the beautiful stove were two large Nantucket style baskets draped with crisp white napkins, open and waiting for the bread that must have still been inside the oven.

"Oh, here, let me help," Austin's mom said from behind her. She popped open a drawer to her left and pulled out a pot holder, before nudging it closed with her hip. She pulled out two pans of steaming rolls.

"Damn. A little too long. I let the staff go early, and now I don't know if I want to guzzle some wine or go double down on their Christmas bonuses. Thanks for taking these into the dining room. Alright, everyone, enough is enough. I said it's dinner time and I mean it. We'll start without you!"

"Geez, Happy Thanksgiving," someone Caitlyn hadn't met yet said from the living room where a football game ran at top volume.

"Fred, I'm a woman on the edge!" She turned to wink at Caitlyn and smiled. Fred sauntered in and put his empty wine glass on the counter.

"You're a beautiful woman on the edge, and I love you, honey." He put his hands on her hips and kissed her on the forehead.

"That's more like it," she said, smiling and leaning into him. "Round 'em up."

Everyone shuffled back to their seats. Caitlyn made her way around the room back to the safety of her out-of-place folding chair in what otherwise could've passed for a museum. Caitlyn hadn't seen this many artifacts since she could remember. Every time she turned around, she was actually touching something historic, and while she was no expert, she was pretty sure all of it was real.

While the antiques were real, the people must have been fake, or Austin came from good stock. His parents, relatives, and even his great aunts all looked great for their ages. Even Aunt Mary, who continued to glare at her like she had peed on the Aubusson rug, had minimal wrinkles. Then again, maybe she just didn't smile all that much.

"Ethan, put that phone down. I only get my family together a few times a year, and I plan to enjoy it. Thank you. Alright everyone, Happy Thanksgiving! I've decided to go informal this year. I've given the staff the rest of the day off, so we'll be serving ourselves after grace. Fred?"

Many of the people around the table looked surprised at what was apparently a new informality. Caitlyn wished helping herself seemed as exciting and different as it did to everyone else.

Austin's dad ambled into the room. He didn't look like the king of the castle, and he didn't look like he fit with Austin's mom. She looked like a model, and he looked more like a retired librarian with his tortoiseshell glasses askew. His rumpled green sweater looked worn with age, and the khakis looked like they were chosen based on comfort, not fashion. Maybe he had been in academia, Caitlyn wondered, but then she eyed one of the forks. Then again, perhaps not. Academia didn't pay the kind of money she was looking at.

"First I'd like to say Happy Thanksgiving!" Fred said, stretching his arms out wide with a distant smile on his face.

A chorus answered him in the same.

"It's great to see everyone. What a wonderful tradition to have carried on for so many years. You know, I really have started to lose count—yes, dear?" Austin's mom touched him on the arm and gave him a strange look. She leaned over and whispered something in his ear while pointing at Caitlyn. "Oh, that's right. A special welcome to Caitlyn who is not from the island. It is Caitlyn, right?"

Every eye turned toward her again. She wished she could hide under the expensive tablecloth. The pause lingered in the air. "Yes, sir. Thank you. I'm happy to be here," she said at last. Once again, always the outsider. She felt like a bug in a petri dish with everyone looking down at her.

His lips lifted in a smile toward her but did little to put her at ease. "Good. Well, I know enough to know sometimes it is better to be seen and not heard, and I believe the food has been tempting us long enough now that today is one of those times. God be praised and let's eat!"

Everyone grabbed plates and shuffled through the line.

"Katie, what's this new dish here toward the end?" one of the many cousins asked Austin's mom.

"Oh, shoot. I forgot. Everyone, Caitlyn brought us a dish to try!"

God, what a mistake this had been, she thought while scooping some mashed potatoes onto her plate. Austin had suggested she bring something Cajun, and clearly that had been the wrong move. She served herself a few glazed carrots and moved down the line.

When she reached the end of the buffet, her plate didn't look like Thanksgiving back home, but instead like Thanksgiving on every TV show she had seen right down to the cranberry sauce. She was almost at the end when she saw her rice dressing. About half remained. Even though people were most likely being polite, it felt better than having to take it all home untouched. Caitlyn smiled to herself and took a full helping. Austin followed behind and did the same.

Caitlyn eased around the large room back to her folding chair. Austin tried to catch her eye. She avoided him.

The family chatted around her, but Caitlyn stayed quiet, absorbing all the details. She had finished her plate when someone coughed down the table.

Across the table, Fred grabbed the glass of ice water. He

drained it in a few gulps before setting it back on the table, the ice cubes clinking together. "Woo, that dressing has got a kick, doesn't it? Katie, let me have your water."

"Do you need more?" Austin's mom asked, handing it over. "Caroline, can you pass me…great, thank you. Fred, here…oh my God!" Katie leaped up from her chair.

Fred's head snapped in her direction. "What's wrong?"

"Your face! Oh my God!"

"My face? What—"

"Holy shit, Dad," Austin said, jumping up out of the chair that clattered to the floor.

"Somebody do something! He's having a reaction to something."

Fred's face had turned bright red. The color rose up from the collar of his shirt and went right to his temple.

"Katie, I feel fine. Honestly, it's just a little spicy. Calm down."

No one listened to Fred. Katie kept insisting her husband should stay calm. Austin ran into the kitchen and came back, bringing a sopping wet hand towel.

"Oh my God, he has hives!" someone said, pointing in Fred's direction.

Sure enough, large lumps now covered Fred's neck and were growing toward his chin.

"Someone call the doctor!"

"I'm fine. I said I'm fine!"

"He needs to lie down!"

"Take his blood pressure!"

"What did he eat?"

"I ate the rice dish. I'm fine!"

Caitlyn's heart sunk into the pit of her stomach. A wave of goosebumps swept down her body, and heat rushed into her face.

"What was in that dish?" someone called out.

"It's fine!" Fred said again. "I'm fine! Katie, stop!"

As always, telling a woman to stop had the opposite effect, and the next thing Fred knew, he was on his back on the couch with an ice pack to his face and three relatives all trying to call the only doctor on the island. Caitlyn squatted on the floor next to Austin's father, holding an empty cup of what had been milk while spewing non-stop apologies.

"Don't worry about it," he said for what must've been the fourth time, but Caitlyn was too busy feeling miserable to count. "I'm feeling perfect now. Katie, no. Stop. It's Thanksgiving. Give the doctor a break. I mean it. Boys, help me up."

Austin and Ethan both knelt down and righted their father, whose color had improved considerably, meaning he no longer looked like a boiled crawfish, but more like a fisherman who had gotten too much sun.

Ethan clapped a hand on his dad's shoulder when he sat back down. "You can't handle heat anymore, Dad."

"Never could," said Austin.

Fred looked up at his boys and eyed them both. "Just wait until you're my age. Old pipes, boys. Old pipes. Now then, where were we?"

At Fred's insistence, everyone returned to eating. He finished what had been the remainder of his plate, including the now infamous rice dressing, which everyone else left on their plate. Caitlyn said nothing for the rest of the meal while she tried to blend in with the wall.

When all the plates were clear, the young adults sprang into action—collecting plates, silverware, and heading in line to the expansive marble kitchen. Scraps were scraped into the compost pail, dishes were rinsed, and both dishwashers were filled. Austin's mom raced in to marshal the troops only to be met with repeated shouts of "Go sit down" and "We got this, Mom." In response, she tuned all of them out and set to making the coffee and laying out the cream, sugar, and various pies. Ethan and Austin had taken over the hand-washing, while Caitlyn fell right into step ushering plates of pies and coffee orders to the elders of the family, who were still visiting in the large dining room.

Every time she came back with two cups fixed to Austin's family member's liking, she noticed something different in the large room. The wood-paneled, vaulted ceiling drew her eye up and made her feel small. Austin's Dad, relieved to not be under the scrutiny of his wife, had gotten up and was stoking the fire in the massive fireplace. Above the mantel, at least a dozen long guns that looked to be very old fanned out on the face of the stone. Interspersed were what seemed to be old handguns, similar to what a pirate might carry, as well as a series of swords.

Caitlyn set the bone china coffee cups down in front of the two great aunts. Only one of them thanked her. Not expecting anything to change, she surveyed the room to see if she had missed anyone before turning to head back to the kitchen.

"I noticed you were looking at the mantel," said the angry aunt. Caitlyn jumped in response and turned back around, not sure if that was an invitation to stay.

"I've never seen anything like it."

The aunt made a noise in her throat that sounded like a grunt of dissent. "I suppose not. Been in the family for years."

"That's incredible," Caitlyn said, looking back over to the display. It was an impressive show of power that, in her opinion, did the trick perfectly. "How old are they?"

"Seventeenth-century, most of them. A few in there are from the eighteenth. Fred keeps the newer antiques in the library."

Caitlyn felt her mouth drop open a bit before she snapped it shut. There were more?

"What do you teach again?"

Caitlyn turned and smiled pleasantly, happy to have something to talk about. "History."

"I see," said the aunt, who then remained silent.

Caitlyn wasn't sure what to do, and after another moment spent admiring the powerful display of wealth and violence, excused herself to get more pie for everyone.

She didn't know a tremendous amount about firearms. Sure, teaching history, chaperoning field trips, and having a natural curiosity had taught her the basics, but she was no expert. Still, the value alone suggested Austin's family had been wealthy for a very long time. She came back into the kitchen and took notice again of how it surpassed anything she had seen on TV. Maybe she could get a tour of the place and see something else. Lord knew, after the making out and the rice incident, this was the last time she was going to be invited here.

"I washed your dish," a voice said in her ear.

Caitlyn only turned half around toward Austin. "Thank you."

"All of the rice dressing was gone. I thought it was delicious." Why did he feel so close to her? If he thought for a moment this was buttering her up again after that little display, he had another thing coming.

"I'm glad you enjoyed it," she said before walking away into the gorgeous living room. Large leather couches filled the light and airy space across from a large TV mounted on the wall. Opposite her, another fireplace crackled happily away in a hearth decorated with a display of gourds and pumpkins. A mostly red Persian rug squished under her as she walked to Ethan, who still stood transfixed on the game. Large paintings of ships at sea and portraits of long-dead family members lined the walls. Many of them had a strong resemblance to Fred and Katie, which of course made complete sense.

Finally, the game went to commercial. Aware Austin stood steps behind her, she walked up to Ethan.

"Your parents' house is gorgeous. Really spectacular."

Ethan's eyebrows raised as if he was surprised she was talking to him again. "Yeah, Mom likes to decorate and all that. Drives Dad crazy."

"I'd love to see more of it if you have a second."

Ethan shot a glance behind her, no doubt to make eye contact with Austin.

"Sure," he said. "Let's walk around here to the library. I think that has the oldest crap— er, stuff. You said you teach history, right? Yeah, okay. Makes sense," he said when she nodded.

Ethan walked with her through the library and the study, which, apparently, were two different rooms. Protected in both were impressive displays of more art and more firearms, along with pieces of furniture named after a variety of French kings in addition to American furniture, which Caitlyn liked better. That wasn't all though.

There were books lined on shelves like soldiers, pieces of silver more beautiful than what had been in the dining room, and even musical instruments. Everything was old and well kept. The rooms each stood as a museum, encased in dark oak and cream silk brocade on the walls. If it weren't for the family photos in silver frames and the newest Apple computer on the desk, Caitlyn would've thought she was on tour in a house museum.

Ethan walked through and explained everything, simply at first, but as she asked more questions, he loosened up and talked more. Austin even chimed in a few times about memories tied to some of the items.

"Do you have anything from World War II?" she asked Austin after he told her about a sword from the Civil War carried at the Battle of Cedar Mountain. "I know you said that was your favorite."

Austin and Ethan looked at each other. A weird exchange passed between them. It was so brief that Caitlyn almost didn't catch it. Just a quick furrow between Ethan's brows before he intentionally relaxed them, creating a passive expression on his face.

"Not really," Austin said, shoving his hands in his pockets while looking at a porcelain lamp of a lady in repose on the desk in front of him. He turned to her. "Hey, when did you want to head back?"

"Trying to get out of Dodge early, huh?" Ethan said, propping up a hip on the same desk.

"We drove together."

"Mhmm." Ethan folded his arms against his chest.

"This is what I get for being considerate. Fine, whatever. Think what you want."

"Yeah, you probably want to go visit with Mom and Dad before you take off," Ethan said.

Caitlyn agreed with Ethan. The more time she spent around him, the more she liked him. He had a damn good point, plus she wasn't ready to get back into the car with Austin.

"Go ahead and take your time. I haven't seen any football yet, and it's not Thanksgiving without it. Do you mind if I watch with you?" she asked, turning to Ethan, who raised his eyebrows for the second time.

"Now you're talking," he said, getting up off the desk and motioning for her to lead the way. She did, not giving Austin a passing glance.

CHAPTER 21

Austin loved his brother, but he also hadn't wanted to admit Ethan was right about anything for his entire life, and that wasn't going to change today, but he knew he didn't have a choice. Bouts of laughter and chatter echoed around the luxurious, bright living room as he headed through. He glared at Ethan, who was sitting next to Caitlyn on the dark leather couch, listening to whatever she was saying. A coil of jealousy wrapped around Austin's stomach. He paused to catch her eye, but she pointedly didn't look at him.

Austin stood there, hoping he was making it awkward. His parents lived here, so what was the rush? Besides, he had an excellent view. Caitlyn commanded attention sitting there on his parents' leather couch, with some sort of orange pillow Austin had never seen before behind her back. She had put her hair up, exposing the slim shape of her neck. Though she would probably deny it, her subtle makeup and easy smile could've turned heads away from the game if she wanted.

A burst of noise came from the speakers around the

room. Ethan leaped off the couch, and Caitlyn cracked a broad smile and threw her hands up in victory.

Austin's breath caught in his chest. The joy overflowing from Caitlyn's unguarded smile filled the room and soaked into his skin. Her chest rose and fell with gasps of joyous, free laughter, lighting the match of desire now burning his spine. Her eyes twinkled as she laughed again when Ethan flopped back down, bouncing her once. While the commercials rolled, the pair of them sat, exchanging a comfortable and relaxed commentary on what had apparently been a stellar play.

At least he didn't have to worry about Ethan making any kind of move. Austin had suspected for years there was something more than work that kept him away from home but hadn't been sure until he had fired that low blow earlier. Ethan's response told him he had more than struck the target. Austin had hit a bullseye.

So what if Ethan had someone? Big deal. Austin wanted his brother to be happy, but more importantly, the navy had taught him to stay in his lane. Not his circus, not his monkeys. Austin had always figured Ethan would get married first, but apparently, that hadn't happened yet, and it was none of his damn business if it ever did. However, all of this meant that though Austin would vastly prefer to be the one sharing the chunk of leather with Caitlyn, knowing Ethan had someone back in New York meant Austin wanted to kill his brother less, which was a good thing. Happy Thanksgiving, everybody. With no other option but to seek out his parents, he left the cashmere and leather stadium and turned toward the kitchen.

The quiet whir of both dishwashers and the sound of the coffee maker were now the only noises compared to the bustling chaos of an hour ago. Pans were either covered with foil or left to drip dry by the sink. The Aunt heap, as he liked to call it, had moved from the dining room, which no doubt was back to looking immaculate, to the breakfast room. Austin headed in that direction.

Compared to the overwhelming kitchen, the breakfast room was cozy. Large floor-to-ceiling windows captured the garden and lawn beyond, but more importantly, bathed the room in light. Austin knew it was his mom's favorite room. The lemon tree Ethan had given her years ago thrived in the corner in a large ceramic pot. Framed on the wall rested the silk fan Austin had brought her from Japan. A novel he didn't recognize rested on one of the tables.

Only Aunt Mary and Aunt Tee sat in plush white chairs, each holding a cup of coffee. Both stopped talking when they saw him. Aunt Mary raised an eyebrow.

"Coming to visit the old bags?" Aunt Tee, whose real name was Charity, asked, her eyes twinkling with humor. "Caitlyn is a lovely young lady. So polite."

"Thanks," Austin said, trying to think through what to say next. "She's a great teacher at the school." He figured that was a safe enough bet.

"I'm sure she must miss her home. When is she heading back?" Aunt Mary asked. Of the two, Mary always came off more stern, but both were equally tough.

"I'm not sure. She's here for the whole school year and maybe more. Have you guys seen my mom?" he asked, hoping to change the subject quickly.

"I think she's in the back, tending to your dad's rash," Aunt Mary said.

"He never could handle pepper," Aunt Tee said to her cup.

"Not at all. James was like that before he died—"

"Great, thanks," Austin said, spinning on his heel before the conversation trapped him.

"Wait just a minute, Austin." Aunt Mary put her cup down

on the small maple table next to her chair. Never a good sign. "Caitlyn doesn't suspect anything, correct?"

"Of course not. John asked me to keep a close eye on her. I know the rules," Austin said, trying to fill the void of silence.

"We were just curious," said Aunt Tee.

"Yeah, I just didn't want to see anyone alone on Thanksgiving," he finished, wondering why his shirt felt too tight around the collar.

"You did the right thing," Aunt Tee added. "That was very nice of you."

"Yes, now go ahead and find your parents. Tell your mother to relax. I looked at the rash myself, and it's nothing," Aunt Mary said, picking up her coffee cup and taking a sip. Austin nodded and went in search.

His parents' room was in the back wing of the house, set apart from the guest rooms and kids' rooms upstairs. Rounding the corner, Austin found the door open. He knocked twice on the doorjamb anyway.

"Mom? Dad?" he called into the large room. Redone a few years ago, the room looked more like a fancy hotel with its custom drapes and bedspread than a place to relax, but then Austin liked his little cottage on the other side of the island. He wondered if his own house would meet Caitlyn's approval.

"We're in here," his mom called out from the bathroom.

"Yeah, we're mostly decent," his dad said.

Austin headed for the marble palace his mother called a bathroom. His mom slathered a thick white cream onto his dad's exposed chest and neck, while he sat slumped on the toilet like a kid with poison ivy in a time-out.

"Jesus, is it really that bad? I thought it had faded," Austin said, craning his neck to try to get a look at the rash.

"Nah," his dad said, smiling and waving his hand.

"We don't know," his mom said louder, clearly overruling him. She dug her hand into the jar, scooping up more of the chalky goo.

Austin picked up the blue jar and read the name. "Isn't this diaper cream?"

"I told her—"

"That's all we had in the house on short notice," his mom said with authority.

His dad offered him a tight-lipped smile of resignation, as his mom frosted the right side of his face like a cake.

"When was the last time we had a baby in this house? The fifties? Is this shit any good anymore?"

"Language, please, Austin. It's Thanksgiving. And it's fine," said his mom, not turning around. "When Laurie used to bring the girls, I kept some in the cabinet."

"Mom, the girls graduated last year."

"Let's go sit down. I need to let this soak in," Austin's dad said. He led the way toward the small seating area, his skin still covered in frosting. His mom ran over and threw down an old towel before he sat.

"You probably know what I'm going to say," Austin's dad said.

"Not a clue, just came in to say bye before I go," Austin lied, hoping to get out of the conversation he didn't want to have.

"It's not a good idea, Austin. You need to be more careful."

"She's just a teacher at school. John is the one who told me to keep an eye on her. I didn't want her to be alone on the holiday."

"Austin, we all saw you," his dad said, his tight smile not reaching his eyes.

"So what? You going to report me?"

Austin's mom jumped in. "Of course not. We're just

worried. She's very nice, and I know you like her, but you know the rules. She's not one of us."

"I know." Austin gritted his teeth to keep a lid on his rising temper.

"Look at it this way, Austin," his dad said in a calm voice. "We all have to make sacrifices to live here. You know that." He folded his arms and crossed one leg over the other as if they were discussing why he couldn't have a dog.

His dad continued in that patient voice he'd used with his students back when he'd taught literature. "Caitlyn's a nice girl, but the closer you get, the more you'll hurt her when you have to break it off. Do you want to do that to her?"

CHAPTER 22

"So you're not going to talk to me?" Austin said after he shut the door of the old truck. Instead of putting the keys in the ignition, he shifted and waited for Caitlyn to fill the silence.

She sat in the passenger seat with her legs crossed, staring out at the woods beyond his parents' driveway. Her hands were folded over the travel bag for the casserole dish she had brought. A mountain of leftovers in Tupperware sat on the bench seat between them. Once his mom had finished fussing over his dad, she had crammed as much food as possible into their hands on the way out.

Caitlyn sighed. "Thank you for inviting me. I had a great time with your family."

"Really? Because you're not throwing off that vibe."

"Well, what do you want me to say?" She threw up her hands before letting her head fall back onto the headrest.

"Listen, about what happened—"

She shook her head. "No, it's okay. It shouldn't have happened in the first place. Not here, and not at the dance."

Austin winced and rubbed the back of his head. "I'm sorry about how I introduced you to my family."

"It's okay. We are coworkers. You didn't say anything that wasn't true."

"I got thrown off. They caught me off guard. Shit, they've always had terrible timing. And you're right. This is inappropriate, and I'm sorry I've put you in that position."

"It's okay."

"So, are we good?" Austin asked, shifting in the seat of the truck. "I don't like it when we aren't. I'm sorry. I fucked up. Can we go back to just being friends?"

Caitlyn turned and studied him. The dark lipstick she had on earlier had pretty much worn away, leaving behind the natural pink he liked. He didn't have anything against makeup, but he was used to seeing Caitlyn a certain way and loved what he knew best.

Her eyes searched his. "Yeah," she said. "We're okay."

Austin started up the truck. "Good. The rice dressing was great, even if it almost took out my dad."

Caitlyn groaned and leaned her head back. "God, don't remind me."

"Hey, it was good! Best thing I've had in years. I've grown tired of the same old bland stuff."

"Thanks," she said in a flat voice. "At least they'll always remember me as the girl who showed up unannounced and brought that spicy dish."

Austin pulled out of the driveway and drummed his fingers on the wheel. Caitlyn had omitted the most memorable moment of the holiday, which told him she wanted to forget it—or at least not talk about it.

The realization stung. He'd been so sure of himself, especially after Halloween when she arrived in that killer Rosie the Riveter costume. Everything that had happened between them back behind the school, which in Austin's opinion hadn't been nearly enough, had felt like a green light.

Even though it was still totally wrong, since the night of the dance, he'd been dying to taste her more. Laurie and John's words echoed in his mind. If it weren't for everyone getting in his damn way and all up in his business and shit, he would've already gotten to know her properly.

Seeing her in the house he'd grown up in stirred up all sorts of feelings. Seeing Caitlyn around his family's collection of heirlooms felt right and made Austin want to include her as a permanent addition. But as his parents had reminded him, that wasn't going to happen.

"Nah, they really did like you. Mom and Dad told me so." Granted, it was right before they mentioned she shouldn't be around. "And I guess you liked Ethan?" Austin knew it was low, but that had been the only bit he hadn't enjoyed so much. Even if Ethan hadn't been interested, Caitlyn didn't have to like him that much.

"He was nice. Told me about working in New York. Sounded really cool."

"Uh-huh." Austin still hadn't turned yet. The drive back to her place wasn't that long, and he wanted to make sure he milked every second of his alone time with her.

"Yeah, we mostly talked about that. I've never been to a city that big. Flying into Logan was a bit of an eye-opener."

"Did you spend a lot of time there?"

Caitlyn looked over at him. "In Boston?"

"Yeah," he said, meeting her eyes. She didn't look pissed anymore, which allowed Austin to let go of the tension in his shoulders.

She shook her head, lips thinning. "No, it was just a stopover. I only saw it as the plane landed. The biggest city I've been to is New Orleans."

"I bet that place is cool as hell."

"Yeah, but you know how it is when you live somewhere. You just can't appreciate it as much. Everywhere else seems so much cooler."

He nodded and eased off the brake before turning onto the road. "Yeah, I get that."

That same exact observation had been part of what had made him want to go into the navy.

"So now that you've met my family, will you tell me about yours? What was it you said? Any crazy cousins? Weird uncles?" he asked with a smile that faded when he glanced over.

The brightness in Caitlyn's face had dimmed, replaced by an ashen look of sadness. "Yeah, pretty much."

The silence in the car stretched, while sounds of the engine filled the cab. Austin braked for a stop sign at a deserted intersection ahead and looked over at her.

"You don't talk about your family."

Pink bloomed on her cheeks before she shook it off and lowered her brows. "Not much to say," she said in a clipped tone.

"Hey, if you don't want to talk about it, that's okay with me," Austin said, holding up his hands.

Caitlyn blew out a breath. "I'm sorry, it's just a long story, and I don't want to get into it, okay? Not right now."

"That's fair. Just know I'm interested when you're ready." Austin glanced over at her. Caitlyn nodded. He should drop her off and be a gentleman. Walk away and do the right thing. He knew the risks, knew his obligations to John, his family, and everyone on the island, but what he said next felt more right than anything else.

"Look, I owe you for my screwup. How about I take you to Boston?"

CHAPTER 23

At dawn, Austin parked his truck in the near-empty parking lot of the marina. Most people would be spending the weekend with their families and not have any reason to run out on the water, which meant it was the perfect time to go. With any luck, no one would realize they both were gone. He grabbed his old Barbour coat from the cab, as well as the brown paper bag, and locked the doors just in case they had to spend the night because of bad weather. Sometimes southwesterly storms came out of nowhere in the afternoon, making the trip too dangerous even in a forty-two-foot cabin cruiser. Years of experience had taught him the power of studying all the weather statements. Today looked mostly clear, as long as they made it back before dark.

The gulls floated overhead, calling down from the crisp purple sky that promised smooth sailing and an easy return trip. It was going to be one of those days that looked warm from the inside, and despite the cold, invited people to leave their comfortable homes.

The boats all sat quietly in the dark, tied to their respective cleats and pilings. Some had already been wrapped and stacked out of the water for the season, to protect against ice and other winter problems. Since the *Bombshell* had a large, closed cabin, Austin preferred to keep her ready year-round unlike the sun seekers with open cabins. While other owners felt better about their boats being carefully guarded against the evils of winter wind, freezing temps, and snow, Austin always felt more at ease with the *Bombshell* where she should be. Most insurance claims filed for boats were for damages that happened to those out of the water, so even with the nor'easters that pummeled them, Austin preferred a bubbling hull deicer and weekly checks even if he had to get out a snow shovel and take care of business.

He also liked to take her out at least once a month to run errands for the family, and he'd told his mom he'd stop by on the way home, figuring it was a great excuse to spend more time alone with Caitlyn. A few times he had even picked up Ethan, who, being in the city, didn't want to keep a boat. In Austin's opinion that just went against family tradition, but his brother had always been a bit of a black sheep.

The thought pulled him back to his parents' house. Austin dragged a hand over his eyes. He had been dying to get to know more about Caitlyn, and then right when he thought he messed up by bringing her to his family's freaking mansion, he surprised himself by fucking up more than usual. It wasn't supposed to turn into a face-eating session. He got hot even thinking about that kiss now. Sure it had been a while since he had been with someone, but Austin could honestly say he had never felt a kiss like that. The truth was it freaked him out.

Of course, he couldn't even enjoy the memory because of what had happened next. Austin wanted to beat his head into a wall again. Dumbass that he was should've taken it on the chin, and owned up to the fact that, hey, maybe they were more than friends. Shit, why couldn't he have just said her name and been done with it? He grabbed the back of his neck and pulled, trying to get the tension to go away.

Still, Austin frowned at the memory as he walked over to where the *Bombshell* waited. He didn't like the idea that Caitlyn was hiding something or that something would bother her. During their late-night talks at school, she always seemed so happy. Sounds of her laughter warmed his skin and drew him back in for more. As he got closer to knowing her, he kept hitting walls. She didn't want to let him in to know the truth about her family. Every time he would ask a question or steer the conversation in that direction, Caitlyn pushed him back, deflecting with a question or other comment that told him nothing. Granted, he had to be the same way with his secret, but that was beside the point.

The car ride home after Thanksgiving told him how much whatever burden she kept weighed on her. When she had rubbed the bridge of her nose in exhaustion, Austin wanted to go beat someone's ass on her behalf and then swallow her in a giant hug. She just seemed tired of carrying whatever weight she bore, which meant today had to be better than perfect.

Like an exotic cat, the *Bombshell* sat at the end of the dock, putting all of the other yachts to shame. New white fiberglass and sweeping hulls couldn't hold a candle to classic American beauty. Her dark blue hull matched the water beneath, answering new flash with refined sophistication. Austin had customized the design, adding a few elements that he had always wanted. The letters of her name, painted in white and outlined in gold like a new bride, called attention to the custom stern platform. Added to that, her gleaming teak, shining chrome, and the brass portholes Austin had installed himself, *Bombshell* drew attention from all sides. Anytime he pulled into port, several old-timers and even the crustiest salt would come over and give her a look.

He pulled out the keys attached to a foam float bearing the number of the Nantucket Boat Basin and let himself into the cabin. Windows exposed almost full views of the bay, which is what Austin had loved about the *Bombshell* when he had first stepped inside. The smell of wool blankets and polish swirled around him to welcome him to what he considered his real home. Sure, the little cottage he had was okay, but most of his money and time went into ensuring *Bombshell* looked her best.

The cockpit sat in the cabin next to the stairs to the galley below with a matching passenger seat on the other side. Austin stepped forward and brushed it off before heading down to the kitchen with the bag to unload his provisions. Caitlyn had seemed impressed by just the little glance they had taken back in September, but walking around someplace for a minute or two didn't compare to staying aboard for at least four hours.

He had taken careful notice of what Caitlyn had eaten at his parents' and tried to pick only what he thought she would like. At Thanksgiving, she hadn't finished her wine, but then that could've been just because she was meeting new people. The packages of cookies crinkled as he took them out of the bag along with a can of roasted nuts and a few other things. He placed all of them in the cabinets which, on a typical day, only held jerky, whiskey, and a lone can of soup.

With that finished, he shoved the brown paper bag under the stainless steel sink he'd installed last year and grabbed a paper towel to wipe off the counter. The rest of the galley looked fine. When he came by yesterday, he returned all the cushions back to their normal positions from storage. Because Caitlyn was coming, he had even taken out the little blue and white pillow his mom had given him that read "Seabatical" in script lettering.

Austin walked through to the single forward stateroom. He had changed the sheets yesterday and put on the blue and white striped linen thing his mom had insisted he had to have along with the worthless decorative pillows. Unfortunately, he didn't plan on them needing to use it, but the idea had crossed his mind more than once late at night. He poked his head in the washroom, still smelling the lemon scent he had used to wipe everything down with yesterday. He had only used the separate shower stall a couple of times but still cleaned the whole thing. Again it wasn't like she'd be using it, but it still needed to be perfect.

Footsteps echoed down from the deck. Austin smiled and went upstairs to greet his new passenger.

"Hi," she said as she took off her coat and draped it over the bench seat.

"Hi, yourself." Austin would've come up with more words, but she looked so good he was lucky he was still upright.

"So, do you drive, er, sail the whole way there?" Caitlyn asked once she had settled in, sitting in the passenger seat next to Austin. In her dark blue sweater and jeans, she looked like the perfect accessory to the *Bombshell*. Austin kept glancing over at her, even more after they'd left the harbor. He engaged the autopilot feature and plugged in the destination before taking his hands off the helm and sitting back.

"No, not really. Ninety-nine percent of the time, she and her buddy Garmin do better without me. It's mostly just in the harbors and docking where I get involved."

Caitlyn nodded, looking out at the horizon. They had left early enough to be treated to the sun cresting above the water. The trip would take almost two hours one way, and Austin wanted to leave them plenty of time in the city.

"So, what do you want to see, eat, and do in Boston? It'll be a little chilly, but we can do whatever you want."

Caitlyn smiled, looking at the water, and slowly turned to him, speaking slowly and deliberately. "I want lobstah."

Austin let out a bark of laughter. "Yeah, I think we can make that happen. Good to see I'm rubbing off on you. Are you more into fine dining or a hole-in-the-wall kind of place?"

"I want it to be good," she said, a woman on a mission, nodding slowly toward the horizon as if he wasn't even present.

Well, didn't that make him feel all sorts of things in all sorts of places?

"And I want lots of butter, I mean, lots," she said, her ponytail swaying with the purr of the *Bombshell*'s inboard engine as she looked longingly off into the sea, thinking about her goal.

"Check. We can do that," Austin said. They were crawling now, courtesy of the town council's unbearably slow speed limit. But once they were in open water, he could really show off.

"That reminds me," Caitlyn said, looking over at him. "Did you bring a chess board?" She frowned and shook her head. "Sorry, dumb question. You probably can't be distracted."

Austin sat up in his chair and looked over at her for a second, processing the question. He totally hadn't thought of that. Dumbass.

"Shit, I totally blanked. I brought snacks though, and there's coffee." He hoped that was enough and waited on her answer, holding his breath. He wanted this to be perfect, and here they were barely out of Easterly Bay, and he had already screwed it up.

Caitlyn shook her head and waved her hand. "Don't worry about it. Honestly, I probably wouldn't have wanted to play anyway. I could stare out at this water for hours without seeing anything else." She sighed and looked straight out the *Bombshell*'s windows toward the horizon. The sun had risen, and pinks started to flood the sky, chasing the retreating deep purple.

"That's one thing I love about living here," she said.

"Ocean views?"

"Yeah," she said with a bright smile. "Sometimes I just come home and sit, looking out at the waves. Like I'll go to sit down and get some work done, but then I'll just stare off out the window." She let out a little laugh and turned to him. "Guess that's one reason I don't get everything done."

"Rest is important. Chicken soup for the soul and all that." Austin shook his head, while he ramped up the throttle to cruising speed, letting *Bombshell* out of the gate like a thoroughbred.

Caitlyn let out a little sound of delight, which widened her smile into a full grin. She leaned forward in her seat and watched as they zipped toward the horizon.

"How fast can she go?" Caitlyn asked, holding on tight and watching the bow with total joy.

Austin shifted in his Captain's chair to face her and leaned back, keeping an eye on the controls. "Oh, she can get up to forty knots, but it'll max out the engine and burn a shit ton of gas. Still, it's fun. Want to see?"

Caitlyn laughed, gripping the armrests. "This is plenty fast for me. Back home, boats can go quick, but I don't think I've been on one this fast, I mean aside from the ferry over, but you know I'm talking about a smaller boat."

"Ever go out in the gulf?" Austin asked, watching her.

Caitlyn shook her head. "No, I mean I knew some people

who had trawlers for shrimp fishing, but the few times I went, it was in a bayou."

Austin was intrigued. Visions of trees with Spanish moss came to mind. "What's that like?"

"Different to this. For one, the cabin isn't nearly like this," Caitlyn said, waving her arms around the expansive space. "I mean, I know I said it before, but this is just a whole other level, kinda like your parents' house."

Austin nodded and waited for her to continue. He loved watching her talk. He couldn't get enough of watching her, no matter how long they were together. Sitting next to her for hours was a dream.

Caitlyn sat back to watch the water. The interior cabin gleamed in the morning sun streaming through the windows, illuminating the mahogany and making it glow from the inside.

Now that he looked at it, the color matched Caitlyn's hair. He probably wouldn't be able to look at it again without thinking of her—not that he minded. Austin thought her hair color was perfect. Still, he frowned at the thought her hair would gray long before his. She looked so perfect sitting there with her legs crossed, now that she'd grown accustomed to the ride, watching the morning light reflect off the waves. Her ponytail swayed gently with the movement, while she sat, hands folded, at peace with the ride.

Austin committed every detail to memory so he could perfectly revisit this moment for the next hundred years and more.

Caitlyn looked over and saw him watching her. A faint tinge of pink hit her cheeks as she smiled at him.

"I'm sorry I'm so quiet."

He shook his head, watching her. "You can be whatever you want today."

She smiled, full of relief.

"You know I haven't thanked you properly for inviting me on this trip."

Austin had a few ideas as to how exactly she could do that but pushed away the image of him and her on the bed below and focused only on listening, so he didn't make an ass out of himself.

"I really appreciate it. It's been a stressful few years, and I'm...well, yeah, it's just really, really nice."

"Of course...shit, are you okay?"

Caitlyn dabbed at her eyes with the cuff of her sweater and waved her hand.

"I'm sorry. I'm just a disaster. Don't...don't worry about me. I'm fine."

"Bullshit," he said crossing the short distance. "Come here." Caitlyn stood and almost fell with the movement from the boat.

Austin wrapped his arms around her shoulders and held on tight, breathing in the scent of her hair. She swayed again, and he planted his feet wide on either side of hers, steadying them against the sea. "It's okay. I got you."

He could've stayed there forever, holding on to her, but Caitlyn sucked in a long breath and leaned back.

"Thanks," she said, wiping her eyes. "I guess I needed that."

"Anytime," he said. Literally, he added to himself.

Caitlyn nodded and looked at the floor. Austin's heart broke. With her tear-stained cheeks and dark lashes, she looked beautiful, but defeated and tired with what she held inside.

Austin so wanted to demand answers, break down the doors she was shutting so he could fix whatever was wrong. He had asked, but she hadn't wanted to get into it yesterday in the truck or right now.

He squatted down a little to meet her eyes. "How about I turn off the GPS and teach you to drive?"

She looked up at him, meeting his stare. "Really?" she asked, looking curious.

"Come on, you take the helm."

CHAPTER 24

Pulling into the marina in Boston had always given Austin a thrill, and today was no exception. The towering buildings looming above them in the cold blue sky might have been a testament to the passage of time, but there was something about coming to a place with so much history that had always made him smile. Today was no exception. If anything, Austin had a broader grin than normal, and it had nothing to do with the atmosphere.

Caitlyn stood and snapped a few pictures with her phone as they entered Boston Harbor. She was resplendent in the morning sun now streaking through the *Bombshell*'s windows. Austin drank in the sight of her and made a mental note to take her out again as many times as he possibly could. The farther away from prying eyes they were, the better. Besides, alone on *Bombshell*, Austin had Caitlyn all to himself with beautiful scenery and privacy only he could provide.

They pulled into the Boston Waterfront Marina and rented a slip before bundling up and leaving to explore on foot. They explored the familiar tourist sights while Austin

THE SECRET ABOUT TIME

explained the famous red line until his favorite restaurant opened.

Steering Caitlyn inside, Austin requested a seat at the window where they had a view of the Boston Tea Party Ships and Museum, which had reopened after a fire. The Barking Crab had always been one of Austin's personal favorites, but not for the decor. Built on a barge, the restaurant's interior was more fisherman bar with mismatched chairs than romance, but the fish was fresh, and they had butter by the bucket.

"This is perfect," Caitlyn said after they'd ordered drinks.

"Isn't it great?" Austin flopped open the menu, which was a formality. He knew his order. "I try to come here every chance I get. Good scrod and good beer."

"Scrod?" Caitlyn looked puzzled over her open menu. "That's a new one for me."

"Whitefish of the day. Could be cod or haddock. Something like that. Kind of like the catch of the day."

They traded opinions on the menu, ordered, and dove into the hot crab dip Austin had requested for them to share.

"I think you're making me a sailor. Well,"—she paused and popped a chip into her mouth—"probably not a sailor, but a fan."

"That was the plan all along."

"Well, you're succeeding. I don't think I could ever get tired of this view," Caitlyn said, looking out toward the tall ships at the museum.

Austin loved his own view of her but kept that to himself.

"So, tell me about the navy," Caitlyn said, eating another chip.

Austin felt a familiar tightening in his gut but brushed it off, more confident around her now. "What do you want to know?"

"What was it like? What sucked?" She took a sip from her drink, her golden eyes watching him.

He stalled by eating a chip and trying to sort through what he could and couldn't say. The good news was she wouldn't know the difference between the navy ten years ago and seventy years ago, as long as he left out the right details.

"Well geez, I don't know where to start."

The server bought him more time. Two full platters of almost everything on the menu with all of the sides landed in front of them, along with the extra hushpuppies and fries he'd ordered. They both settled in, munching away before she asked the question again.

"I'm curious," she said, prompting him while digging into her coleslaw.

"The food was just okay." Austin hoped she'd be satisfied. Fewer details worked in his favor.

"Yeah?"

"Yeah. Had to use condiments to add flavor to it, and sometimes we'd be out to sea for ages, so we'd lose touch with back home a little bit."

"I guess that's true. There's no cell service on the water, right?"

When he'd gone into the navy, his parents had only just gotten a phone in their house, but he wasn't about to bring that up.

"Yeah, so that sucked. It was monotonous. Same shit, different day. People got on each other's nerves. Fights broke out."

"Did you ever get in any?"

"Oh yeah, sure. Had an ax to grind when I was younger. Chip on my shoulder with something to prove."

"Is that how you got your scar?"

Austin reached up to his chin and ran his fingers over the

familiar line, now a part of the road map of scars telling his body's story.

"Yes and no. Wasn't on the ship. Beer bottle in port. Got ugly with a group of local guys. To be fair, we were all drunk."

Caitlyn nodded while chewing. "What was your favorite part?"

"The guys." Even now, he could see all of their faces, etched in his memory forever.

"Do you ever get together?" she asked, looking down at her food. "Or keep in touch?"

A stab of pain lit up his chest like a shock. "Ah no. No, we don't really keep in touch."

Austin had tried for years following up, and even going to a few weddings and baptisms, but time had marched on for his friends. During his last visits, which had been at least fifty years ago, more than a few had remarked on how he hadn't aged a bit. That was when Austin knew the time had come. He called a few times a year and caught up with them, listening to stories about how their kids had kids. A few had gone into nursing homes, and Austin had attended the funerals, standing way in the back as one by one, they all passed along without him. When asked, Austin had merely said he was the son of a fellow veteran and left it at that.

"You okay?" she asked. Her golden eyes were large, filled with concern. "We don't have to talk about this."

"I'm okay," he said, but his voice was gruffer than he meant. Austin focused on stabbing a scallop with his fork and didn't look up. She didn't need to know about the screaming in his head that kept him up at night, or the memories of the moments before the ship went down.

"Your family must be really proud of you," Caitlyn said.

If they were, they were wrong, but Austin couldn't

correct them. "Dad was pissed when I signed up, but he and mom needed money."

Caitlyn's eyebrows rose in shock. "Really? No offense, but they don't look like they're hurting."

"Yeah, just because the house is like, whatever, you know, they didn't always have it." God, why did he sound so dumb?

"I get it. So, they didn't want you to go?"

"Well, it was mostly the money, but I figured I'd better volunteer before I was drafted."

The second the words left his mouth, Austin wished he could take them back. He glanced up at Caitlyn to see if she'd noticed his mistake. A slight frown made his heart sink.

"The last draft was Vietnam." She plucked a French fry up and dunked it into a cup of ketchup. "I don't think they'd do another one. So unpopular."

"Yeah, well, I never said I was the smartest kid on the block. So anyway, yeah, it was everything I'd expected and more," he continued, hoping if he kept talking, she'd forget his screwup.

"Once we had to do some stealth drills or something like that, and they killed all the lights onboard, like everything."

Caitlyn munched on her food while transfixed.

"And the stars were unbelievable. You know how we get used to seeing just a few because of all the lights and shit? Yeah, well, without that in the middle of the ocean, it's spectacular. I mean, the constellations really look like stuff. They actually stand out. The Milky Way is incredible."

"That's my favorite candy bar," Caitlyn said offhandedly.

"I'm more of a Snickers guy. Anywho, yeah, the stars were great."

"I love looking up. I've always wanted a telescope."

"We should totally bring one next time. When it's warmer, you know." Austin relaxed as the conversation continued without Caitlyn pushing on the boneheaded draft comment.

"What was the scariest part?" she asked after they had finished talking about each other's zodiac signs.

"Of the navy?" He thought when she nodded. How could he tell her the sound of the Japanese planes circling around them like vultures, or the booming sound of the anti-aircraft guns? As far as he knew, no navy ship had been involved in anything quite like that recently.

The sound of Japanese fire hitting the sides of the Astoria echoed through him. The fatal shot had hit the boiler room, making the heavy cruiser an inferno. Austin rubbed his hands at the memory of grabbing a bucket in his part of the brigade as a frantic attempt to save their home while the Japanese continued to attack, sending a barrage of deadly accuracy into the sides of the burning ship.

They had started to list, the subtle shift a deadly sign that only sped the panic into a frenzy of action. He could still smell the gasoline as it burned in a cloud of smoke and hear Carmichael's frantic swearing in front of him, passing buckets forward to drive the flames back on the gun deck while the cross around his neck swung with each movement. Convinced of certain death, the crew continued trying to fight the blaze while under continuous bombardment. The deck felt like a furnace, heated from the fire below. It shook with each hit, drowning out the cries of the wounded carried along with the dead to the forecastle.

What happened next was most certainly a miracle. The Japanese halted their attack and retreated, leaving the Astoria to burn in the water. The crew continued to fight for their lives as other ships moved alongside to assist when the call came to abandon ship. Austin had fallen, hitting his head on the deck now drenched with seawater. It had been Carmichael who had grabbed his dazed ass and helped him get to a raft before they could board the nearby destroyer. Within hours of the attack, all evidence of the Astoria was gone, sucked down below to live on only in their memories.

Austin's throat felt dry, and he closed his eyes for a moment, trying to shake the images he fought hard to ignore.

"Austin?" Caitlyn's voice was small, tentative.

"Sorry," he muttered, shoving some fish in his mouth to cover the gravel in his voice.

"Don't apologize. You respect my privacy. I respect yours."

They ate in silence, Austin wishing he could tell her everything and share his stories with someone, but also grateful she didn't push.

"Yeah, sorry, I just got to thinking about something," he said after they had finished eating. "I meant for this to be a nice lunch."

"Oh, it was great," Caitlyn said, wiping her mouth.

"Yeah, well, you know. Still—"

"Nope. All good. You have things you'd rather not talk about, and I understand that more than you know."

Her golden eyes watched him from across the table. Flat and serious, they held the mark of tremendous anguish and a heavy burden. With a deep breath, she smiled, putting what he now knew to be her mask back firmly in place, shielding from view the pain he had just seen.

"So, how about dessert?" she asked.

CHAPTER 25

Mark Schmidt stood at the edge of the pier,
loading baggage onto the ferry for the trip from
Hyannis to Nantucket. He shoved his hands
into his cheap old work coat when the icy wind rushed off
the water, reminding them all that winter was around the
corner.

"Alright, Schmidty, go ahead," said Scott, who had
finished taking inventory of the boxes. The young kid in his
thirties flashed a thumbs-up and hopped down to get out of
the way.

Mark dug in his pockets. He pulled out the old key and
started the forklift, loading everything from fine furniture to
toilet paper just as he'd done for the last forty years. Muscle
memory walked him through the steps, but now arthritis had
settled into his joints, making the familiar moves stiff and
awkward. The doctor had advised against working with his
hands or in the cold, but people who didn't have to work for
a living had no idea what the rest of the world went through.
Mark didn't have a choice.

When the work was finished, his hands were frozen in

the position of the controls, and it took a minute for them to free back up. Climbing out of the forklift, he started the process of loading the luggage by hand. Compared with the summer season, the neat cluster of bags was a fraction of the usual heap of crap they had to deal with. As always, lifting each one onto the boat strained his arm, which had never been quite right after a bad break in his youth.

A familiar hand slapped his back, making him wince. "Hey, Schmidty, don't worry—we got the rest." Scott and the young guys all moved as fast as he once had, but that had been a long time ago. Though they never said it, Mark slowed them down, and he knew it.

"Coast Guard's worried about the weather. This'll be the last run for today," Scott said, looking out to the water and back at him. "It'll be good to get some Dunks. Warm up, you know?"

Mark nodded once and watched Scott walk on board to run final checks. He moved with such speed—a speed Mark hadn't known since Vietnam.

The need for warmth curled in his body, but unlike Scott, it wasn't coffee he needed. In his pockets, his hands trembled. Mark tried to remember if the bottle under his seat in his dad's old truck was empty yet.

Shouts of questions and answers in the affirmative echoed around the high-speed ferry as the engines fired up. The young kids scrambled all over the boat with an ease they didn't notice. Mark hauled himself up the gangway and headed to grab his scanner to check tickets. There were only a few people on board, a sure sign the schedule would get cut back.

While he waited for the damn digital scanner to load, Mark looked out a small window in the staff area. Yachts and fishing boats bobbed with the swells in the harbor. One stunning cabin cruiser with a dark blue hull pulled into an open dock. A blond man in a nice coat tossed fenders over the side before hopping down to tie the beauty off to the cleats. Satisfied with his work, the man stood up with his hands on his hips and turned toward the ferry.

Mark froze when he saw the face.

"Scott, give me a minute," Mark called out before shuffling down, not waiting for an answer. Mark headed to the gangway and looked out.

He had seen that face before. It had been years, back before his old man had finally done him a favor and died. Mark's hands shook as he squinted, forcing his aging eyes to work.

The blond man jerked as if he heard something and turned around to stand next to…. Mark blinked. It was her. The woman with the one-way ticket to Brightrock stood next to a man out of Mark's childhood memories.

The ferry blasted its horn, ready for departure, while the growling engines frothed the ocean below. Flashes of his dad looking at his old navy pictures with a scotch next to his hand came to Mark. As a child he had clung to those images, studied them, hoping he could find the secret in them to someday be the person his dad would want. Not the kid who was always in the way.

Without thinking about it, Mark rubbed his arm, finding where the bone had been snapped years ago. He had seen the face so many times he was sure it was the same, except that wasn't possible, was it? Mark rubbed his eyes and watched as the man helped the woman on to the dock and walked back toward the streets of Hyannis without taking his eyes off her.

It was him. Mark knew it in his gut. He had the same broad chin, same grin, but he couldn't be sure until he got back to the house. As the ferry started pulling away, Mark clambered back to the edge of the boat to watch the couple, desperate to confirm. There would be no way to know for sure until he got home and pulled out the old bastard's albums. Mark watched them until they turned past a corner.

Shaken by what he had seen, Mark stood at the edge of the rail, watching the harbor shrink with distance. His dad had died years ago. There was no one from that war still alive outside a hospital or nursing home, but Mark knew that face like the back of a bottle. Scott called for him, pulling him out of his head. Mark turned around and saw him waving the scanner in question. Determined to pull out the image when he got home, Mark stumbled back to his job with the man's face frozen in his mind.

Everyone had always talked about something weird on Brightrock. Rumors of witchcraft and criminals had circulated around the secretive island for years. Mark's hands shook as he tried to work the scanner.

Now, he believed.

CHAPTER 26

Caitlyn planted her feet wide in the galley, still trying to get used to the increasing rocking sway of the ship. They had left Boston a few hours ago, then headed to Hyannis where Austin picked up a few things for his mom at a local specialty food store. The store had been packed and took longer than expected, but now they were heading home after what had proven to be a day to remember, and she wasn't just talking about the lobster.

Spending time with him had been easy, filling in cracks she hadn't known were there. Soaking up the history and feeling of a new city with a good friend had been the therapy she probably needed. She hadn't laughed like that since she could remember. Probably before Amber had died.

Caitlyn shook off the memories and went back to focusing on washing her hands in the galley. The floor rolled beneath her, and she caught herself against the edge of the sink.

The clouds now blocked the sky, and the wind had picked up, but Austin felt they could still make the run back to the island before dark. The sooner they were back, the less likely someone would've realized they were both gone. Overnighting it with the boss was not a good look, no matter how many times she caught herself staring into his bright blue eyes. She wished she could see into him. For all their conversations, Austin still hadn't opened up about what had bothered him.

After lunch, Austin had bounced back from when he had gotten lost in his memories. Caitlyn wished she could ease whatever haunted him, but she wasn't prepared to tell him about her past and had no business getting into his.

Still they had a great afternoon. They'd talked about school and laughed away a few hours before walking the historic red line through a few places Caitlyn wanted to get pictures of for her classes. They had passed by the Old North Church, Faneuil Hall, and Paul Revere's house, which matched her lessons on the Revolution, their current unit.

Caitlyn smiled to herself at the thought of the kids walking over the cobbled streets, following the red line like a scavenger hunt, and getting the chance to see the historic sites.

She laid out the cookies on the granite countertop. The galley in the *Bombshell* was truly a thing of beauty. The stainless steel appliances adorned the mahogany and teak space like jewels in a golden crown. Everything on the yacht seemed customized. Only the best of the best.

Even the bathroom on board included a spacious shower, window, and a shiny chrome sink. The bedroom next to it seemed almost as large as an average room, with what looked to be a queen-sized bed in it. It even had windows cut into the sides of the triangular walls matching the bow of the boat. With its fluffy duvet and blue and white striped pillows, Caitlyn wondered what it would be like to lie down and wait to be rocked to sleep by the waves.

A vision of her and Austin in that bed flashed into her

head, sending a thrill of warmth down her chest. Austin sat at the helm up the wooden stairs. She turned to the side to get a glance of him from down below. He had taken off his Barbour coat and tossed it onto the little sitting area behind the helm and shotgun seat, as Austin had called it.

He sat in a long-sleeved sweater over a collared shirt. The color matched his eyes, tropical blue, and set off his blond hair perfectly. He had a firm set to his jaw as he looked outward with one hand on the joystick to his right.

He really was one of the most intense and beautiful people she had met in her life. Another wave of heat bloomed over her skin, hitting her face, making her cheeks feel warm.

Sharing the bed behind her on a boat like this, surrounded by just the waves, seemed like the most sensual fantasy. Just them and the raw power of nature with no one around for miles. She stared ahead out the small window over the sink, letting herself imagine what it would feel like for him to pull her collar to the side and slide his lips over her skin, grazing her with his stubble. Maybe he would unbutton her shirt and slide his hands inside, cupping her before easing her onto the bed. After that, he might take her in his arms and slip them both under the covers so they could warm back up with the heat from their bodies.

Caitlyn felt her mouth water, and she swallowed on reflex before looking back down at the package she was trying to slice open without taking off a finger. Because that wasn't going to happen—the finger slicing or the bed warming. She wasn't ready for that kind of connection, and hello, he was her boss. Caitlyn wasn't that kind of woman. The kiss—make that kisses—had been too much, and as nice as this trip was, Caitlyn knew it would end here. It had to.

She had almost declined this trip for that very reason. Being alone with Austin or anyone for that matter with no way to escape or call for help didn't seem like a smart idea, but the temptation to get lunch in Boston and explore the city a little had proven too great. Add to that, he'd been a perfect gentleman the entire time.

Caitlyn frowned at the bread. No doubt that was because of how Thanksgiving had gone down. She shook her head trying to get her thoughts straight. After Halloween and Thanksgiving, it was clear he liked her, but after the way he'd introduced her to his family, assuming it was anything serious would be foolish. She was not going to get fired and risk her heart for a fling that wouldn't last.

Caitlyn glanced at the bed behind her. It didn't look like a bachelor's bed, and she wasn't stupid. Austin had never talked about exes, but she wasn't naive. The chances she was the first woman to stand in this galley, on this boat with him, were about as low as the balance in her bank account. Jealousy clawed at her chest, but Caitlyn was so used to burying her feelings, she just shoved it down deep so it could fade away like all the others.

Anyone who was invited on this boat and didn't take a shot at Austin was an idiot. The confidence with which he handled the helm and the gentleness of his thoughts, wrapped up with the heat of his kisses was too tempting. As much as she didn't want to acknowledge it, Thanksgiving had been some of the best kissing she'd ever experienced.

She savored the memory of Austin pulling her close and enveloping her, the heat rising inside her. Caitlyn had wanted more, and that was the dangerous bit. Getting interrupted had been the best thing to happen. Still, she knew she would cherish the memory of standing in the autumn chill, pressed against his strong, warm body, to the grave. Even now, the thought made heat bloom on her skin.

A swell almost knocked her off balance, tugging her back to the present. She focused on the task at hand again, trying to get back to normal. When they got back home, she was going to thank Austin and walk away, with a firm talking to herself.

Besides, the last thing she needed to be doing was getting involved with someone. Especially given how her previous relationship ended.

Another swell lifted one side and pushed her into the wall.

"You okay? Here, let me get that," Austin said, reaching down to take a cookie and clasping her hand in his. The warmth of his touch, with the fantasy fresh in her mind, sent a shot of heat up her chest. Using his arm and the wall for support, Caitlyn made the climb and reached out for her seat to steady herself.

"Glad you're not getting sick from this."

"Me too," Caitlyn said, sitting down. The sun eased down toward the horizon and would have created a perfect sunset if it weren't for the dark cloud obscuring most of it. Though it was only four in the afternoon, it had gotten much darker than when they had left Hyannis.

Caitlyn glanced over at Austin to her right. His jaw jutted out a little, and a thin line of concentration formed between his eyebrows. Unlike before, he had both hands on the helm and slowly guided it in both directions in a series that didn't make sense to her but seemed to create some sort of pattern for him.

Waves churned in the water, rocking them back and forth in a pattern she hadn't noticed before. Whitecaps formed, and sea spray showered the bow and windows. A seed of anxiety formed in her gut. Austin shifted in his seat and leaned forward, activating wipers she hadn't noticed before.

If anything, his quiet concerned her. Austin never seemed to be without words or his happy-go-lucky style. Now he watched the waves in front of him, sitting quietly with a laser-like focus on the path. A stark departure from his default, Austin gripped the wheel and leaned into this goal, looking straight ahead and frowning, the sailor in him clear as he turned the bow partially with the waves every time they rose.

Rain started splattering against the window in thick, fat drops before coming in rapid succession. The wind got louder, and the waves got higher. The bow of the boat rose and then fell, sending more of a spray up above the windows. Some of the sea came over the bow and slid off in all directions.

"Caitlyn," Austin said without looking in her direction, mouth tight in a thin line.

The sound of his voice concerned her. Deeper than normal and without his usual smile.

"Ah...yes?" she said.

"I need you to go into the compartment under the bench behind you. Inside there is a black harness. I want you to put it on."

The tone of his voice didn't leave any room for debate or question.

"Uh...sure," she said, standing up and promptly getting thrown to the left. She hobbled her way toward the compartment, clinging to the furniture as she went, trying to hold herself upright. The boat rocked back and forth with violent sways. Without another handhold, Caitlyn hugged the wall as it pitched up and down before dropping to her hands and knees and crawling over the smooth wood to get to the little cabinet door. She opened the small brass circle and pulled out one of several harnesses that matched Austin's description.

"Do you need one?" she called above the sounds of the wind and storm around them.

"Just put it on," he said, standing now and fighting to keep them on course in the crashing surf ahead. Caitlyn unhooked the straps and pulled them on like a jacket before clipping the belt back together. The word inflate stood out in bold letters over a whistle dangling from a small cord.

Without asking again, she pulled another one out of the cabinet and tried to stand up, taking two tries to do it. Clinging to the sides of the cabin, she eased her way forward to the seat, one harness on and one in hand.

"I'm going to do everything in my power to make sure you don't need that, but I can't have you without it. I just can't," Austin said, not facing her. His jaw had a firm set to it, as he pulled the helm while the waves crashed into the *Bombshell*'s hull.

"Give me your arm," Caitlyn said, standing behind him while bracing herself on the back of his seat.

Austin looked at her, pissed for the first time. The normally warm eyes were cold and intense. His brow was furrowed low, creating a nasty snarl that took away all the charm. "What?"

Caitlyn met him in the eye. "Give me your damn arm. I can't have you without one either."

Austin blinked at her a couple of times as if trying to process what she just said. A massive wave crashed into them, spraying water all over the bow. Austin swore and returned his focus to the front with a white-knuckled grip on the helm. He pulled back on the little joystick and kept cranking the helm left and right.

Caitlyn grabbed one hand off the helm and slid the black harness over his arm. She had to get in close and reach around him to the other side, bringing her body in full contact with his as the *Bombshell* rode the angry waves.

"Hand!" she yelled at him, pissed he would even think twice.

Austin glanced back and didn't say anything but lifted his

hand just enough so she could slide it up over his shoulder before reaching around to his waist from behind to clip the two belt pieces together.

"I've never worn one before," he said over the crashing water. "I mean not since the navy."

"Well, if I'm wearing one, so are you," Caitlyn said into his ear over the noise. Her arms were still around his hips, holding on as the cabin lurched from side to side. The clanging of something that sounded like pots and dishes in the galley came from below. An eerie howling started outside as the wind pummeled the windows and flybridge above the cabin.

The window wipers batted away, but outside, Caitlyn had trouble making anything out in the pitch blackness.

"I can't see a damn thing," Austin said through gritted teeth. "I need to cut the lights in here, okay?"

"Okay."

Caitlyn was still holding on as Austin hit a button that sent them into blackness. Instruments glowed in the dark on the other side of the helm. She blinked a few times, letting her eyes adjust. The boat rolled and pitched back and forth even more with one side lifting far above the other. Rain poured down onto the windshield in sheets, while the wipers tried to beat them back, struggling to keep up with the pace.

"I'm going to need you to help me look around," Austin said, raising his voice over the noise.

"What am I looking for?" Caitlyn let go after a strong swell and threw herself across the aisle, timing her jump with the sway of the boat. Arms outstretched, she made contact with the arm of the chair and paused before hauling herself into the seat with the next swell.

Austin swore again. "Anything with a light, and anything without a light."

Caitlyn blinked a few more times and braced herself on

the railing in front of her seat. Nausea rolled in her gut with the boat, so she stood back up and spread her legs wide trying to ride the floor.

"That doesn't make any sense!"

"A large black spot without light—fucking shit—that's something, and we don't want to hit it."

"Got it," Caitlyn said, watching. "How close are we?"

"Close. I don't know if I can...Jesus. I don't know if I can enter the harbor with this storm."

The inky darkness spread ahead, but gradually, shapes stood out to her. The horizon was a shade lighter than the water but by the barest shade. Waves higher than she had ever seen churned ahead, tossing the *Bombshell* around. The bow of the cabin cruiser pitched up before slamming down, rattling everything in the galley below. Surf splashed all of the windows around them.

Austin swore again as another wave crashed into the side, pushing the boat and rolling everything around her. Caitlyn stood and braced herself, squatting down to take the waves of the boat while staring at the horizon for minutes that stretched into what felt like hours, the silence punctuated with Austin's curses and the blowing gale outside.

Her eyes stretched in the night, everything starting to look the same, when off to the right, she saw a glint. Caitlyn closed her eyes and rubbed them once before opening again and searching the spot she had seen it only to be met with dark. She stood and angled herself to get a better look.

The seconds stretched to minutes in the violent dance with the waves. After what felt like the better part of an hour, Caitlyn saw something glint in the distance. She leaned forward and pointed.

"What?" Austin said, glancing at her while still guiding *Bombshell* on the waves through sheets of rain.

Caitlyn shook her head and remembered he couldn't see her. "I thought I saw…Holy shit, Austin, look!"

"What? What? I can't see it."

"It's a light. Wait. What the hell? I saw a white light, and now it's gone."

Caitlyn thrust her hand out to point the direction, waiting.

"Oh my God, there it is again! You see it? You see it? Right here!"

"Thank you, sweet little baby Jesus. That's the fucking lighthouse." Austin's voice was like a sigh that let all the breath he had been holding out in a rush. Caitlyn almost wanted to jump up and down on her toes with joy, which made her realize how terrified she had been. Just the thought of seeing the island and her tiny apartment above the ice cream parlor was enough to sag with sweet relief.

But they had to get there first.

"You'll see a red light next," Austin said. "That's the light we need. It's the entrance to the harbor."

The strain had come back to his voice again. "Can we go in yet?" she asked.

Austin stared straight ahead, still steering *Bombshell* with the waves, muttering curses only a sailor would know under his breath. If anything, the intensity of his focus had only grown after seeing the lighthouse ahead.

"The bay should be calmer. I won't know until we get there."

Caitlyn nodded to herself and continued her post, watching ahead. The journey toward the bay felt like hours had stretched by when she knew it couldn't have been that long. As they passed the lighthouse and rounded a small piece of land jutting out, Austin's swearing really came to life. The waves kept wanting to push them away from the bay, and they shifted at the last moment, pushing *Bombshell* right toward painted pilings that marked the shoals.

In the dark, she couldn't see them, but Austin knew where they were from memory and the chart plotter screen he had covered up with a towel to shed more light.

Finally, *Bombshell* passed the lighthouse on the starboard side, and though the waves were still choppy, they were nothing like the open Atlantic.

Austin sat back against the seat for a moment, breathing hard, lines of stress and exhaustion etched on his face.

"Fuck."

That about covered it, Caitlyn thought before sending up a silent prayer of thanks. She still stood, riding the smaller waves and watching the wipers beat back the rain as she had been for the last hour.

"I'm so sorry," Austin said in the dark.

"Thank you for getting us back safely. You were incred—"

"I should've known better." Austin looked haunted and terrified. "I'm so sorry."

"It's okay. The storm wasn't your fault."

Austin turned to look at her. In the dark, she could just make out the lines of his face from the glow of the instruments. The boat rose and fell under them like it was breathing in a steady pattern. Rain pounded on the windshield.

"We could stay on board for a little bit and wait out the storm." His voice was soft, inviting, rising in invitation. A swell of heat bloomed in her chest. On reflex, Caitlyn squashed the feeling.

"I had a great time," she said, trying to ignore every part of her that wanted to go jump in his bed.

He stared at her for another moment, then he nodded once and put one hand on the joystick, pushing them forward toward land.

CHAPTER 27

ustin tossed his bag into the visitor's chair and fired up his Mr. Coffee the second he walked into his office. He slammed down in his old chair, leaned back, and breathed in the scent of caffeine brewing. He had tossed all night, getting tangled up in the sheets and regrets.

The trip to Boston had been stellar and would've been perfect had it not been for the storm and his weird little trip down memory lane while she had been sitting across from him at lunch. He hadn't expected her to climb into bed with him, but the rejection had still stung. Austin knew he should turn away, but naturally, he was more obsessed than ever after she turned him down and politely thanked him at the dock.

The coffee maker beeped, and Austin scrubbed his face, feeling old. Out of habit, he started doing the math to figure out his actual age. He didn't feel that old in regards to his body of course, but it was his mind that was exhausted. Some days he had so much energy he felt the need to get out and run. When that wasn't an option, he balled his hands into fists and could feel the energy vibrating through his body.

In his younger days, Austin had punched the wall regularly, much to the irritation of his parents. Not in a weird way, but in a boxing cardio sort of way, which had come in handy in the bottom of the USS Astoria's hull when someone wanted to pick a fight. It just felt satisfying to feel the solid plaster under his knuckles. Sometimes, when he was alone in his office, he still gave the wall a few taps, just to show it who was boss. But not today.

No, this morning was slow going. Austin heaved himself up from the chair and found his silver tumbler, the only one that kept the coffee hot until lunch, and poured in the beautiful dark liquid. He had stopped counting scoops long ago and never had added any cream or sugar.

Austin was just letting the first sip slide down his throat when there was a knock at the door and Principal John's face poked around the corner.

"Hey, knew you would come in early. How was your break?" John asked. Today he was wearing an open suit jacket that was the same brown as his thinning hair.

"Short. You?"

"Good. Same," John replied.

"What's up?" Austin made a point to be the first in the building every day, and John never came in early.

Instead of saying anything, he pushed through the door and shut it behind him with a soft click. Austin was tall, but John had another six inches. He also had another fifty pounds on him, making the large principal awkward in the tiny, cluttered space. John shuffled around some stacks of files on the floor.

"Want to sit?"

"Won't be able to get back up. Don't get old."

"We should put that on T-shirts. 'Come to Brightrock. Don't get old.'"

"Funny, but I doubt the council would get the joke."

"I'd buy one." Austin smiled as the smile fell from the Principal's face, letting the wrinkles show.

"I heard you invited Caitlyn to your family's house."

Austin felt his jaw tighten but kept the poker face on. "Yeah, wanted to be neighborly. She didn't have anywhere to go." He wondered how much John knew but wanted to bet he didn't know about the kiss.

"Right. We're having a special council meeting tonight."

Oh, shit.

"Oh, yeah?" Austin asked, taking another sip of coffee as if he didn't care where this was headed.

"Yeah, and you need to come."

"Why's that?"

"Look, Austin, you know I see a lot of great potential in you. The teachers like you, the kids like you. You're my rock around here. Part of what keeps this place going. We don't know what we'd do without you."

Discipline kept Austin quiet during John's pause. It gave him time to notice the principal looked sick to his stomach.

"They're putting in an order against you."

"Bullshit. For Thanksgiving? That's totally asinine, and you know it."

"It's not just for Thanksgiving, Austin." The principal's eyes told Austin how much he knew. Austin played it like it was a bluff.

"If we can't even invite—"

He held his hand up to stop Austin. "I warned you this might happen."

"You called the meeting then?"

"No, but Austin, I've been burned by this kind of thing in the past. I can't let it happen again. I can't lose any more good people. The council wanted to verify some concerns brought to them."

"What's to say I'll stay at a place that blows the whistle on me?" Austin said, leaning back in his chair. He knew his jaw was jutting out, but he didn't give a fuck. "Thought you said you needed me? I guess not that much, huh? This was all your idea, wasn't it?"

"Austin, don't do this."

"All I did was try to be nice, and hello, aren't you the one who told me to keep an eye on her? Get her to trust me?"

"Austin, I didn't think it would go this far."

"When's the meeting?"

"Six."

"Got it. Did you need anything else, or is the knife in my back it?"

John looked like someone had killed his favorite puppy. "Shit. Don't be like that."

"So that's it then? Great way to start off the week," Austin said, taking another sip of coffee before he stood. His shoulders were too high, and he had rolled up his sleeves like he was ready to throw down. Turns out old habits did die hard. "If that's it, I'll see you later. Got shit I gotta do." Austin stood and propped his hands on his hips.

John was halfway out the door when he turned around and said, "You know, Austin, I didn't make the rules. She's a nice girl, but it is what it is."

Austin didn't say anything, holding the fury with a firm grip. A few seconds later, John left. Austin waited until the man was out of earshot and slammed his fist on the desk.

CHAPTER 28

Caitlyn tossed the last project on the stack and breathed a sigh of relief. Next to her desk lamp, Caitlyn studied the folded chess board that lay untouched. She hadn't exactly been waiting for Austin to come up after how things had ended, but she had stayed at school longer than necessary. She hadn't seen him all day.

Probably not a surprise. After Austin had parked the *Bombshell* and tied her off in the pouring rain, he had come back into the cabin only to be met with a polite thank you. After a great day together on board and a harrowing return trip, it had been a cold move in hindsight.

A weird sensation twisted in her gut when she thought about him. She shouldn't get involved, couldn't afford to, but Caitlyn missed his company as a friend. Most of the staff still weren't chatty with her. By now she thought that would've changed. Caitlyn thought she was friendly, but she'd been wrong before.

On her way out of the room, Caitlyn hoisted up her over-sized bag and glanced at the clock. For once she was leaving at a decent time, even though it was late, but when she came out into the hall, Connie's door was already shut, as were most of the doors in the upstairs hallway.

Caitlyn's footsteps echoed off of the old painted brick walls and down the empty stairwell. When she reached the first floor, all of those doors were locked up for the night as well. Caitlyn went by the office, which was unusually dark.

Her footsteps were the only sound around her, echoing off the walls in the silence. The hairs on the back of her neck rose. She peeked down the electives wing hoping to get a sight of James the custodian. There was no one.

The lights above her were on, but that didn't mean anything. Thanks to the energy-saving initiative, they would go off without anyone hitting a switch. No one had to be here to lock up.

Her low heels clipped on the linoleum. Sweat prickled in her palms. Caitlyn pulled her purse a little higher on her shoulder and pushed through the front door then stopped.

The little Ford Escape sat alone in the lot, illuminated by a lamppost in the dark.

An icy chill that had nothing to do with the wind seeped into her bones. On a whim, Caitlyn was tempted to run for the safety of her car but instead settled on a brisk walk. Her ears strained for any sign of children running around outside or cars on the road. There was nothing.

Caitlyn hustled toward the car, hitting the button on the key, opening the doors. She fought the urge to run the last few steps. Slamming the door shut after she had clambered inside, Caitlyn punched the lock twice. Something wasn't right.

Caitlyn fired up the engine and pulled out of the barren parking lot, trying to calm her rattling nerves. The roads were deserted. Unease slid back into her as she searched for another pair of headlights and found none. Caitlyn's hands shifted on the wheel.

Reaching her apartment over the ice cream parlor, Caitlyn parked her Escape in her spot behind the building. She clutched her keys in her hand and eyed the alley around her. Throwing open the car door, Caitlyn hoisted her bag and jogged over to the exterior stairs, taking them two at a time up to the door. Key in the slot, jiggle, twist, push and she was inside. Caitlyn threw the deadbolt behind her and felt her shoulders sink with relief of being in the warm pool of light from the lamp on the table in the small foyer.

When she had first moved in, Caitlyn had bought a timer from the hardware store and set up the light to be on when she came home, turn off after she fell asleep, and back on in the early hours. Something about having the light on when she woke up made living alone a little homier. She kicked off her shoes and moved them under the small table with her toe before shrugging out of her green wool coat and hanging it up in the tiny closet in the hall.

Caitlyn knew there must be a logical reason why everyone had left early. As an outsider, there had been a steep learning curve when she had moved here, and there was nothing to suggest the curve had leveled off. She pulled open the fridge and took some of the Thanksgiving turkey she had fixed for herself on Saturday, threw it on a plate with some mashed potatoes, and popped it into the microwave before heading to the bedroom.

She washed her face and swiped on the same brand of lotion that her mother had sworn by before pulling on her favorite gray pajamas and a white waffle robe. A braided rug cushioned her bare feet as she padded over to the bed to plug in her phone.

The temptation to flop down onto the cream-colored bed called to her, but at that moment, the microwave beeped. After a quick debate, Caitlyn rose from the bed and grabbed her food and a can of Coke before heading to the couch. For once, she craved the sound of the TV after the weird drive home.

That thought reminded her that she still hadn't seen anyone since the last bell released the tide of students from the building. She took a quick bite and grabbed the remote, clicking through the channels to find some people, so she wouldn't feel so alone.

Too late for the news, and with nothing else of interest, Caitlyn settled on the Home Shopping Network for the company if nothing else. A lady with big hair and too much makeup demonstrated the ease of a new pan, which held what looked to be some sort of bubbly casserole. Caitlyn settled in and polished off her dinner. A few callers called in, one of whom made a point to say that she lived alone and needed to cook for one. Caitlyn could sympathize.

While the TV droned on, she felt her lids lower. As the kitchen products she was never going to buy flashed in front of her, Caitlyn felt herself slide down into the throw pillows on her couch. At one point she started resting her eyes, comforted by the ongoing voice whose words she could no longer identify beyond the sounds they made.

Voices undulated, punctuated with sharp bouts of laughter. Even with her eyes closed, Caitlyn could tell they were smiling. Though it was surely a marketing technique, Caitlyn smiled to herself. The woman's voice almost reminded her of her mom's, but the accent was wrong. Still, Caitlyn succumbed to the rise and fall of her slow breath while letting the woman's voice wash over her.

On the edge of sleep, a knock at the door brought her back to full attention. The TV droned on, now with a tall gentleman demonstrating something else. Caitlyn listened.

Three more knocks echoed from the front door down her small hall. Caitlyn sat up and eyed the door, wishing to God she had a damn peephole.

Maybe Austin had come to fill her in on whatever it was that she had missed, she thought. Who else could it be? Emboldened, Caitlyn marched forward and grabbed the knob.

"Hey! I was wondering where—" Caitlyn froze.

Dark tousled hair that matched a scruffy beard and glasses stared back at her.

"Hey, I guess you weren't expecting me," Caleb said in a soft drawl that dragged her back to Louisiana. "I need to talk to you. Tried to call."

The pounding in her chest made it hard to, and it wasn't until she tried to drag in a breath that she realized her mouth was open.

Caitlyn clipped it shut. "What about?"

"Can I come in?" he asked.

"Why?"

"Caitlyn, come on. I just flew on three different planes."

"Why are you here?"

"I told you I need to talk to you."

"What about?"

A gust of wind blasted through the open door. Caleb hiked up his shoulders, and Caitlyn pulled her robe shut while holding the door with the other hand. It was then that she realized he was just wearing a sweater.

"I didn't realize it would be so cold in November."

"Yep." She didn't budge. Good manners yelled at her to let him in, but Caitlyn couldn't. She didn't see any luggage.

"Where's your bag?"

"At the bed and breakfast. I booked a room there, and they let me know where to find you. Look, I don't want to spend the night or anything. I just wanted to talk to you."

"Why didn't you just call?"

"I did. You never picked up or called me back."

Caitlyn remembered seeing his name on her missed calls,

but for the life of her, she couldn't remember how many times.

"I've been busy."

"Yeah, I know, with school and all. I texted too."

Another gust of wind howled through the alley, and she could see Caleb shake a little in the cold.

"Fine." She pushed open the door and let him pass. "Do you, um, want anything to drink or whatever?"

Caleb stepped inside the small foyer. He glanced around at the nautical touches on the walls and shook his head. "When did we become strangers?"

"When I left."

Caleb looked pained at this comment, and Caitlyn felt bad enough to look down. She needed something to do other than stand near him. "Coffee?" she asked.

"If you're making it. Don't make a special pot for me."

"It's not Community," she said, referencing the premium brand from south Louisiana.

"That's okay."

Caleb stood in the living room and looked around her tiny apartment. He stopped once to study a painting of a whaler. The Mr. Coffee started bubbling away, so she went back to the couch and flopped down. He eased into the chair across from her, before leaning forward to prop his elbows on his knees.

Caitlyn didn't say anything. She wasn't sure what to say.

"So how is it up here?" he asked.

"It's nice. Different."

"Looks a lot different from back home."

"Yeah."

"Small."

"Yeah."

"Quiet?"

"Oh yeah, it's quiet." Especially tonight, she added to

herself, thinking back to the weirdness of the entire faculty vanishing. She had wanted company, but this was not what she had in mind.

The coffee maker beeped, and Caitlyn jumped up. Caleb stood on reflex and accepted the cup she brought him. They sat back down. Both of them took a sip.

"You look well," Caleb said quietly. He was cradling the white mug in his hands.

"Thank you." Caitlyn still wasn't sure where this was going. "What's going on?"

Caleb smirked into his mug before looking at her. "Parrain asked me to say hello. He's been asking about you. You left without saying goodbye."

Guilt stung her chest. Caitlyn had always liked Caleb's grandfather, Mr. Broussard. The old Cajun was a relic but had a sense of humor about him.

"To either of us, that is," Caleb added.

A sigh escaped her. The guilt turned into raw pain in her chest and wore her down. Exhaustion hit her like a truck. Looking down at her hands, she realized they were clutching the mug of coffee. She wanted to hurl the thing against the wall.

"You didn't give me a chance. Didn't you think we could get through this? You didn't think for a moment I could help you? Shit, that any of us could help you? You're not alone." His voice was desperate and pleading.

"I can't go back there. Maybe to visit. Someday. But not now," Caitlyn said, staring at the coffee table.

"Why not? We want you to come back. I want you back."

Pain turned to anger, and her voice rose. "You don't get it. Everything about that place. All of it—it's just too much."

"What do you mean? You've lived there your whole life."

"Don't you think I know that?" she snapped.

Caleb winced in pain, and Caitlyn felt terrible, but she couldn't stop.

"Your accent is too much for me right now."

"My accent? You have the same one!"

"Caleb, if I went back, every accent, every corner, every tree, church, and house would remind me of them. Oh, and let's not forget the people all coming up to me to talk about them. How do you think that would make me feel?"

"Caitlyn, it should make you feel good because everyone loved your parents. They loved them, and they miss them. The people who bought—"

"Don't." She scrubbed her face. Her hands were wet. It was only then that she realized she was crying. Caleb looked determined.

"No, stop. You need to hear this. The people who bought the house are a young couple. They love it. They're going to have a baby."

"Great. Good for them," Caitlyn said, very much wishing she had left him outside.

"It is good for them," he said, his voice pleading again.

"Please leave."

"Shit, Caitlyn—"

"Please. I can't do this now."

Caleb swore under his breath. "I didn't mean to make you cry. Listen, if this is about that girl, no one blames you."

Caitlyn wiped her face and stood. She really couldn't deal with this now. "It's fine. I'm fine, but I need to go to bed. I have to work tomorrow."

Caleb sighed and stood too. He looked older than when Caitlyn had last seen him at the funeral. There were more lines on his face. "I didn't mean to mess this up again. I'm just worried about you. Can we talk another time?"

"I don't know. I'll have to check my schedule," Caitlyn

said, knowing full well that she had absolutely nothing going on.

"Okay, fine. Please let me know when you're free."

"When do you leave?" she asked to be polite.

"I don't know. I didn't buy roundtrip."

Her stomach sank. "What do you mean? You can't stay here that long."

"Why not?"

"Uhhh…I don't know. Your job? Money?"

Caleb's lips formed into a thin line. "Want to get rid of me that quick, huh?"

"You're the one who barged in here."

"Just check your schedule and let me know. Please. I promised my family I'd find out if you're okay."

He looked like he always had, but older. Maybe it was just jet lag, but the lines near his eyes stood out to Caitlyn more. Still stubborn as a mule.

"Fine," she said at last.

He nodded once and walked to the kitchen.

"You don't have to do that."

"Well, I am."

Determined as always, he rinsed the cup before opening her small dishwasher and placing it inside on the top rack.

Caitlyn stood with her arms folded, watching him. When he came out of the kitchen, he paused and looked as though he was arguing with himself.

"If you don't call again, I'll be back," he said in his soft drawl. It sounded more menacing when Schwarzenegger said it. With Caleb, it was just his old reliable self, like a dog with a bone.

CHAPTER 29

Austin jerked around in the old truck as it jostled him over the dirt road in the area he had lied to Caitlyn about being merely a refuge. It was a refuge, at least according to the Commonwealth of Massachusetts, and the biological reasons for that classification were legitimate, but they would never know the secrets about what was there. Not that he cared.

Rage pumped through his veins now, and the only thing keeping him on the dirt road with a laser-like focus was anger. John had no business outing him to everyone. He was the one who had stirred his behavior in the first place.

Austin gripped the old steering wheel as he turned onto the main road. When John had stood in the old meeting-house and addressed the council of elders, Austin had been tempted to throw a chair, but figuring that would get him no brownie points, he'd instead sat in the old pew and ground his molars. The well-meaning principal had explained how the new history teacher had become very close with the residents and should be considered dangerous and avoided.

There was too much risk in revealing information about Brightrock and its residents.

After that little bomb had been dropped, non-disclosure agreements had been reread along with the consequences for violating those contracts. All of it a large dog and pony show designed to intimidate him and other residents who had solemnly sat and nodded in the pews as if listening to some cult-like gospel.

Austin's parents had nodded slowly and tried to catch his eye, but he wasn't in the mood. An emergency town hall meeting, his left foot. It was a bullshit move.

The shitty thing about living on the island was how much control it had over him. All of the other residents sat and voted calmly on matters that affected his daily life on a quarterly basis. He couldn't get pissed anymore because he was stuck with the pack of them until he wanted to leave and die. He chewed on his cheek again and hit the gas to get to Caitlyn as fast as possible. Fuck whoever saw him and wanted to say something. Yet more proof Ethan had the right idea after all.

Austin made a mental note to ask him more about life off the island when he saw him next at Christmas. Fake IDs were nothing new to the residents here, but day to day life would get tricky after a while when other coworkers aged and he didn't. Still, if his brother could do it, he sure as shit could.

The old truck rounded around the main road until Easterly Bay came into view. The dark landscape melted into the horizon of the Atlantic, where waves crashed and cooled his rage a little. Austin craned his neck to see the windows above the ice cream parlor. The rest of the shops were dark, closed down early because of the so-called emergency meeting. Austin turned to pull into an open space when out of the corner of his eye something moved in the dark.

He braked and slowly pulled into the space. In the darkness, the tide moved but nothing else. He had lived here for almost one hundred years. He wasn't scared.

The old engine idled over the rushing of the slow, languid waves. A gust of wind rocked the cab, demanding Austin's attention and asserting Mother Nature's authority as only a New England winter could. Fall had come to a close, and soon, the beach would be buried in snow. Austin sat in the heat a little longer, letting his rage cool.

John knew better than to approach Austin after the meeting. Austin knew how to disappear at work, so that wouldn't be a problem. He needed to do classroom observations anyway, and wouldn't it be rude if his walkie went off during a lesson? Satisfied with his plan, Austin shifted and reached to cut the engine when he saw it again.

On the other side of the road, the outline of a man walked down the stairs from Caitlyn's apartment. The darkness hid his features, and the wind forced him into a jacket that apparently wasn't keeping him warm. He stalked away from the ice cream parlor with his hands shoved in his pockets, back braced against the wind. Austin watched him walk along the sidewalk until the darkness obscured him totally.

The glow of the light in Caitlyn's apartment suggested she was okay. He waited until he saw her shadow move around before relaxing his grip on the door handle. It hadn't taken long, which is why he wasn't stomping up the stairs and banging down her door to make sure she was safe.

Something seemed off, but Austin stayed put. John's earlier accusations floated in his head, which pissed him off again. He couldn't care less what John thought of his relationship with Caitlyn. Besides, after the way they'd left things on the boat, he wasn't sure there was much of a relationship left anyway. What bothered him now was John's last suggestion.

The principal's voice echoed in his head. "We don't know

Caitlyn. All of her information checked out, but at the end of the day, we can't take a chance on an unknown. We must take caution around her."

Austin's fingers curled around the steering wheel until the fingernails bit into the palms of his hands. Everyone else was at the Town Hall meeting, and he hadn't seen a car come this way. He had been the first to leave. Austin racked his brain for a missing face at the meeting and came up empty.

Someone had visited Caitlyn tonight. Someone not from the island.

Though he hated himself for doing it and would for a long time after that night, Austin put the key in the ignition and reluctantly drove away.

CHAPTER 30

Caitlyn plopped her purse on the swivel chair behind her desk and tossed down the random papers someone had shoved into her mailbox. Even though Thanksgiving break had been just days ago, Caitlyn's shoulders remained tense with anxiety. Rolling them back, she took a gulp of coffee out of the stainless steel tumbler bearing the seal of the school. It had been part of a welcome gift she'd received on her first day along with a few pens and a desk calendar.

While she waited for her computer to load, she popped open a little white bottle of pain pills, swallowed some with another swig of coffee, and set up her room for the day. Thanks to standardized testing, she wouldn't see students until after lunch, and though it probably wasn't a good use of time, Caitlyn felt like a little socializing to take her mind off of Caleb's unexpected pop-in.

Stepping out of her classroom and into the hall, Caitlyn poked her head into Connie's room. The veteran English teacher sat at her desk, reading over the testing instructions. Today she wore red-rimmed glasses that matched her earrings and shoes. The accessories gave a pop of color to the crisp white shirt and black and white scroll-patterned pants Caitlyn wished she could pull off.

"Hey," Caitlyn said. "How was your weekend? I didn't get a chance to ask you yesterday."

Connie glanced up and offered a quick smile before shuffling more papers on her desk. "Hey, yourself. Yeah, I had to duck out early." More shuffling. Connie plucked a pencil out from her pencil caddy and made a note on a sticky note. "No, my weekend was good. Short, you know the drill." She shrugged. "Hey, can I email you if I need a bathroom break today? These testing blocks kill me."

"Yeah, sure thing," Caitlyn said, leaning against the door. "How long do you think it will go?"

Connie shoved the pencil behind her ear and answered without looking up as she read over what looked to be the writing prompt. "Considering the fact this will determine their growth scores in the spring?" She clicked her tongue. "Gonna be a while."

When Connie didn't add anything, Caitlyn figured the conversation had gone about as far as it could. Promising to check in on her later, she headed down to Austin's office. It wasn't unusual for people to be quiet around her, but Connie typically talked more. Blaming it on testing, Caitlyn descended the stairs.

A few teachers holding coffee cups chatted in the main hall on the first floor by the overstuffed trophy case. Pat, Laurie, and Sally talked, but when they saw her, they each stopped and offered a polite smile.

"Morning," Caitlyn said, walking forward to join them. "Ready for testing today?"

"Yeah, I think it'll be a long one," Pat said.

Sally nodded in agreement while Laurie took another sip of her coffee.

The pair of them started to walk off, when Caitlyn asked, "Hey, have you guys seen Austin?"

They exchanged a quick glance. Sally clenched her silver tumbler with both hands, looking panic-stricken.

"Sorry, haven't seen him," she said in a rush before she spun on her heel and sped in the other direction toward her classroom.

Caitlyn turned to Laurie, who looked worried. She was chewing on the inside of her lip. "Is everything okay?" Caitlyn looked from her to Sally, hustling to her room, and back.

Laurie turned to face her and gave a smile Caitlyn didn't believe. Where there should have been brightness, concern echoed. In her old school, people who had that face were usually on the verge of quitting.

"Everything's fine. We're all just a little tense before the holidays. Testing and all that." She paused and looked as if she was debating saying something. After a quick sigh, she said, "I saw Austin go into his office a few minutes ago. He's probably still there."

"Okay, thanks," Caitlyn said. "I'll head there now. Let me know if you need anything, okay?"

Laurie gave her another sad smile and headed into the library as the bell rang. Caitlyn turned and went down the hall, heading in the direction of Austin's office. She was rounding the corner when he came out, looking grim.

"Hey, I was looking for you. I tried to find you yesterday, but everyone took off." She paused, getting a look at him. "What's wrong?"

Austin's face looked like it had been chiseled from concrete. A gray pallor had taken over, and his normally tropical blue eyes seemed cold and flat.

"Maybe you should start by telling me who came to your apartment last night?"

She jerked back in surprise and felt her eyebrows shoot up. So much for ignoring it today. Caitlyn sighed and pulled a hand through her hair, trying to ease a persistent headache.

"Guy from back home. It's a long story."

Austin stood unmoving, silent. When she didn't speak, he did. "Oh, I'm sure it is."

"Listen, it's not like that. Caleb and I used to date."

Austin raised his left eyebrow. His chin had a hard set to it, giving him an almost predatory stare.

"I didn't ask him to come here. I don't know why he came."

"I can think of a few reasons," Austin said, taking a pocketknife out of his pocket and sharpening a pencil the old way. It seemed to make the other teachers nervous, but if they brought it up, he pointed out that shop had saws and won the argument.

"No, it isn't like that. He wants me to go back to Louisiana. Says the people there miss me." Guilt gnawed at her stomach, polishing off what it had been wearing away all night.

"So why don't you just go back?"

"I can't. Not right now," she answered, watching the students start to amble in. Laurie's voice boomed overhead through the loudspeaker, reminded students about the testing schedule and where to go.

Austin gave her a penetrating stare.

"Too many memories," she added, looking away.

Austin flipped the blade closed and pocketed it before propping his hands on his hips, looking down as if he were boring a hole in the tiled hallway.

"I'm sorry if you got the wrong impression," Caitlyn added.

Austin sucked air in through tight lips before blowing it out in a rush. "I've got to run—"

"Where was everyone yesterday?"

He looked up at her, suspicion in his eyes. "What do you mean?"

"What do you mean what do you mean? Literally, everyone was gone. I tried to find you. The whole parking lot was empty." Caitlyn threw her hands wide and let them fall with a slap on her navy pants. "Actually, I initially thought it was you knocking on the door to tell me what had happened."

"Town hall meeting," Austin said, looking away.

"Oh, that makes sense. Should I come to those?"

Austin shook his head. "Residents only." Before she could reply, he kept going. "Look, I got to run—"

"Wait, I feel like you and I need to talk. A lot has happened since Thanksgiving and..." she tried to find the words with gestures but couldn't. "There's just been a lot, and I miss our talks."

"Hey, Mr. Brooks," a senior Caitlyn didn't know called out.

Austin raised his hand in reply. "Look, I can't talk here."

"Okay, well then, where?"

"I'll send you a text later once I figure that out, okay?"

Caitlyn nodded and waved him off as he jogged toward the main office. Restless, Caitlyn headed back to her classroom, trying to think through what might be happening. Teachers usually sent texts when they wanted to keep something off the email. Which was never a good sign.

CHAPTER 31

Mark stumbled up the cracked walk from his old truck. The normal, high-speed ferry had seemed to tread water on the way back, stretching Mark's patience to the limits. When they finally pulled into port, Mark had hurried for the old truck and went straight home as opposed to stopping at the liquor store like he usually did. He needed to know for sure.

As he pushed through the piece of shit screen door on the crumbling front porch, he regretted that decision. Letting himself inside shielded him from the wind but did little to warm his freezing, stiff hands.

He didn't shed his coat as he shut the old front door, shaking the pitiful walls of the small house. Smells of coffee, booze, and old cigars floated with the dust in the air. A thin path of brown carpet patched with duct tape wound through the stacks of take-out boxes, bottles, and junk. Old furniture buried under unopened mail, mostly bills, sat around the small living room. The once-green couch peaked out from under old towels that covered where the upholstery had deteriorated next to a worn brown chair covered with a thin quilt for the same reason. His dad had often passed out on one. His mom had passed away on the other. As much as Mark loathed the memory, he was repeating the same pattern. He hated the old house, but never got up the strength to walk away from the only home he had ever known. God, he was weak.

Mark shuffled to the kitchen in the back, down a narrow hallway filled with old clothes and bundles of toilet paper. He didn't stop to scrounge for food, but instead climbed the creaking stairs to the bedrooms he rarely visited. He preferred to sleep downstairs on the chair with the TV for company.

The stairs strained under his weight, and he slowed at the top to catch his breath between two open doorways. Stacks of old shirts lay on the bed surrounded by a cluster of furniture hidden under a layer of dust. A haphazard tower of boxes that had been tossed in the room obscured the path to what had once been his own room. Mark went into the other.

When his dad had died, Mark had no interest in emptying the old bastard's nest. Now inside again for the first time in he didn't know how long, it was like his old man had left yesterday. The large bed dominated the small space. The bare, stained mattress sunk into a pit in the middle. When the paramedics came, they couldn't get the gurney up through the house and instead took the sheets to carry him away. Mark had never bothered replacing them.

Thin lace curtains shrouded the view of the street below. Boxes of papers, cassettes, and VHS tapes littered the small space. In the open door of the closet, clothes hung straight like emaciated, forgotten soldiers.

He shuffled around, hearing the click of the radiators he couldn't buy oil for this year. The thermostat couldn't be any lower, and what little oil remained would no doubt be gone soon. Not that he cared about the pipes in this shithole hell. He could walk away tomorrow without a thought.

An old metal box poked out from the side of the bed, bringing a grim smile to Mark's wind-burned face. He lowered himself down to slide the thing out. Planting a hand on the bed, he hoisted himself up and carried the box downstairs.

Mark settled into his mom's chair. His hands trembled. On instinct, Mark rummaged down around him for a bottle with something actually left inside. Finding one, he took a pull, emptying it, and tossed it down, hearing the hollow ping as it hit the carpet.

Mark took a breath and opened the box, revealing newspaper clippings, photographs, and notes from his dad's time at sea. Feeling like a child again, Mark took a moment to mourn the wasted time he had spent combing through this box only to fail time and time again. The last time he had opened it, he hadn't heard his dad come up behind him.

Mark winced at the memory of his arm being jerked away from his body, the large hand snapping the bones like the twigs they were. His dad hadn't even bothered to come to the hospital. His mom had taken him there without the car. Mark had walked, cradling his arm in the coat sleeve, letting the cold dry his tears.

Even now he shuddered at the memory of when the nurses had asked what happened. The cold stare his mom gave him from across the room while waiting for him to speak told him exactly what to say. He had been playing where he shouldn't have and gotten hurt. Their kind words and warm bed did nothing to soften the disappointment on his mother's face. His father had been her world, and when the prayers didn't stop the violence, she blamed Mark and started drinking too.

Mark pushed the dark memories out of his mind and

looked at pictures from a lifetime ago. Worn with age, the images looked back up at him. His father still had the same glint in his eye, a mean streak even from the grave. Mark flipped it face down without a thought.

With the man's face from the harbor burned into his head, Mark shifted the papers around until the same face looked back up at him from the bottom. A group of men all stood next to an anti-aircraft gun in their dress uniforms. The old bastard stood on the edge, with a smirk over cold, hard eyes while the rest of the crew beamed as the camera caught them all midjoke.

Mark held the picture in his shaking hand and studied the face in the center. A broad happy smile with a scar on the chin looked back up at him. It was a perfect match.

CHAPTER 32

Caitlyn sat in the sand on an old blanket and let the sea breeze fill her lungs. She faced toward the dark water and let the air wash over her. The moon above Crescent Beach resembled more of a sliver, but the stars shone high above her. The Milky Way swept across the sky like flour on a dark counter. Caitlyn stared up, listening to the waves. The chill in the air bit through her coat, keeping her awake. She could see why people never left Brightrock. As far as she could remember, she had never seen the stars so clear and defined. Postcard perfect by day, Brightrock was exquisite at night.

The tide had gone out since she had been sitting here. She hated being late. In this case, having this time to herself before Austin arrived calmed her. The annoyance had melted away into the sea. If anything, they needed to talk and set the record straight. That, of course, meant that Caitlyn had to figure out her thoughts, a task easier said than done.

First, they were coworkers, then she had felt they'd become friends. His blue eyes and blond hair made her chest tight. His hands were scarred from God knew what in the

THE SECRET ABOUT TIME

navy, and his chin jutted out when he was ready to take on a fight. His laugh though. It started as a giggle and dove down to the belly so his whole chest echoed the deep rumbling roar. His eyes lit up. His face turned red. Everything about him captured her attention.

God, she was screwed. Caitlyn hadn't been able to go into work for weeks without seeking him out. Stupid idiot that she was, she wanted him to like her and believed he did.

The make-out session, which in hindsight was such an obvious mistake, had led her to believe for a moment they were headed toward "something more" territory. Once his family had caught them, though, Austin had almost pulled a muscle getting away from her so fast. Then their trip to Boston had been so damn perfect, she hadn't known what to think. Spending the day with him had been everything her life had been missing for the past six months—happy, light-hearted, and easy. Austin was fun and relaxing, and they just fit together like red beans and rice, which was what had freaked her out.

Her last relationship with Caleb had blown up in her face. Being close to someone after the grief of losing her parents followed by Amber's suicide had been too much. Every compliment Caleb had tried to give her just felt like salt in the wound. She shouldn't have left him like that but couldn't bear to find the words to make him see what she endured. Escape had been the only way out. Everyone had said it wasn't her fault her parents died and *that* she could accept. The timing had been so close and the pain so raw and real, but no one else had been in the classroom when a shy, talented student came forward with her notebook filled with cries for help and cuts on her wrists.

Caitlyn squeezed her eyes shut and then forced them open. The rolling waves in the darkness in front of her barely registered in the dark, cold night. The absence of sight made her feel safe, giving her permission to retrace her steps in that awful moment. Caitlyn hadn't been prepared—she'd been caught off guard. Maybe it was because she was still reeling from her dad's death just two weeks earlier. Should she have taken more time? Would Amber have reached out to someone else? All of her training had told her to go find an administrator or counselor. She should've reached out and hugged Amber, grabbed her and pulled her close, human to human in a primal show of love, affection, and value. But she hadn't.

Amber had given Caitlyn a half-hearted smile and waved goodbye after they'd walked down to the counseling office. Procedure had been followed, boxes had been checked, and they sent Amber home on the bus. The survey didn't indicate a threat, but who answered those questions honestly? The next day, Amber was found on the floor of the bathroom in her apartment next to a notebook filled with details of an abusive boyfriend and stepfather.

Candles lit up and tears fell, and Caitlyn shattered. She put in her notice and cut all ties, including Caleb. Caitlyn took a deep breath of the salty air. She would not cry. She would not cry.

She flicked the first tear away. It wasn't fair, but Caitlyn couldn't change the past, and the only thing she had in front of her was the present.

Austin had never said anything about them being together, and after Caleb had shown up, Austin's usually happy demeanor had gone right down the tubes.

Caitlyn frowned and pulled her blanket tighter around her, imagining Caleb in the Cedar Inn, sitting by a fire, thinking about what in the hell he was doing there. Why else would he follow her to a tiny island no one had ever heard of and ask her to come home? An image of his rough hand holding a ring floated through her head. Her gut twisted at the thought. She hated to say it was her and not him, but it was. Caleb represented everything a Cajun girl should want. Handsome, hardworking, caring, the list went on. But it wasn't right. Not for her. She didn't even feel she could talk to him about all the shit in her head. How could they possibly be right for each other? Just his presence reminded her of pain.

Caitlyn wanted different. Hell, she was the one who had left to come to this tiny island. It wasn't her home. She knew a few people, but not well. At least not as well as she knew Caleb. Austin's face puzzling over a chess move came to mind.

Caitlyn looked at her hands in the dim moonlight. Unremarkable, stubby, and a little wrinkly. She wasn't young, and everyone knew teachers didn't age well. Public school had a way of chiseling wrinkles into a forehead. Her parents were gone. Her home was gone. People had reminded her for a while at weddings and baptisms about the ticking clock. Archaic, but people didn't know when to shut up. In the past, she had laughed it off and changed the conversation before rolling her eyes. Now, she heard it ticking too.

Her parents' funerals had been the first two times Caitlyn felt this way. Pushed right up to the front of the line for who would die next. When she had stood in the back of the church at Amber's service, the profound sense of loss was like a banging drum that wouldn't stop. It was no wonder she felt the urge to cling to her youth. Caitlyn now felt it again.

The waves rolled in, and the breeze blew. There was no one left to judge. She liked him. He liked her. In the dark, Caitlyn drew in a breath as she reached her decision. She didn't give a damn anymore. Time was ticking.

Caitlyn glanced over to the parking lot. Two headlights swept up over the dunes. Perfect.

A car door slammed, and Austin's silhouette stood on the

bank. At that moment, Caitlyn absorbed the sight of him. His broad shoulders stood firm against the icy breeze. Even in the dark, she knew what his face looked like as he scanned the shore for her shadow in the night. Just seeing him calmed her soul. Tension eased in her shoulders as he approached her, hands in his pockets.

In her heart, she knew this was the right decision and now was her time. She couldn't bother with worries, maybes, and what ifs. For the first time, Caitlyn didn't care about what the future looked like. She just wanted to live now for however long that was.

The wind rushed into her face, spraying her with drops from the surf as it crashed into the sand. She couldn't hear Austin approach, but she could tell when he was near.

CHAPTER 33

"I'm not sure you could've found a colder place on the island."

Caitlyn turned to him. His broad shoulders stood unflinching in the icy blast. The coat he wore wasn't as heavy, but she knew he would sooner freeze to death than put on something as fluffy as her coat and blanket.

"You said you wanted privacy."

"Can you even feel your fingers?"

"No," Caitlyn said. She stood up from the sand and turned toward him.

"Caitlyn—"

"Don't. Listen. I don't care anymore."

In the dim light from the shred of the moon, Caitlyn saw his eyebrows shoot up, then crinkle together. "It doesn't matter. I know you have secrets, but it doesn't matter anymore."

"Caitlyn, I—"

"Austin, stop. Do you like me?"

The gust of icy wind slammed into them, pushing them both off-balance.

He cleared his throat.

"Because I like you." Caitlyn closed the gap and pressed her lips to his. A declaration without words. A commitment to whatever happened. His arms locked around her, pulling her to him. Caitlyn pushed higher into his mouth and willed him to lift her away. At first, their mouths had been cold, and now they were on fire.

The waves crashed behind them, but Caitlyn wouldn't have noticed if the whole ocean swallowed them up. She didn't know how long they kissed. Every breath and tug pushed her higher and higher off the ground.

Austin's hands roamed over her, rushing against the fabric of her coat, cupping her body underneath. He pulled her in tight against him when the wind blew cold and hard against them both, and he bent low to nuzzle her neck, exposed by the collar of her coat.

Thick, strong hands she knew would catch her swept up over her lower back, caressing through her coat, pulling her tight, encircling her. The heat inside her had nothing to do with the layers she wore. It raged and burned hotter than the brief interlude in November. Caitlyn wanted to rip her coat off now, just to feel his hard, muscular body against hers. She wanted that connection; the ache in her chest was real.

Austin pulled back, panting for breath. His blue eyes glowed like tropical waters. "Come on," he said, his voice hoarse and rough.

Caitlyn didn't ask where. They crossed the beach and hustled up the sand dune held together by his firm grip. When she stumbled in the dark, his warmth held her fast like a steel girder. In her gut, she knew that if anything popped up in the dead of night, Austin would be lethal.

He ripped open the door to the old truck and would've tossed her in had she not leapt for the warmth.

"I didn't see your car," he said, pulling the door shut.

"I walked," she said, still panting and watching him.

He hadn't shaved, and his lips were swollen and parted. Those blue eyes burned into Caitlyn with desire she'd never felt or seen. Yes, everything about this felt right.

"Caitlyn, do you want to go home with me?"

"How long is the drive?" she asked. Her voice sounded low, husky, and entirely foreign.

"Maybe five minutes."

"That's too long," she said, breathing heavy. God, just looking at him made her want to weep. His strong arms draped over the wheel, and his thick jaw was everything she had ever wanted.

"No."

"What?"

Austin cranked over the engine. "I said no. That's not too long." He threw his arm over the back of her seat and backed out with ease. "Need a bed. Too damn old."

"Oh yeah?" Caitlyn said, sliding over. In the dark, she slid her hand down over his thigh, finding her target with ease.

He groaned and lurched upward, his neck snapping back. "God, are you trying to kill us?"

"I want you and I want you now," she said, working some magic in the dark. Caitlyn found his mouth. Austin threw the truck in park and kissed her back hot and hard. His stubble rasped against her chin as his tongue penetrated her mouth, searching, claiming, knowing.

Heat rose between them. Caitlyn tugged at her coat in the dark, pulling it down behind her. Her arms tangled, pinned, Austin took control and pulled her onto his lap before flinging the coat away, freeing her. Her hands locked to his face, hungry for more. Desperate. Enough time had been wasted. This needed to happen now.

Caitlyn found the hem of his sweatshirt and tugged. Austin broke the kiss and tore the shirt off so fast, she thought he had ripped the fabric. His hands roamed underneath her sweater. She wished she had the abs he was rocking. Austin nuzzled her neck, biting where the skin met her shoulder and giving her little nips. Her spine sizzled with a burning need. She could feel his hard length straining against the fly of his jeans, pointing right at her core. His hands roamed underneath her sweater, caressing and cupping her curves. Nimble fingers kneaded her skin, sending a flurry of goosebumps over her body. Caitlyn panted with need. Austin sucked in a breath without leaving her skin, teasing her with air, stoking the fire that burned inside her.

"Off," he said against the skin under her ear.

Caitlyn had the same idea and flung the top away into the darkness of the cab before finding his lips again. The chill of the air hit her skin, but only for a moment. Her skin against his, the heat of their bodies melded them together. Her hands fisted into his hair, tugging it from his scalp, begging for more and urging him to go faster.

Austin looped his hands under the straps of her bra and eased them down. Impatient, Caitlyn ripped the damn thing off, tossing it aside.

"God, you're so perfect," Austin said, his voice hoarse with need. "I wish I could see you."

"Later," Caitlyn said, turning his mouth back to her and claiming it.

Still straddling him, she lifted herself to undo his jeans. Austin set to work on hers as well and tugged them down. Caitlyn welcomed the cold air on her thighs and pulled Austin's waistband. Getting the message, he hoisted himself up and finished the job. Caitlyn slid off to the side, still kissing him while shoving her jeans down. She kicked off her boots and rid herself of the too-tight-anyway-pants before launching herself at Austin again.

He had made quick work of his own clothes and when

she hopped on him again, the ridge in him pushed against the thin layers of cotton between them. His tongue did the same dance before he pulled back and cupped her breasts with his hands, suckling each nipple. His teeth nipped at her while strong arms held her in place. Caitlyn threw back her head and opened herself to him. He could have all of her, take every part, do everything. Inhibitions gone, she fisted his hair again and pressed his face into her breast while she rode him hard. His shaft between her legs felt like the shifter on the floor, it was so hard. Austin's hands pressed into her back before he got the gist and cupped her ass, helping her slide against him through the fabric.

Heat swirled inside her chest and filled the old cab. She couldn't see outside anymore through the fog on the glass. Kate Winslet came to mind, but Caitlyn wasn't about to take her hands off the hottest thing she'd ever touched. This was the night she had been waiting for. Caitlyn felt alive and in control. Her hands started to quiver. Muscle spasms that she hadn't felt in years began in her hands and spread to her core. Fatigued with effort, Austin felt the change and pushed her on, helping guide her, stroke her, to the finish.

Caitlyn clung to him, on edge, afraid to drop, scared of letting go and giving up control. His fingers gripped her ass. Their skin wet with sweat and need slid against each other. She knew she had soaked them both. So close, but unable…

Austin's arm snaked around and pressed the one spot as if he had been there every night for a hundred years. With one touch, Caitlyn lost control. The wave ripped through her body like a tide held at bay for years. Her muscles flailed as she went boneless, giving way to the female energy that bloomed from her core through every crevice of her body.

When the shaking stopped, she collapsed onto Austin's torso, where he cradled her, running his hands over her back, warming the now cold, damp skin. Caitlyn could've slept there against his shoulder, feeling his breath in her hair. She couldn't remember when she had been this relaxed. Everything about this felt right. In the dark, she smiled to herself for the second time that night.

She sat up and looked at the man she knew had carved a place in her heart, whether or not he knew it. Leaning forward, she pressed her lips against his, tenderly thanking him and stoking the fire that she knew still burned for him. Caitlyn slid off him like a siren. She wasn't a virgin, but she wouldn't call herself an expert either. Tonight, however, Caitlyn wanted it all.

In the seat next to him, she ran her hands over him, feeling his warm skin pulse under her fingertips. The ridges of his muscles flexed as she explored each scar on his perfect body. Their mouths melded again, and Caitlyn could feel the heat rising once more in her own body, the tension still threaded through the fibers of Austin in the seat next to her.

Emboldened, Caitlyn broke the kiss this time and kissed his chin and neck, working her way down over his pecs and farther to his abs. A groan escaped him, and without looking up, she knew he had thrown his head back exposing the long column of his neck. Caitlyn couldn't see much in the dark, but that only spurred her on. She wasn't sure she could've done this in the light. Using touch as her guide, she found the waistband of the last remaining barrier and drew it up and over what was the largest man she had seen.

Hot need rose between her legs, begging for her to rush and get down to business, but Caitlyn forced herself to go slow. Austin sucked in a breath above her. She ran her finger over the shaft of his cock from the base to the tip, feeling every vein and ridge. The tip was damp. She swirled the bead of moisture around the head, while it bobbed up and down like a dog begging. Caitlyn palmed the length and stroked upwards, softly at first, using Austin's sounds and short breaths as a guide.

His hands were elsewhere, and she wished they were against her so she could feel his need. As if he had heard her thoughts, a firm hand clamped down on her wrist like a steel vise, speeding her up and coaxing her on.

If he thought he could be in control, he had another thing coming. Tonight was her night. Caitlyn bent down and swept her tongue upwards, causing Austin to jackknife off the seat. She took him them. She couldn't fit him all but made up for the difference with her hand. Now it was Austin's turn to grab a fistful of her hair, but he was careful not to pressure her. She set the pace, slowing to torture him and speeding up to drive him crazy. The strong muscles in his thighs strained and quivered with effort.

"Oh God," he said. "You're going to kill me." His voice cracked with dryness right before his hand started to shake.

Caitlyn dragged her tongue upwards before releasing her hold. She sat up and looked him in the eye, sitting next to him in the foggy, hot cab.

"I need you," he said, panting.

"Take me," she said breathlessly.

Austin crashed into her lips. One arm swept behind her while the other cradled her shoulders. He threw them down on the seat while their mouths sucked and claimed, gasping for breath and stealing each other's. Caitlyn knew she was slick with need. The cab was hot, but Austin's skin felt like fire. His breath rasped against her as he swept it over her neck and down to her breasts, tasting each one before sweeping lower.

He returned the favor tenfold when his lips pressed between her legs. Caitlyn gasped as his arms locked around her thighs and his tongue swirled against her, prodding and urging her on the same path. Caitlyn gripped the dashboard.

Her hand scraped the window, giving her that Kate Winslet moment after all. The tremors started, but Austin held fast. Caitlyn threw herself over the edge and into the sensation, shrieking when the shatter came, forcing her torso off the bench seat for a moment.

This time, however, there was no cuddling. Austin straddled her now and looked into her eyes. He kissed her hard but didn't move any closer.

It was a question, and Caitlyn knew the answer.

She wrapped her arms around him and positioned him just so. His hard length touched her tender lips, still swollen from Austin's tongue.

"Oh God, yes," Caitlyn said pulling his mouth against her right as he plunged inside, filling her with everything she had wanted and more. A groan escaped Austin again as he covered her with his powerful torso. In the darkness, she could see the muscles on his shoulders and biceps as he looked down at her. His breath rushed out over her in a wave of warmth.

They held there for a second, connected. She couldn't make out the expression on Austin's face. Caitlyn cupped his face with her hands and brought him down to her, kissing him gently. Her tongue probed his lips and begged for entry again.

A shudder ran through Austin. He pulled back and dove into the corner of her neck and shoulder, pressing his lips against her skin, branding her with a hot kiss. His stubble grazed her skin, stoking the flames for what would be a new personal record. He still hadn't moved in her, though his hard length held fast as she felt herself stretch to accommodate his size. Caitlyn squirmed, trying to get him to move. In response, his teeth took her earlobe and nibbled on it, sending a ripple of pleasure skittering down her spine and through her toes.

His name escaped her mouth in a moan she didn't expect. Austin murmured something she couldn't hear into her hair. Caitlyn wanted to ask what when he claimed her mouth with his own. Their lips melded and danced together, each breathing in the other and exploring. Caitlyn rocked her hips again and scraped her fingers along his broad back.

A deep grunt came from Austin before he kissed her hard, pressing himself into her again. The dominant thrust rocked Caitlyn to the core, sending sparks through every nerve in her body. Austin did it again, and for a moment Caitlyn wondered if he might tear her in half. Panting now, Austin pulled back an inch away from her face and looked at her.

"You're perfect," he said in a hoarse voice, thick with lust.

Before she could answer, Austin propped himself up on his forearms and pummeled into her, sending them both on a path, racing toward oblivion. His hips pistoned up and down so Caitlyn could only cling to his shoulders. The flames burst back to life within her, and with every thrust, he sent her higher. Her muscles spasmed and wrapped tight around her bones. She gripped his neck and pulled him down to her, urging him on with her own hips, spreading her legs as far as the cab would allow to let him have her. Austin took the invitation and pounded harder still. Caitlyn's head reached the passenger door. The energy spun her out of control. She couldn't have relaxed if she wanted. Harder and faster the thrusts came. One arm locked around her waist as he held her to him. Their hot slick skin glided together. The air in the cab filled with heat from their breath. Caitlyn climbed higher and higher, clinging to Austin, her only tether to the world, keeping her from exploding.

The delirium was too much. Her head swam. Caitlyn held on for dear life, but the muscles in her arms burned with the effort. Stuck on the precipice, Caitlyn cried out, begging for a release only he could offer her. Hearing her cry, Austin hiked up higher against her, changing the angle. With one final thrust, he sent her over the edge. Caitlyn shattered. Her aching muscles spasmed again, gripping her bones and locking her onto Austin like a life raft. Waves of ecstasy coursed through her body, sending pulses of energy. With the last bit spent, Caitlyn collapsed, limp and boneless.

Austin propped himself up on his hands on either side of her, showing off an impressive set of shoulders, and finished with two more hard pumps before lifting out. Warm jets sprayed on her stomach before Austin flopped down on her, only slightly bracing his weight.

There, in the cab of the truck, they breathed in unison. Caitlyn hung between sleep and consciousness by a thread. She tossed an arm over his back, letting it lie there. She would've been perfectly happy to stay in that moment with Austin forever. It had been the best, and nothing could compare. As Austin's breath slowed, settling into a slow, steady pattern of slumber, Caitlyn smiled again to herself in the dark. This was living.

CHAPTER 34

No stranger to meetings, John Clarkson sat, drumming his Mont Blanc pen on the yellow notepad before him while he listened to the council of town elders debate. He didn't care what they were talking about, but his position as principal dictated his attendance.

The fireplace crackled in the small conference room at the back of the new town hall. Established in the 1750s, the "new building" as it was called by the elders, operated most of the daily minutiae that came with local government. Payroll, insurance claims, and the bimonthly meetings of the council of elders and the principal all took place in the beautiful brick structure. Because of consistent use, the interior didn't have to be preserved but instead gleamed with polish and wax. Part courthouse and part office building, the carved oak interior walls held candelabra that had been updated from beeswax all the way to LED. A thick Persian rug the color of blood cushioned John's aching feet while a gleaming chandelier hung above them, casting speckled light on the Philadelphia walnut table.

"I disagree. The fact remains we are due for a hard winter. The leaf removal budget must be cut." Timothy Chappell pushed up his horn-rimmed glasses and twirled his fountain pen as if it were a duel of the minds. One of the few original founders left, he sat ramrod straight despite his age. Though he appeared to be in his eighties, simple math suggested he was no less than four hundred years old. His English accent remained on principle, whereas many of the other original settlers had let it go and gradually adopted the more American speech.

Born in England far before Jamestown, with several Ivy league degrees, Timothy often voiced strong opinions on matters of education, budget, and strong conservative action. When the other members of the board had suggested Brightrock's students needed laptops to remain competitive candidates for college, Timothy had become so upset he excused himself from the remainder of the meeting and abstained from the vote.

"I hear you, Timothy," said Mary Brooks, sitting opposite him. "I would remind you that if we have a strong winter like you are suggesting, the leaves will mix with the snow and hinder any removal. They will also make things more challenging in the spring, which will overload the budget for landscaping."

Mary had been on the same boat with Timothy, but that's where comparisons stopped. Older than Timothy by at least six years, she eyed him while he responded, listening to his argument and no doubt preparing her rebuttal. As founding members, women had been offered the opportunity to vote from the arrival, a rare opportunity which Mary had taken full advantage of.

Mary sat, full-figured and plain-faced, tacitly debating the fine points of the budget like a master politician. Her short black hair was a sharp departure from what he had heard she had looked like in her youth back in the seventeenth century. As someone who had witnessed every step of the women's rights movement, Mary was a full participant. John had heard that she'd even fought alongside her now deceased husband in a few battles long ago. Judging by the way she took on Timothy every meeting, John had no doubt Mary knew the business end of a gun, and if dueling pistols ever came out, he was putting his money on her.

While the pair continued talking, John slid a glance to his new smartwatch that he didn't fully understand how to work. At least the damn thing had the time in big numbers so he could actually see it. He knew better than to bring up that the school could just revert to e-commuting, which would save money, but would send the more senior residents of the island into a tailspin at the thought that the children should, in their view, miss school because of weather. Trying to explain to the stakeholders that education looked different than it did even twenty years ago was like bashing his head into a table. Nothing was going to give, and it only gave him a headache.

Sarah Smith, another founder and the acting secretary, interjected. "I'd like to point out that those contracts have already been paid for the next two weeks. I propose we table this issue and for the sake of time, reevaluate it later." From her seat near the center of the table and opposite the fireplace, Sarah cast a glance around the room to confirm. Everyone nodded in agreement.

Of everyone on the council, John had to admit Sarah Smith was probably his favorite. Subtly, she directed the conversations and kept the meeting moving. Class, poise, and elegance were all window dressing to the brain. Sarah was quiet, but she was smart. That she knew how to manage people well made the politically correct pillar of the community even more valuable to John, as so often matters around the school provoked a long-winded and fierce debate.

In a cream sweater and tan cashmere scarf, Sarah looked like the dutiful wife she had been for three centuries. But after her kids had left and women marched into Harvard, Sarah stepped in right along with them, earning herself an MBA later in life.

Perfectly manicured hands opened a leather-bound folio. "Next on the agenda is the news and search history report. Given that the trend we saw the last time we met has continued, I've prepared a report for everyone."

Papers shuffled across hands. John accepted his last and looked over the charts and graphs.

"I'll summarize, but those are yours to keep. Any questions or feedback can be added to next week's agenda—"

Timothy cut her off. "Next week? With these numbers, we'll be overrun by then."

"I'm sure we can still meet and discuss this, though I agree it is concerning," Mary said. She had pulled out a pair of plain readers and furrowed her brow in scrutiny at the paper.

"Is this correct? Seventy-five percent growth?" Timothy looked at Sarah over his glasses, now perched on his nose.

"Yes, however our numbers had been so low we are under five hundred hits on all of the major search engines." Sarah paused and looked concerned. "Still I admit the numbers were unexpected. Hence the copies for all of you to take."

"We need to figure out what is causing this," Timothy said, throwing his paper down on the beautiful wood.

"I'm not sure we can put a stop to curiosity," Mary said, still studying the paper in her hands.

"There is another matter that could be related," Sarah said.

"What?"

"Sal and Alex shared with me that there is a man who has recently checked in."

Timothy shook his head. "I was against the inn when they opened it."

"Please let me finish," Sarah said, stopping the beginning of a vicious cycle of disagreement. "When I discussed it with them, they reported that his comings and goings mostly involve walking around on the beach and touring the island. He doesn't have a rental car."

"When is he checking out?"

Sarah shifted in her seat. John sat up. Sarah never looked uncomfortable. She looked down and straightened the papers in front of her. "He hasn't said."

Mary sat forward now and leaned over the table. "What do you mean he hasn't said?"

Sarah cleared her throat. "He purchased a one-way ticket and is staying indefinitely."

"We need to figure out who this guy is and get him out of here."

Sarah flipped open the portfolio again and passed a paper around. "I looked him up. His name is Caleb Broussard. A resident of the state of Louisiana."

All of the elders stopped passing papers and looked at John.

"He must know Caitlyn," John said, sitting forward himself. He rested his arms on the big table, turning one of the papers toward himself and studying the face of the copied driver's license photo.

"I didn't agree with bringing in an off-islander," Timothy said. "There's too much risk involved."

John drew in a breath. "We didn't have a choice, Mr. Chappell. We had to meet federal standards, and Ms. Brooks has been requesting leave for years now, and the cause is more than reasonable."

"Did she invite him here?" Mary asked.

"Caitlyn? I'm not sure, but I'll find out."

"Sal and Alex also reported that he mentioned he was here to visit a friend from home," Sarah said.

"He's probably researching the island," Mary said. "That could be what is causing these numbers to go higher."

Sarah cleared her throat. "That brings me to the next report."

"There's more?" Tee asked, her eyebrows raised. She leaned forward from her post across the room. Unlike her good friend, Mary, Charity, who went by Tee to those close to her, spoke only through her vote unless the matters were about annual festivals. A few of the other elders looked up as well. The council included a dozen members, some of whom John knew better than others. Just like his teaching days, the quiet ones were the hardest to read.

"Yes, I have continued the practice of doing a name search for the residents on the island—"

"All of them?" asked Jane, Timothy's wife who rarely spoke.

"Yes, it is a basic search to see what pops up so that any issues can be addressed. I have also organized a report on search engine hits for our residents."

"I'm sorry," Timothy said, leaning forward. "Do you mean that you have these computers search if other people are researching each of us individually?"

Sarah folded her hands on her folio of surprises. "Yes, most of the time the results are hits on other people with the same name. For example, Ethan Brooks has one of the highest numbers of searches likely due to his business in New York."

Mary eyed Sarah. "Okay, so who is being researched? I get the feeling it isn't Ethan."

Sarah cast a quick apologetic glance in John's direction. "Almost all of them are for Austin Brooks."

Every head in the room once again turned in John's direction. His shoulders knotted with tension as he clenched his jaw. One bad decision on his part now risked exposure. He was determined not to let things slide on his watch. Austin wasn't thinking with his head, John knew, and it was up to him to find the solution before things got any worse. He was the principal. This was his job.

"I'll see that this is taken care of." John pulled out his phone and dialed.

CHAPTER 35

A ustin stretched in the tiny bedroom decorated in blue and white. The sun streaked through the windows, illuminating Caitlyn's private space.

They had barely made it back to the apartment this morning. God, was it really last night? He felt like he had met her at Crescent Beach a lifetime ago, and given his age, that was saying something. After what had been a pleasantly unexpected turn of events, Austin had mustered up enough energy to drive the truck back to her place. The stairs had damn near killed him, but wouldn't you know that somehow a second wind had come at just the right moment. They had gone to sleep, but it had taken a while.

Waking up this morning, he felt younger than he had in decades. The knots in his shoulders that had become routine were gone, and he was filled with energy he hadn't known in a while. But after last night, who wouldn't be ready to swim Massachusetts Bay?

He pulled on his jeans commando style since his drawers had gotten lost in the shuffle and looked at Caitlyn. Perfect. The rise and fall of the fluffy, white duvet told him how deeply she slept. Her hair covered the pillow while her lips and eyes were soft and relaxed. It was a damn good feeling seeing a woman asleep like that.

Austin stretched and looked around, desperate for info she hadn't shared. It wasn't like he was trying to creep around, he just wanted to know more about her and that guy he'd seen around town. A wave of possession churned in his gut. Yeah, he definitely wanted to know what the hell was up with that dude.

His eyes shot over to the nightstand. A small lamp, her phone, and a picture of who appeared to be her parents sat alone. There was only one phone charger, a plus in Austin's book. He walked around taking in the jewelry tray on her dresser which was sprinkled with earrings and charms he had seen her wear often, as well as a bottle of perfume. Austin looked over his shoulder and brought the small glass bottle to his nose. He recoiled immediately and looked at it before setting it down. It wasn't bad, but it wasn't Caitlyn's smell. The rest of the room, though feminine, was sparse. It almost felt more like a hotel than anything else. Her sweaters and cardigans were tossed on a chair in the corner, shoes hid under the dresser, but there wasn't much else.

Austin headed to the adjoining bath. The small marble space was clean as well. Inside the drawers were cosmetics she didn't need and toiletries. A half empty bottle of Oil of Olay sat on the counter, which was otherwise bare. He pulled open the glass door to the shower and popped the top off her shampoo. Inhaling deep, he went back to the night before when twice he fell asleep in her hair while breathing in her scent. This smelled like his Caitlyn.

His Caitlyn? Austin shook off the thought. He didn't want to get all up in his head, but it felt right. Shoving that thought away to puzzle through later, Austin opened one drawer revealing one toothbrush, one deodorant, and one razor. Pleased, he went back out and checked that she was still asleep before heading into the kitchen. Closing the door behind him, Austin went around the small kitchen, living, and dining area in search of answers that weren't there.

Well, he had confirmed one thing at least—the only thing male in this apartment was him. Everything was white, clean, and fluffy. The most personal things he could find were a few photographs, recipe cards, a half-burned candle, and a couple of pieces of furniture he could tell were handmade. It reminded him of people in the military who weren't putting down roots on purpose.

A bubble of disappointment floated up. Austin wanted to see more of who Caitlyn was—but all memories of her past were hidden away. Austin headed back to the kitchen area and did the Mr. Coffee thing. While he listened to the caffeine trickle away, he looked around the space and considered his plan.

What if it didn't work? Could he even do that? The rules were simple. No outsiders could ever know. But then he had been prepared to tell her everything last night. He had been ready to spill about the well, the rules, and even his actual birthdate. God, what would she think?

He had been ready for that too. In the truck, under his seat, were some photos of him from the navy during the war. He knew the risks. Shit, he had already been warned.

A click from the bedroom door brought him back. Austin wanted to drop to his knees and worship the sight before him. Caitlyn stood wrapped in a white robe, hair tousled, lips swollen. Without makeup, she looked fresh, young, and utterly delectable.

"Morning," she said, looking at him with a shy smile. "I wondered if you'd left. You know, walk of shame and all that."

Austin closed the distance and wrapped her up in his arms. "Would that bother you if I did?"

Caitlyn stretched back her neck to look at him. "Maybe."

He planted a kiss on her lips and pulled her in close. "Good. I was hoping you'd say that. I made coffee."

"It smells good."

"You smell good." Austin tucked his head up into the corner of her skin where her shoulder met her neck and pulled her even tighter. God, the scent of her shampoo intoxicated him. They stayed in the kitchen, holding on to each other for not nearly long enough when she pulled away. The change was small, but when you were focused on someone's every move, shit got noticed.

"Sorry, I need coffee and maybe an Advil," she said with a siren smile, shooting a sultry glance.

"I'm not sure how to take that, but I'm going to take it as a compliment," Austin said while helping himself to creamer in the fridge while she got the mugs down. He didn't usually use creamer, but he was willing to learn.

Caitlyn laughed. "Yeah, you go ahead and do that."

He wanted to ask if it had been a while, but the idea that it had ever happened before was enough to make him want to jump in the truck and go beat the shit out of the guy at the inn who they still hadn't talked about. He watched her pour the coffee. Desperate to know all of her, his eyes were hungry for the information denied to them the previous night.

Her hair hadn't been brushed, but to him it was perfect. So often at school Caitlyn appeared put together, not a hair out of place. A lock of it fell forward into her face. In response, she swept her hand up and over her head, sending a fresh cascade to settle below her shoulders. The color mixed somewhere between gold, bronze, and whiskey. Hints of red glittered in the morning sun streaming through the window. He knew she hadn't colored it, not because of the color, but because that didn't jibe with her personality or what he had seen in the bathroom. While she fixed the cups of coffee, Austin's eyes skimmed over her back in the white terrycloth robe, all the way down to her exposed calves. Her slender legs stirred him up again.

Caitlyn spun around with two cups of coffee and held one out to him. Austin stood there frozen. He wanted to remember this moment. He ran his eyes over her features, her expression, even down to the slender hand holding out the mug.

"Austin?" she said. "You okay?"

"Yeah, yeah. I'm good." He shook himself out of it and accepted the cup.

Caitlyn arched a perfect eyebrow and sipped along with him. Immediately, she pulled back and frowned at the mug. "Jesus, this could wake the dead." She coughed. "I think I'm going to need some more creamer."

Austin gave her a sheepish smile with a shrug. "Sorry, I don't measure. I just sprinkle it in until the souls of the damned cry out." He took another sip. Yep, sure enough, the dark liquid could peel paint, which was just how he liked it.

"I thought you would've liked it strong," he said, watching her graceful hands take the mug over to the sink where she added a bit of hot water and then another splash of cream.

"I do like strong coffee. That's the only way it's served in Louisiana." She spun around and propped herself against the sink as she held the cup to her lips with both hands, taking another sip and this time, savoring it. "I don't like motor oil."

Austin brought a hand to his chest, feigning offense. "My coffee? Motor oil? I prefer jet fuel. Thank you very much."

She broke into a grin that made his whole world click into place. Austin had seen a lot of things in his life. Some places he had seen, thanks to Uncle Sam, were too beautiful for any postcard or camera. At this moment though, he knew he would never see anything as breathtaking as Caitlyn right now. Her tousled hair swept over her head in chaos that seemed just right. The robe split at the thigh, giving him an excellent view of what he had known so well last night. Her eyes twinkled at him over perfect, smooth skin that was flawless. Her lips, still swollen from so many kisses, were curved in a knowing smile that made Austin want to grab her caveman-style and head back under the fluffy white duvet to do all sorts of fun things.

As if she read his thoughts, Caitlyn lowered her mug, and they did just that.

CHAPTER 36

Lizzy Brooks uncrossed her legs and unfolded herself from the back of the cab she'd hired at Boston's Logan Airport. One manicured hand held her phone, and the other held a giant cup of Dunkin's finest coffee. The young driver hustled around to the back to get her oversized bags out of the trunk and heaved them onto the cracked sidewalk where they landed with a clumsy clatter.

A few minutes and several swear words later, she had her bags next to her, while she sat in the Hyannis Port Ferry terminal savoring the last of her Dunkin.

Terminal was a generous word to describe the small building with plain, sturdy, linoleum floors, fluorescent lighting, and two sliding-glass windows cut into the wood panel walls. The red plastic chairs inspired the few people also inside waiting for the ferry to lean against the wall instead of sit. A wall of windows overlooked the port. The boat to Nantucket by way of Brightrock was docked but not ready for boarding. Crew members scurried about, loading and unloading all of the day-to-day items that were not available on the islands.

She was exhausted. When she had been earning her undergraduate degree followed by her Master's at Columbia, the trip hadn't taken this long. Now that she was studying at the Curry School of Education at the University of Virginia, a few more hours had been added. The drive to Dulles, the fight through the traffic, the flight to Logan, and then the cab ride to Hyannis had taken the better part of the day, but she wasn't in a rush. She didn't want to go home. She had just left after years of asking.

The PhD road was a long one, and the leave of absence from Brightrock had just started, which was why she had been surprised when John Clarkson had called the other week asking for her to come back early for the holidays and perhaps teach the remainder of the year. Thankfully, her supervisor and mentors had agreed to let her come, on the condition she begin her research at her school.

With such a small population, she was in a great position to study the mechanics of how small schools functioned in different ways to support diverse students. The hope was that this new research could be applied in similar environments, like reservations and rural schools, and help target where funds should be spent to get the best results.

A few minutes later, Lizzy held out her phone to the crew member checking tickets and headed up the gangway leaving her luggage in the small cluster waiting for the crew. With the tourism season over, getting a window seat was not a problem. Lizzy headed for the front, knowing it would have the most movement but not caring. Getting seasick had never been a problem. She had ridden in boats since she was a child and had grown used to the feeling.

She settled in and tucked her coat around her legs, snuggling into the warmth when the thrum of the engines growled underneath her. The gray waves outside churned up with more white water, showing a sign of sure departure.

"Excuse me, miss?"

Lizzy turned to see an employee. Worn by the waves, deep crevices lined his forehead and cheeks before disappearing under gray hair. His hands on the seat back looked like baseball mitts with scars. "May I please see your ticket?"

"Oh, they already scanned it," Lizzy said, looking back but reaching for her purse anyway.

"I'm sorry. The system's down, and we're just double-checking." He offered Lizzy a cold smile she didn't believe, and she could see his front right tooth was chipped. "Can't trust these computers."

"Um, yeah, okay. Here, let me just pull it up on my phone." She passed him the screen. In his large hands, her phone, which was oversized and in a glitter case, looked small and ridiculous.

He squinted and studied the screen with a frown. The crease on his forehead deepened.

"Is there a problem?" The engine rumbled beneath them both, and with a lurch forward the ferry starting moving away from the dock.

"We don't get many people to Brightrock. Thought you might be someone I was looking for." He nodded once before ambling away, muttering something that sounded like a pleasantry.

Lizzy watched him go and noticed the other dozen or so people on board were either on their phones or looking out the window, and one was already asleep.

There was no one else checking tickets, and none of the other passengers were approached. A ripple of unease slid over her skin.

Lizzy tried to settle herself by watching the horizon, but within a few minutes, she was restless and on her phone. Paranoia had never been her default. Shaking her head and twirling a lock of her dark and curly hair, she focused less on the weird man and more on her social media. Maybe she was just being peculiar, but she was out of protocol here. Usually, Lizzy would've called her cousin Austin for a lift on his beloved cabin cruiser, but when she called last night, he hadn't picked up.

Brightrock Islanders only took the ferry when it was absolutely necessary, which was next to never due to the airstrip and the fact that most of the families owned yachts the size of a small house and sometimes even a private plane. Even those who worked for other families as butlers, cooks, gardeners, and maids could buy the state of Wyoming if they ever got the urge.

Over time, logging had turned into whaling and whaling had turned into shipping. After a while, Brightrock's residents had so much money they stopped thinking about it. And that was of course long before any of them had gotten into the stock market. Once they did, all bets had been off. Sure, textbooks talked about captains of industry like Carnegie, J.P Morgan, Vanderbilt, and Rockefeller, but those men were way behind Brightrock. No high school student would ever learn anything different, though, because of the need for discretion. Hell, the Commonwealth of Massachusetts was damn near giddy from the amount of tax money it got from Brightrock, but that sum was pennies compared to what they could be getting if totals in offshore accounts were ever revealed.

Lizzy watched the waves as the high-speed ferry raced across the dark blue water. That kind of money made things happen—and people suspicious. And that was just the cash. If anyone found out about Brightrock, the consequences would be dire. Lizzy could almost see the newsflash in the glass window in front of her: "Fountain of youth found in America! Millions race to small New England island. Residents taken for questioning." Her lips thinned at the thought.

The unease lingered. Lizzy hunched down in her seat and eyed the other passengers, most of whom were now asleep. Of course, staying on the island was easier day-to-day. Everyone knew her, and there wasn't a need to lie to people in the same boat, but Brightrock didn't have a college, and there was the rub. Most of the students were being encouraged to complete their studies online. Only Ethan officially lived full-time off-island and came back just for the seasonal Renewal ceremony since he worked in New York. She couldn't imagine the stress of that. Lizzy didn't talk with her cousin enough to ask him, but she figured that eventually, he would need to change apartments, jobs, identities, friends, and shit, even his coffee shop.

Lizzy peered over her shoulder to eye the bar in the middle of the boat behind where she had sat. The young bartender leaned on the bar and scrolled aimlessly on his phone, giving her a good idea how refreshment sales were going. She pined for another cup of coffee but knew better than to drink whatever it was that claimed to be coffee on the ferry. Her thoughts floated back to the mystery man looking so closely at her ticket.

It probably was just because she had the only ticket going through to Brightrock by way of Nantucket. Maybe it was so rare that the staff wanted to verify. It didn't sit right, and nothing Lizzy did made the uneasy feeling disappear.

Looking out the window and ignoring her phone again, she craned her neck to see if land was on the horizon yet. God, she couldn't wait to get there and see why she was being summoned so she could handle whatever it was and get right back to her life in Virginia.

Even though she was super vigilant, the rest of the ride and the following ferry trip was mercifully uneventful. Seeing her home on the horizon through the streaked window of the much smaller, much older ferry, a swirl of dread filled her stomach. The gray, rocky shoals of Easterly Bay looked like claws reaching out to grab her as the ferry rocked in between the buoys to ease its way to the destination. Despite the frigid air, her palms were slick with sweat, and Lizzy moved from foot to foot waiting for the gangway to be cleared for her departure onto land. The crew hustled, but Lizzy was on edge, and her impatience had nothing to do with wanting to be on the island. In fact, it was the total opposite.

Sure, Brightrock was quaint, cute, with its ice cream parlor, general store, old houses, beautiful gardens, and pristine beach. At least that's what the tourists who usually rode the ferry must've thought when they arrived. To Lizzy, it felt like a prison.

Her family was here, and the school was excellent, but after having been in one place for what would have been the average person's lifespan, she was more than ready to seek out greener pastures. Hence the PhD. The new federal law had been the tipping point the council needed to give her the break she had wanted for years.

Other than college, Lizzy had never left for more than a few days. Now that she was trying to strike out on her own, being summoned back even before the Renewal made her skin itch. If anything, it reminded her of how much of a hold this place had on her.

The crew finally cleared her, and Lizzy swept forward in her Manolos, thanking each person and tipping the person who carried her bag. She might be a self-important bitch in a bad mood, but at least she tipped often and well.

Lizzy hadn't even reached the end of the pier when she noticed him. The hiccup in her steps caught the heel of her shoe on a board, nearly sending her into a somersault. Thankfully, she recovered and pulled her Canada Goose coat around her even tighter as she continued the march forward with narrowed eyes.

The weather above her matched her mood, and the slap of the ocean waves against the dock grated on her nerves. She kept her eyes on the man seated on a bench as she moved forward. She had never seen him before, which wouldn't have made a difference anywhere else in the world, but on Brightrock it made all the difference, especially after tourism had died down. She had already had one odd encounter, and that was after she had been traveling since dawn, thanks to Northern Virginia's traffic. Plus, of course, Lizzy knew she would have to contend with an onslaught of visiting once she got to her aunt and uncle's house, which was why she hadn't called them yet. Figuring the apartment over the ice cream parlor was still occupied, Lizzy couldn't go hide away immediately but had decided on at least having dinner alone at Kate's Diner before calling her cousin Austin again.

Lizzy left the pier and officially touched Brightrock right when a huge gust of wind smacked into her as if the island was saying that her feelings toward it were mutual. Lizzy kept the man in her peripheral vision while she tugged around her two rolling bags in a most ungraceful way over the clattering pea gravel to get to the parking lot. Her heels teetered in the rock, jarring her ankle a new direction with every step.

Why in the hell didn't the town pave this shit? She was about to hit the pavement when she lurched forward, free of her weight, and fell face first into the rocks. Holy exfoliation, Batman.

Footsteps came running. The off-islander.

Lizzy scrambled up and tried to wipe off the gravel still embedded in her skin. Pockets of pain howled when the wind raced across the bay and plowed into her. She wasn't sure what had happened when she still realized she was holding one of the stupid luggage handles, now nothing but a u-shaped piece of metal, torn from its larger half.

"Hey, are you okay?"

Lizzy flung the piece of metal away from her, not caring where the piece of shit landed. She made a mental note to burn the luggage as soon as possible. Shit, she might even dance around naked as it turned to ash. Why did all luggage suck so bad?

"Yeah, I'm fine," she said, not wanting to linger. Visitors and tourists came, but were carefully avoided by the locals other than a "Hi, how are ya?"

"Hey, you're bleeding a little. Do you want me to call someone?"

His voice was everything Brightrock wasn't. The southern drawl in it curled around her and steadied her, so she stopped trying to get away from him as fast as possible, instead looking up at him, and suddenly felt herself go still. Woah.

She knew she had never seen him before because she would remember those eyes. They were green with little gold flecks surrounded by lashes that looked like they cost more than that piece of shit luggage she was going to burn later. His skin was smooth and tan, but not in a fake or beach boy way. His dark hair curled out a little from underneath his ball cap like he hadn't gotten a haircut in a while.

"You okay?" That voice again steadied her. He spoke deliberately and gently. Maybe it was slower, but that wasn't the right word. There was something about it. It wasn't the harsh New England clipped accent she had known forever. It was more Southern than Virginia and a little different.

"Come on," he said in a gruff tone. "Let's at least get in out of the damn cold." Without asking and quick as a flash, he reached and picked up her purse and dusted off the stupid gravel. Gently, he looped it through the remaining working bag's handle and set the pair upright on the pavement.

"Oh, don't worry. It's heavy."

This man picked up her oversized, you-need-to-pay-extra-ma'am suitcase that she knew weighed every bit of seventy-two pounds and held it, looking at her. He jutted his chin toward the bag. "I can come back for that one if you want. I'm staying right in the inn there. You can use my room to check your face. They've probably got Band-Aids."

"Okay," Lizzy said in a small voice that surprised her. She took the other bag and headed toward the only inn on the island, wondering who this man was and what had brought him here. She also couldn't look away, convinced he would hurt his back, but no. He walked next to her across the deserted, cold street.

When they reached the steps, Lizzy slung her black leather purse to her shoulder and lowered the handle of the second ma'am-you-don't-need-this-much oversized bag.

"Here, I got it," the man said, plucking the bag up like it weighed nothing. With one in each hand, he climbed the steps at an easy pace and set them down to open the door into the small foyer that acted as a lobby. "Go ahead. I'm on the second floor. Here's the key. I don't think they have a bathroom down here. I'll bring your bags."

"No, it's okay," she said. "They're ridiculously heavy because I pack too much crap."

"You sure? I don't mind. I wouldn't want someone to mess with your stuff."

The wind howled in the gray skies outside, slamming into the cedar shingles of the house. Literally, no one was around. The ferry had already left. Inside the little foyer, this man stood, waiting with a bag in each hand. It was warm and homey with a patterned rug over gleaming hardwood floors and pale yellow walls.

Lizzy had intended to call her family for a lift when she arrived, but cleaning up first couldn't be a bad thing.

"I'm Lizzy," she said and stuck out her hand.

CHAPTER 37

ustin pulled the Ranger into the frigid parking lot
of the marina and hopped down into the icy wind.
Caitlyn's apartment over the ice cream parlor sat
at the other end of Easterly Bay. Memories of waking up in
her private space warmed him and sent a shot of arousal
through his blood. Austin straightened his worn Barbour
coat and headed in a different direction. Maybe he'd have
time to catch up with her later.

The Cedar Inn stood tall and proud against the mighty
Atlantic winds, its three-story facade gleaming in the fading
light in a festive display of lights and wreaths. Candles twinkled in each of the red-shuttered windows, and through their
golden glow, Austin could see a Christmas tree decorated
with all sorts of fancy ornaments. What caught his eye,
though, were the few second-story windows in the turret
that were lit from within, occupied by one guest who wasn't
from around here.

Austin had called the owner, Sal, earlier to find out
about Caleb. Sal and Alex lived in what had been the old
kitchen around back, and there were no other guests.

Austin and Caleb would have the whole place to themselves for the evening, which was good. Tonight Austin intended to make a new acquaintance. He needed to get to the bottom of this and figure out if he was a threat to Caitlyn or to the island. Maybe then the council and John would get off his back.

Austin hopped up onto the porch and barely noticed the fresh wreath on the door. He let himself into the tight foyer and shut the door behind him, ringing the little bell overhead. He stood, waiting and listening. Sure enough, footsteps somewhere above him padded around the room. The place was empty, and an arrival would be sure to trigger Caleb's interest.

Austin headed into the living room to wait. A fire crackled away in the fireplace next to the large tree Austin had seen from outside. Scents of banana bread and balsam floated in the air. In the state-of-the-art kitchen, a candle burned on the island. Chairs and tables sat around the space, creating little nooks for guests to sip coffee while watching the seascapes or gardens during the summer tourist season.

Anticipation clawed at Austin. Like before a fight in the navy, his hands twitched, ready to go. He looked down at his hands, still red from the cold. Thin, white scars traced his fingers, hands, and forearms. He had lost count of the number of bar fights he'd been in. It had been years since he'd planted his four worn knuckles against another man's jaw, but if push came to shove, he'd welcome the chance. Coming here would likely not end in a fight, but more information, which experience had taught him was more valuable.

A door opened, and the floor creaked somewhere up and behind him. Austin could feel his jaw tense when footsteps came down. He watched the fire, intentionally giving Caleb his back to see what would happen. Austin shifted his weight to the balls of his feet and took his hands out of his pockets, bringing them together in front of him as a precaution.

The footsteps came into the living room, muffled by the large rug, and stopped.

"Good evening. Are you looking for the owner?" His southern accent outweighed Caitlyn's. Austin turned around.

"You must be Caleb. I'm Austin," he said, extending a hand without a smile. Caleb took it with a firm grip. His hands were rough and tanned, showing signs of work. Caleb stood shorter than Austin by at least four inches, but the navy had taught Austin how tall a man was had nothing to do with the force of his punch.

Caleb's army-green eyes watched him like a cat. His dark hair stood in direct contrast to Austin's blond. Caleb released his hand and crossed his arms in front of his chest. Worn work boots peeked out from below the hem of his jeans.

"I heard you know Caitlyn," Austin said.

"I do," said Caleb, not moving. "What's that to you?"

"Wanted to stop in and find out why you're here. Heard you didn't have a check-out date. Don't they have a policy against long-term guests?"

Caleb raised an eyebrow and unfolded his hands to start cracking a knuckle. "Sal and Alex don't seem to mind. Caitlyn took off without telling anyone where she was headed. Wanted to make sure she was okay. She's been through a lot."

Austin watched Caleb for a minute while he made up his mind. "She hasn't said much about Louisiana," he said, testing the water.

Caleb shrugged. "That doesn't surprise me."

"Why?"

"After her parents died, she was pretty bad off. The bills were unreal. She had to sell almost everything. Broke her heart to sell her parents' house. Her dad had done so much to it you would've thought he'd built it by hand. Then a student died. Suicide."

Austin leaned back and folded his arms, listening. "What does it matter to you? Don't you have somewhere to be back there?"

Caleb's eyes flashed, and his head cocked to one side. "Not that it's any of your damn business, but I work on an oil rig. Thirty on, thirty off. So for the next twenty days, I'm free to roam anywhere I want. And besides, I like to keep an eye on people I care about."

Keeping his hands to himself was an exercise in total self-control. "Didn't she dump you?" Austin asked, raising an eyebrow and looking for a fight.

Caleb squared his shoulders, facing Austin. "Also none of your damn business. She was upset, left without saying goodbye. I wanted to check in on her."

"Well you have, and you didn't need to," Austin said, his voice flat, making his intentions clear.

Caleb watched him, green eyes narrowed. To the man's credit, he didn't shrink back from anything Austin said, but instead stood his ground and looked him square in the eye. Had to respect the hell out of that, even if he wanted to knock the guy on his ass purely on principle.

"Yep, sure did." Caleb's eyes were hard, calculating. "Funny thing was, she didn't mention you when we talked."

Austin shoved his hands in his pockets and rocked back on his heels. "Yeah, I guess she doesn't like to share her personal business with strangers."

"I've known her for years. I wouldn't call me the newb." Caleb wasn't backing down a bit.

Austin studied him again, waiting. Caleb met his cold stare right back with one of his own. At this rate, they were going nowhere fast. "Tell me why you really came here,"

Austin asked. "That's a long way to go for a woman who doesn't want you."

Caleb winced and made a face. "I came to find out what the hell happened. Everything was fine. She didn't say much at her dad's funeral, but that's to be expected, you know?"

Austin nodded.

"A few days later, I texted. Wanted to give her some space and all that."

"Were you two serious?" Austin asked, wanting to know the answer for a variety of reasons.

Caleb shrugged and lifted his hands. "Her mom had died, and her dad wasn't doing too good. Put a damper on things. Listen, I get that you're interested in her. I just came to see what happened." Caleb shifted his weight to one foot and looked off at the tree. "She suddenly stopped answering my calls, and the next thing I knew her house was up for auction along with almost everything inside. Shit, she didn't even say goodbye to my family. They all came to the funeral, by the way. Imagine how that makes me look when they all want to know how she's doing, and I don't have a fucking clue."

Austin rubbed the back of his head. "Yeah, that really sucks."

Caleb popped a few knuckles. "Yep. Sure did. Once I figured out where she went, I wanted to check in. Talk about shocked when I was there at her door, but hey, that's what happens when you don't pick up the damn phone. At least now I can tell my family what happened."

"Did she give you a reason?" Austin asked, now curious. He could see where Caleb was coming from. Said a lot about him for coming all this way when he had been shut out. Austin couldn't say he would've done the same thing. He was much more of a "Fine, fuck you then," kind of guy.

Caleb folded his arms again and twisted his mouth into a humorless smirk. "You mean aside from, 'It's me, not you.

Back off'?" He shook his head. "Grief. Couldn't handle living there with all the memories. Too painful."

After Austin and Caleb had traded enough information for each to be satisfied, they walked away with a handshake. Austin had to respect the shit out of the guy for being that loyal when he had been dropped without a thought. He could also report to John that Caleb wasn't a threat to them.

His heart ached at hearing about Caitlyn's past. She must have suffered more than anything he had ever known in his life. The way she dropped all contact with Caleb struck him as so unlike her and indicative of her raw need to escape. The story had been heartbreaking, and even though it was a school night, Austin left the Cedar Inn and walked along the shops to the other end of Easterly Bay where above the Two Scoops Ice Cream shop, the lights glowed on, summoning him like a beacon.

After hearing from Caleb, Austin wanted to make Caitlyn smile, even if she had no idea why.

CHAPTER 38

Caitlyn crouched down over a group of students.

"So wait," Charles asked. "Who actually said fire?" He picked up the other testimony from the court case following the Boston massacre with a puzzled expression.

"Well, what do you think?"

"They both say the other person did it. But—" Charles opened his mouth to speak when the intercom went off above him.

"Code blue!"

Charles and the other kids all stood and rushed to the back corner, designated as a safe zone. Papers scattered and a few pencils fell to the floor. Caitlyn checked the door, killed the lights, and closed all the blinds before joining the huddled pack of twelve-year-olds crouched in the corner.

The room fell silent. In the dark, the sound of a sneaker squeaked against the waxed linoleum, causing a murmur among the students. Caitlyn shushed them all, and the quiet resumed and started to stretch.

At her old school, the class had been so large they had

barely fit into the so-called safe zone, usually the farthest place from the door. Also, getting thirty-plus kids to stay quiet had been an exercise in Whack-a-Mole.

Caitlyn itched to grab her phone and text Connie to confirm how long the drill would last, but it was in her purse at her desk across the room. She couldn't leave the kids, so she shifted on the hard floor and watched the time tick by on the clock.

After a few minutes, Caitlyn frowned to herself as she counted on her fingers. They had hit the minimum number of drills required by law last month. Surely, this was just another drill.

She stretched, trying to alleviate the pinpricks of numbness in her foot, sending a silent prayer of thanks up that she had chosen her stretchiest black work pants today. The floor was hard enough, but at least she wasn't in a skirt and could sit somewhat comfortably on the cold, uncomfortable floor.

The eerie silence persisted in a building that was rarely quiet. Caitlyn turned around to eye the students. Squirming, the class of fifteen sixth graders, less than half of the size of her classes in her last school, had folded themselves almost in thirds, hugging their knees. The cluster of them reminded her of how small they actually were. Charles, though the brightest, was the smallest and had managed to fit himself into a space smaller than the one-foot square tile on the floor. In the dark, the children started to exchange glances.

Something slammed into the door. Kids screamed as the door shook with a violent pummeling. The children cowered in the corner, shaking, eyes wide and hands pressed to their mouths. Caitlyn crawled in front, putting herself between them and the door. Her heart raced while possibilities ran through her mind. Angry parent? They'd have to get through the office first. Troubled child? Not likely here. Where was the admin? How did this person get to the second floor? She reached into a book bag and pulled a laptop over, ready to throw it if the door gave way. Her heart pounded. She gauged the distance and raised her arm to throw as the heavy oak door shook with each hit.

The familiar scraping of a key entering the lock was the only thing that didn't have her throwing the computer.

Austin poked his head around the door as the kids all shrunk behind her with a gasp and some whimpers.

"Everybody good in here?" Austin asked, walking in with a clipboard. "Ms. Landry, do you have your badge?" He looked at her, holding a pen ready to check her off some form.

Caitlyn unfolded herself off the floor, stumbling once on her numb foot. Instead of flashing her badge around her neck, she marched forward, doing her best to hide the limp.

"Can I speak with you in the hall? Stay there," she said when the kids started to get up. "No talking. None. Do not move until I get back."

Austin followed her out into the hall where Caitlyn rounded on him when the door clicked closed. "What in the hell was that?" she hissed in the silent hallway.

Austin held up his hands, the ridiculous clipboard still in one, pen in the other.

"I know. It's the safety committee—"

"That was out of line, and you know it."

"They're the ones—"

"I don't give a shit. You just terrified a bunch of twelve-year-olds for no damn reason."

"Caitlyn—" Austin looked down, the ghost of a smile forming on his lips.

She narrowed her eyes and stepped in closer. "Do you think this is funny? I grabbed a computer to throw at you."

"I know—"

"That was unnecessary."

"They want us to simulate a real attack. I'm sorry, okay?"

"No, it's not okay! You want kids to take this seriously, and they are. They haven't done anything wrong. This isn't a joke!"

"Listen, I have to finish or—" The walkie at his back cut off the rest of what was bound to be a bullshit escape route. "Green section almost done."

"Also, why did you go talk to Caleb behind my back?" Caitlyn leaned into his face, hissing low.

"Caitlyn, this isn't the time—"

"You have time to scare the shit out of my kids. I want an answer. Now."

Austin's blue eyes narrowed to slits. "How did you know?"

"Because he called me last night, saying so. Said it didn't feel right to talk about me behind my back and wanted to apologize." She folded her arms in front of her chest and tilted her head to one side. "At least he owned up to it."

"Your ex-boyfriend shows up, and you don't mention why because you can't get into it? You don't think that's suspicious?"

"That's none of your business."

"Oh really? I think it became my business after the other night. You sure got into it then, didn't you?"

Caitlyn wanted to slap him, but instead she leaned in and hissed. "You're an asshole."

Austin shrugged with a swagger that infuriated Caitlyn even more, spilling gas on a burning blaze. "Been called worse."

"So your secrets are yours to keep, but you get to go into mine?"

Austin jerked like she had just slapped him. "What in the hell are you talking about?"

Caitlyn leaned into him again putting her finger in his

chest. "Don't give me that crap. You know you never talk about where and when you were in the navy."

Austin's face reddened with a deep color. "I've told you plenty," he hissed back at her.

"Or how about where you were when everyone left? Or what everyone always seems to be whispering about around this damn school? Shit, even Charles mentioned his parents had gone to a secret meeting."

Caitlyn knew she had him. The steely silence he returned was as damning as a conviction. A muscle tensed in his jaw, then started pulsing as he gritted his teeth, trying to think of something to say.

The walkie squawked at his back again, calling him back to the library.

"Exactly," Caitlyn said as she turned on her heel and grabbed at the key around her neck to open her door. "I don't know what it is about this place. All the old shit, all the money, and all the damn secrecy. I thought we had a connection. Guess I was wrong. Probably just another notch in the belt for you."

Austin's hand landed on her shoulder. She flinched away.

"Don't touch me. You can act all nice, but at the end of the day you're just like everyone else here. You broke my trust."

Austin swore under his breath and ran his hand over his head as he thought about what to say next. Under his white dress shirt, his bicep flexed with the movement.

"I want to make this up to you. I have something I need to tell you."

"Well, spit it out. This had better be good."

Austin shushed her, a move that sent her into a flustered rage until he grabbed her by the shoulders and pulled her close, so his head was next to her ear.

"I can't tell you here, and you must tell no one."

His voice was hoarse, and when she didn't respond immediately, he gave her a little shake.

"Promise me?"

"Uh, okay. I promise. Where?" The rest of the question didn't need to be said between them. This was not a safe space.

"Beach again. Tonight. I'll tell you everything."

He pulled back and stared at her until she nodded. He looked different than before, and then Caitlyn realized she had never seen him this scared. Even on the boat during the storm, Austin had been haunted, but now whatever had just happened and whatever he was going to tell her terrified him. Austin nodded once, and pulled the walkie around to the front, talking into it as he turned and walked down the hall.

Goosebumps rose on Caitlyn's arms, as a chill went through her. Pulling her sweater around her, Caitlyn turned and let herself back in the classroom as the announcement came over the PA.

"Thank you, students and staff. This was just a drill."

CHAPTER 39

M ark Schmidt's vision swam courtesy of the cocktail of cheap liquor and no sleep. He'd been at it for days now. Scott had called to check on him when he missed work, but Mark hadn't even bothered to answer the phone.

Mark sat in the chair, barely awake, watching the blue glow from the TV. An image of a smiling man stood on a stage over a phone number. Mark picked up the paper in his lap. He had been studying it when he had finally fallen asleep.

None of it had made any sense. Mark had set out to find the truth, and what he had learned haunted him day and night.

Empty bottles tangled with the printouts of the man named Austin Brooks all over the piles of clothes and trash. Most were from the navy, but a few others—the ones that had been so hard to track down—came from websites covering school sports. And they were recent.

Once the librarian had gotten Mark a name from Veteran's Affairs, he had set to work, navigating the web to find a new image of the person he'd seen. The librarians had been patient with him and helped him to track down pictures and a few tag-lines from various websites saying he now taught and coached on Brightrock, which matched up perfectly with the woman Mark had seen with the one-way ticket a few months ago. It had been so easy to convince them he wanted to meet the descendant of the man who knew his father.

Mark shifted to sit up in the weak chair his mom once occupied, knocking a bottle out of his lap, which hit the floor with a dull thud. He pulled a rough hand over his face, scrubbing his eyes, trying to force them to focus. A puff of breath clouded his view of the blurry picture in front of him. The house was cold.

He squinted in the dark, not bothering to reach for the lamp next to him. The pictures were the same, and not just the scar on the bastard's chin. Two images side by side showed a birthmark on the inner forearm. The ugly, red mark looked like a blood stain and made Mark's lip wrinkle in disgust. The first picture was a clip from a newspaper in which Austin worked on a large piece of equipment Mark didn't recognize. His arm had been outstretched so that half of the embarrassing mark peeked out from under his sleeve. Whatever that bastard was, it was clear he didn't want that mark to show. In almost all of his other pictures, though there weren't many, his sleeves hid the mark from the camera's lens.

But then, a few years ago, when the wrestling team had won regionals, the photographer had caught Coach Brooks, mouth open, in midjump, his arms outstretched above his head, revealing the same ugly blotch of skin.

When Mark had put the two images side by side at the library, his hands shook so badly the librarians had offered to call for a ride. Mark had waved them off and driven straight to the liquor store and then home, where he drank away the shakes and passed out for, judging by the clock radio next to him, what had been at least a few hours.

Looking at them now, it all came back. The tremble started in Mark's wrist, jerking his fingers up and down. He pulled another hand over his face, smelling the alcohol on himself and wishing his credit card could handle more. Any day now, he would hit his limit.

The pay from the ferry was dismal despite forty years of service. Social Security didn't cover much, and while blowing up grass huts in Vietnam had fucked him up, it was not enough to get a check from Uncle Sam.

A booming voice from the TV ripped his eyes away from the printout in his hands. Mark jumped in his chair even though he was less than sober.

"God has a plan for you! Are you listening? I said, God has a plan for you."

Mark watched as the man on the screen spoke like thunder. His black jacket and purple vest looked expensive, like the kind Mark had always wanted to wear but had never owned. "Every one of you has got problems. The people you hate got problems. The people you love got problems. All of you got problems." The man paused to stretch out the silence before he started pacing, the gleam in his shoes catching the light from above as he strutted with confidence. "I'm here to tell you, there is a purpose in your problems. God knows, and he needs you to overcome for a purpose." The way the man talked through perfect, white teeth, sharing his words like a beat of a drum, hit Mark in the chest. The man thrust his finger at the crowd, flashing a large gold watch. "He needs you to serve a higher purpose. God's purpose." At the last word, he pointed his finger up and waited. The crowd hung on his last word. Mark did the same.

Breaking the spell, the large man walked again. "Maybe

someone doesn't like you. Maybe somebody's got it out for you at work. Maybe somebody is lying to you or about you."

Murmurs of assent came from the faithful sitting in pews as they nodded. Mark glanced down at the crinkled paper in his hands and leaned forward, despite the groan of the old chair.

"Maybe you got bills you gotta pay. They won't even let you get back up after you fall, just keep throwing you back down. Man, I tell you." His arms flailed up above him as he turned his head up to the ceiling.

"You try, and you try. Workin' hard, but no matter what you do, you just get knocked back down. Am I right?" He dropped his hands and looked back out at the crowd, shoulders low, defeated.

A few yeses called out from the crowd as the preacher nodded. "Mmhmm. Maybe you have some mistakes in your past. Things you ain't proud of. Things you've done"—he paused and looked at the crowd—"that you just can't get over. They haunt you. Won't leave you alone. Well, I'm here to tell you, God has a plan for you!" A thick fist pounded a shiny podium with a force that punched through the microphone on his lapel and echoed throughout the space.

Weak applause and sounds of appreciation peppered the speakers as the preacher walked again. "All of that distraction, all of that noise, all of those problems, your problems—everything that's keeping you down, holding you back. All of it. That's the devil trying to break you," he continued, leaning forward and looking at the crowd.

With sweat on his brow, he dropped his voice to a whisper in the microphone, "So you gotta be strong."

He jumped back to life, raising his deep voice again. "Because why? Because God has a plan for you! You gotta be strong. You gotta fight. All of this, all of these problems, all of these obstacles in your life are the Devil, and God needs you.

You are his soldier. You gotta be strong. You gotta fight. Are you gonna give up?"

On its feet, the crowd shouted a no. "I said are you going to give up?" the preacher said, stoking the fire.

"No!"

"Why? Because—say it with me now—God has a plan for you! We gotta stand up and fight for the Lord. Matthew 10:34 tells us, 'Do not think that I have come to bring peace to the earth. I have not come to bring peace, but a sword.' We are at war! We are God's soldiers."

The crowd erupted into wild praise and applause. The minister strutted back and forth across the stage. "There is evil in this world. Evil we cannot imagine. We are at war against evil, and we must remain strong! We must fight back!"

As the crowd on the TV cheered, Mark's hands were shaking. The images around him were unnatural. Whatever it was he had noticed, it wasn't right—it couldn't be— but he was the one who had noticed and figured it out. He had seen this evil thing that had tried to hide from everyone else. All of the fuck-ups, debt, and the wasted time he had in his life didn't matter anymore because what Mark had discovered made it all worth it. He had found this thing masquerading around with all of his wealth. Mark crumbled the printer paper in his hand with rage at the memory of the beautiful yacht that thing and the woman had sailed into Hyannis. It wasn't fair that he was sitting in this bullshit squalor when that bastard had money.

"All of those problems and all of those things in your past you don't like to think about. Everything you're ashamed of. Everything that makes you feel weak that knocked you down has prepared you for this moment! You have a purpose! God's purpose!" The preacher pulled out a rumpled cloth and wiped his brow as he strutted along, fueling the cries of his flock.

"Don't believe me? Hear Ephesians 6:12. 'For our struggle is not against flesh and blood, but against the rulers, against the powers, against the world forces of this darkness, against the spiritual forces of wickedness in the heavenly places. Therefore, take up the full armor of God, so that you will be able to resist in the evil day, and having done everything, to stand firm.' The devil walks among us. He is here in our world. We are at war! Are you ready to fight? If you ain't up already, stand if you're ready to fight for God!"

The crowd jumped up. Mark tried to stand, but the liquor made him stumble and fall. He clawed his way over the stained carpet through the empty bottles to get to the TV where he kneeled and put his hand on the screen, inches away from the preacher.

"Oh boy, we better be ready! This is going to be the fight of our life! We are serving God's purpose! Do not be afraid! We are doing God's will! We are ready to fight evil on behalf of the Lord! You were made for this moment! Everything in your past! Everything you are! Everything you've struggled with! Everything you've done has prepared you to fight the evil in this world for the one, true God in Heaven!"

Mark's face, bathed in the blue glow of the TV, sat inches from the screen, listening to the cheers of the crowd. He watched until the screen faded to black and a woman's voice read out a phone number to order the sermon.

Mark sat still on the ground. The evil face looked up at him from the papers littered around the room. Dark, cold fear clawed in his chest. His whole body shook, whether from fear or excitement, he couldn't tell anymore.

In the dim light of the screen, he turned to look at the clock radio and watched it count down until the library reopened the next day.

CHAPTER 40

A few minutes after the last bell rang, Caitlyn tucked in a few chairs in her now empty room. She rounded the corner of a table, crouching down to grab stray pencils as she headed to snag her purse. She didn't want to be late to find out whatever it was Austin tried to tell her earlier.

A knock at the door got her attention. Principal Clarkson stood in the doorway.

"Hey, I need to speak with you. Is now a good time?"

"Um, sure. Do you want to head to your office?" Caitlyn asked, starting to put down the coat she had slipped over one arm.

He held up his hand and ambled in before leaning against one of the other tables in the room. His dull brown suit looked overly large as usual and reminded Caitlyn of a walrus when combined with his goatee. He set his walkie-talkie on the table and turned down the volume before folding his arms.

"So, I've got some news."

Caitlyn braced herself. "Okay?"

"The teacher who had left to go to UVA returned home last night."

Caitlyn felt her face get warm, but she tried to fight the panic that bubbled inside her. "I thought she wasn't going to be back for at least a year—"

"Yeah, we all did." He blew out a breath and looked at her. His blue eyes met hers with clarity. He spoke calmly, but Caitlyn wasn't listening, though she could feel herself nodding and making what she hoped were appropriate sounds to suggest she was following. Panic gripped her, making her squirm in her seat. Fighting the urge to get up and pace, she twisted her hands in her lap.

"Mr. Clarkson—"

"John, please. Mr. Clarkson was my father," he said with a smile.

"My contract says I'm working here through the entire school year."

He closed his eyes and nodded. "I know. Listen, you've done a great job here. You really have. I hope it's okay with you. I made some calls around Nantucket to see if they have any openings right now. They don't, but one of them knew of an opening on the Cape."

All of this was happening so fast. Nausea tossed around the pasta salad Caitlyn had for lunch like a dingy in the harbor. While John said words like "recommendation," "accredited," and "great guys," Caitlyn tried to process what was happening.

Thoughts of Louisiana and Caleb poured into her mind. She had wanted to escape the memories of her family and see the world, so what did it matter where she went? It wasn't even Christmas yet, and she felt like she had settled in enough to put down roots. Roots that were now being torn out of the ground.

John stopped talking and stared at her. She had no idea what he had just said. "What about the kids?" she asked.

"We're going to treat it like a normal board sub situation, like FMLA, so you and she will teach together next week and then she'll take over. This way she'll know where you were at, and the kids won't feel jostled around. There'll be some sense of continuity," he said, nodding with a smile as if that settled all of the problems.

"I'm sorry, this is very sudden. What about my apartment? Where will I live on the Cape? I'm not sure I can afford something that isn't subsidized."

"Denise assured me there is a program that most of the staff participates in. It offers a reduced rate for police, nurses, and teachers. Public servants. That sort of thing."

Caitlyn sat stunned. In a matter of five minutes of simple conversation, her life had been ripped away as if she was being recycled like an old purse. Totally dispensable and replaceable.

"I know this is a lot. I just wanted to let you know so you can start to make arrangements. Don't worry about the cost of moving your things. I've called a company to help load everything onto the ferry and move you in. I'll have Denise send you the email with those places that are available so you can pick out one that you like."

John talked a bit longer, offering praise, apologies, and best wishes before he slid off the table, picked up his walkie-talkie, and ambled out the door. Caitlyn waited for the door to the stairwell to shut before she launched herself up and out of the room.

In less than a minute, she rounded the corner to Austin's cramped office on the first floor.

"Did you know about this?" she said, marching into the doorway.

Behind his desk, Austin looked up from his laptop and

raised his eyebrows. He, too, had been on his way out. Despite piles of paper, growth measure charts, and a deconstructed pencil sharpener strewn about his desk, Austin already had his coat on.

"Know about what?"

"I just got fired."

Austin bolted out of his chair, his jaw jutting out, ready for a fight. "What? Are you kidding me? How?"

"John just stopped by and casually let me know the other teacher's come back and I'm being transferred to the Cape."

"Lizzy's not supposed to come back—"

"Well, guess what? She's back." Caitlyn stomped around the small space and didn't know whether to kick something or cry. "I mean I guess they can do that. I'm a probational employee. At my old school I'd been there so long they'd have to work to get rid of me, assuming I didn't mess with money or honey." Caitlyn slumped into Austin's visitor chair and ran her hands through her hair, stopping at her crown and tugging in frustration.

She frowned and looked up at him. "You don't think this is about us...?"

Austin had apparently reached the same conclusion, judging by the grim set of his mouth. His fists were planted knuckle first onto the desk, and if looks could kill, the wall opposite him would have been toast.

Caitlyn blew out a breath and slumped even farther down in the visitor chair. There was nothing she could do. Everything was all wrapped up. What was she going to do? Sit in the classroom and refuse to leave? Staring at Austin's cluttered desk, she felt the fight leave her shoulders.

"At least I'll be on the Cape so we can still visit. Assuming you want to, that is."

When he didn't answer, she looked at him. Austin stood motionless and stared off into his overfilled bookcase.

Caitlyn sniffed, trying to hold back the tears. God, would the new school be enough to pay her debts? "It has to be me. I really tried to do a good job. I thought I was doing a good job, but now... What?" she asked, looking from him to the old binders and back again.

He swore under his breath and grabbed his keys out of a drawer. "I need to show you something. Now."

CHAPTER 41

Ten minutes later, Caitlyn pulled the Escape into a small oyster shell driveway big enough for just two cars. Austin got out of his Ford Ranger. She did the same and was hit with a frigid wind off the sea. The small cottage was more like an oversized garden shed or converted garage. Still, the view was nice. One weathered Adirondack chair sat on a postage-stamp-sized lawn overlooking the water on the other side of the street. In the summer months, it would have paired nicely with a sunset, a glass of wine, and the briny air.

"Welcome to my humble abode," Austin said with a smile that Caitlyn didn't believe. He looked jittery with nervous energy. Pumping his jaw, he motioned for her to go ahead toward the door.

"This is so not what I expected," Caitlyn said, walking on the winding brick path while looking at the small cottage. Thorny sticks clung to the gray cedar-shingled structure. In the spring, she was sure it would be full of roses, but now, in the twilight of fall, a pumpkin sat on the freezing stoop surrounded by a heap of dried leaves. The wind off the icy blue ocean slammed into them. Caitlyn sank down into her coat until Austin opened the door into a small space.

Her first thought inside was that it was cozy. Her second thought was to wonder how Austin managed to maneuver around the tiny cottage. Austin tossed his coat onto the coatrack by the door before taking hers. An old, rumpled couch sat against one wall next to a tiny wood stove, which would make the space even cozier on a blustery day. Above the sofa, an oil painting of an old, masted ship hung on the plastered wall facing a TV on the other side of the cramped room. Caitlyn could've touched the low, sloped ceiling but instead followed Austin past the cedar chest that acted as a coffee table back a few feet into the smallest kitchen she'd ever seen.

Austin passed a small tabletop Christmas tree on the counter. The ornaments were little buoys and signal flags.

"That's really cute," she said, admiring it.

Austin gave it a passing glance as he headed for a cabinet. "Yeah, Mom dropped that off. You know how she is."

Better suited for a boat, the small space consisted of a handful of small, old pine cabinets. The counter gleamed with a varnish, making the grain of the pine stand out. Austin picked up the coffee pot and headed to where the countertop jutted out to make room for a tiny sink.

"Coffee?" he asked, already making the preparations. "I know how to work this machine," he added with a small smile, referencing the debacle at her place.

"Yeah, sure," she said, only because he seemed like he needed something to do. Austin still seemed off, but then it had been an off day with her being fired out of the blue.

It was so different to know someone at work than it was to be invited into their private space. After seeing his parents' house, Caitlyn hadn't known what to expect. She wandered the few feet back to the living room and examined the old bookshelf. Well-worn books on World War II and the navy stood in rows like sailors on deck. Judging by the spine, each looked like it had been read at least twice. There were a few old pictures in frames too. Most were shots of a battleship. All seemed to be original to the forties.

The smell of dark coffee floated around the small space, while the floor creaked underneath the worn Persian rug beneath her boots. Something about the little cottage felt like home. Austin passed by and handed her a cup of coffee, and Caitlyn went to sit on the sagging orange couch. From her vantage point, she could see the water and the sunset. It would be dark soon.

Austin set down his cup but didn't sit. Instead, he went into a doorway that led to the back. The whole house couldn't be more than two tiny bedrooms at most. Caitlyn sipped her coffee and didn't notice the lack of cream and sugar.

The couch just begged her to take her boots off and tuck her legs underneath her before curling up with the throw behind her. Instead, she contented herself with leaning back and watching the light fade. Caitlyn sighed and wondered what it would be like to get snowed in here with Austin.

She really did love him. Even though he had broken her trust and refused to open up to her. Whether or not he shared that opinion didn't change hers. As heartbreaking as it had been to let go of the house her dad had maintained all those years, this place felt more like home than anything had since her mom had died. She never expected to feel that feeling again. Hadn't set out for it. To make matters worse, she had only been inside for two sips of coffee and already felt at ease. Leaving was going to shred what was left of her battered heart.

Caitlyn heard Austin rummaging in the back. He hadn't answered when she'd mentioned visiting once she left for the

Cape. She wasn't twelve anymore. She knew what that meant. Drawing in a breath, Caitlyn took another sip of coffee and committed every corner of the little house to memory until he came back. This way she could revisit what could've been in her mind for years to come.

"Okay," he said in an oddly shaky breath. Austin's jaw was tense, and he wouldn't look her in the eye.

Caitlyn sat forward, concerned. He was usually so forthright.

"Austin," she said when he had paused, holding what looked to be a photo album. He didn't look up from the old book when he swallowed hard.

"Austin," she said again, this time standing up. "What did you want to show me?"

Austin's hands shook as he held the album. Cracks ran up the binding where the leather had split from age. A rubber band held the whole thing together.

"Hey," Caitlyn said, taking a step forward. "Let's sit down." She didn't know what was going on, but sitting down seemed like the right thing to do.

Without a word, he nodded and sank down next to her. He eased into the couch like an old man, tired and sore. Austin swallowed again and pumped the muscle in his jaw as he ground his molars before drawing in a shaky breath. Caitlyn touched his knee and put her hand on his back. This was his goodbye to her, she realized. A last parting gift to earn back her trust and explain everything.

Seeing him like this shook Caitlyn to her core. Usually so strong and full of life, Austin now seemed scared and fragile.

"Hey," she said again. "It's okay. Do you want your coffee?" she said, noticing that it sat untouched on the small kitchen counter.

He shook his head and went to slide the rubber band off the cover. With a pop, it snapped, sending the cover up in a flurry of memories. A picture escaped and floated to the floor.

Caitlyn bent down to get it and turned it over.

Another picture from the forties. Judging by the size and the age, it matched the collection of originals on Austin's bookcase. Two sailors stood side by side, each one with an arm flung around the other. Caitlyn squinted at the one on the left.

"He must be your grandfather. You look just like him," she said with a smile. "No wonder you're fascinated by World War II."

Austin sighed. The sadness inside him seemed to melt his bones so that he sagged even lower. He reminded Caitlyn of a dog waiting to be kicked.

"I have something to tell you," he said, the apology thick in his voice.

"Yes?" Caitlyn took a deep breath and put the picture down on the cedar chest in front of them. She'd been waiting for the big reveal since they had left his office.

"Do you see the scar on that man's arm?"

"Your grandfather?" she asked.

Austin pulled his mouth into a thin line and swallowed. "Look."

His finger guided her eye toward the inside of the man's arm. "You have the same birthmark?" she said. The chances of that were almost unreal but not unheard of. She thought of her cousin who had the same beauty mark as her mother and brother, in the exact same place. Why that would make Austin so sad didn't make sense.

Austin's eyes met hers. The sadness in them would've drowned anyone.

He opened the old album and revealed a lifetime of memories, all from World War II. Newspaper clippings, letters, and more photographs scattered out. Austin flicked through the pile and pulled out another photo of the man with the birthmark, only this time it was his portrait.

"It's remarkable how much he looks like you," Caitlyn said, admiring the picture as he handed it to her.

"Turn it over," he said in a sad voice. He looked like he was in absolute agony now. A man at war with himself.

Caitlyn looked at him, wondering what was going on. She was the one that had just been fired, and she didn't see what any of this had to do with it.

She could feel Austin's gaze as she held the picture with her fingers on the edge and tilted it to the side.

Caitlyn frowned and turned the picture back over. The hairs on the back of her neck rose, and a ripple of unease ran up her arms. Caitlyn felt her face get hot as she turned to him.

In a small voice, she looked at Austin and asked, "I don't understand. Are you named after your grandfather?"

Austin shook his head no, sending Caitlyn's blood pressure into a tailspin.

"Austin," she said, trying to remain calm. "Who is this?"

He looked as though he wanted to throw up. While Caitlyn waited for an answer that she could make sense of, Austin lifted his gaze from the portrait and looked her dead in the eye.

"That's me."

Caitlyn felt the blood drain out of her face. Her heart raced, and blood pounded in her ears. "That's not possible," she said in a whisper.

In response, Austin unbuttoned his shirt. Caitlyn scooted back as he removed it. He pointed to his birthmark and the first picture that had fallen out of the album.

"No," she said to herself. "That's...that can't be. It's not true."

"Caitlyn," he said in a sad, pitiful voice. "I'm sorry I didn't tell you until now. The rules—"

"Don't be ridiculous."

"I was born in 1920."

"Austin, you're scaring me." She didn't take her eyes off him.

"It's the water," he said, now desperate. His eyes looked strung out, like someone who had been away at sea on the edge of dying from thirst.

"That's why we can't leave. The water in the refuge keeps us alive. We start drinking it at age eighteen. The kids don't know, but then they find out. Every seven years is like one for us."

Caitlyn could feel herself nodding. Her chest was ice cold, and fear froze her muscles. "Like a fountain of youth?" She could hear her teacher voice, the one she used when a student had concocted a fantasy story and needed a sympathetic listening ear. Inside though, she was holding back a dam of panic. He was crazy. He'd lost it.

Austin grabbed her shoulders hard. His fingers bored into her skin. "Exactly," he said, panting. "We can't tell anyone. That's why no one talks to you. They're too scared they'll fuck up and be exiled."

Caitlyn knew better than to make a run for it. Her best chance was to calm him down. "Please let me go," she said, her voice firm and stable.

Austin withdrew his hand. "I'm sorry, but you gotta listen to me. I've never told anyone. They're trying to get rid of you because of me. They warned me we were getting too close. I didn't want you here, but now I do, and they're trying to take you away. Caitlyn, I've never known anyone like you."

She could feel the surprise hit her face before her brow lowered. The quick flash of anger burned away a little of the fear. "You told them we were together?" Which in hindsight had apparently been a terrible idea for more than one reason. Caitlyn wanted to slap herself the second she could get in the car and drive the hell away for even thinking she loved him.

"No, no, no. Of course not. All those nights playing chess. That's why I had to stop coming around. They've been on me, putting my balls in a vise." She wrinkled her nose at his description. The crazed look in his eyes made her swallow the bile that was rising up her throat.

"Okay, Austin," she said when he sat back waiting on her response. "If this is true, then why are you telling me this now?"

"I need you to know. I can't let you leave. I want to be with you. You're the best thing that's ever happened to me. I'm sorry I broke your trust. If we go to the town council and tell them that you know—"

"Wait, I thought you said no one was supposed to tell? Exile?"

Naked from the waist up on the orange couch, Austin nodded in earnest like a puppy, eager to please. "Yeah, but if you become one of us, you'll stay here and never leave. I'll get you the water somehow. We can live together. Here. Forever."

That got her up. "Austin, you're freaking me the hell out. I need to go. Now."

He grabbed her arm. She yanked it back. "Get your hands off of me!"

Austin dropped his arm again, looking frantic in the small space. "No, Caitlyn, please. You gotta believe—" Devastation clawed at his face.

"Believe what? That you're immortal? You're out of your damn mind, and I'm getting the hell out of here." Caitlyn headed for the door. Austin launched himself in front of her. "Don't you dare," she said, shouldering past him.

Shaken to her core, she reached for the handle and pulled

open the door before running to the car. Austin called after her but thankfully didn't pursue. She wrenched the door open, jumped in, slammed it shut, and cranked the engine. Her foot slammed the pedal, and a spray of gravel peppered Austin's tailgate in a cacophony of pings.

Her tires squealed as she turned out of the driveway and sped off into the night.

CHAPTER 42

Mark stood on the same dock he had known his whole life and watched as the high-speed ferry he had served bobbed in front of him. The Atlantic winter winds sliced through the old army coat he had picked up years ago from a secondhand store.

The young crew hopped around and danced with the ropes wearing just hoodies, oblivious to the luxury of their youth.

Scott had been messing with the ticket scanner when he looked up, did a double take, and jogged down the gangway to meet him.

"Schmidty!" he said, his smiling face unmarred by lines of worry and debt. The tanned young skin and blue eyes looked handsome and full of life. "How's it going? Tried to call and check in on you, but you never called me back. What's doing?"

Mark looked down. Scott had been one of his coworkers he had almost liked, even though he wore fancy clothes and had a good family. Unlike the others, he didn't lord it over people. "I called the office and let them know I'd be taking some time off."

"Yeah, they mentioned that. You back now?"

Mark looked at the ground and shook his head. "Passenger today. Going to take some time."

Scott nodded. "Well, you deserve it. Can't remember when you last took some days off."

Never happened, which is why you don't remember, Mark thought to himself. He shifted his legs and nodded, wanting to get this over with as fast as possible.

Scott reached out to take the ticket. "Brightrock, huh? They just got that one place to stay—the Cedar Inn, right?"

Mark nodded again, hoping not to draw attention to himself or his bag, which he gripped tightly. Even though he wore wool gloves, the cold bit through and froze his aching joints into position.

Scott frowned at the ticket. "Wait, this is just one-way. The office must have fucked up again."

Mark watched, holding his breath. If things went to plan, he wouldn't need a return ticket. Besides, if it hadn't been for the employee passes he never used, he wouldn't have been able to afford the overpriced trip.

"We'll get this straightened out. Come on in before we freeze to death out here. Hey, you get to sit in the front today," Scott said with an easy grin.

"Yeah, I guess I do," Mark said, hauling his service duffle bag on board.

As he sat himself down like one of the fancy people he had shuttled to luxury all his life, Mark looked out toward the horizon.

The Island of Evil as he had taken to calling it lay beyond, only a few hours away. Between it and him, the choppy, rough sea churned beneath the waves. The skies above were gray and cold. The sun would be down soon, and Mark would arrive in the dark, like the angel of the Lord he knew he'd been called to become.

After hearing the word of God, he had become transformed. All the pain and suffering in his life made sense now. None of it had been his own fault. All of it had been by design for him to witness this manifest of evil, so that he alone could destroy it.

The calling had scared him at first. He had waffled for days, scouring the computers at the library for any word of Brightrock through the years. But now that he knew what to look for, the signs were easy. People had always talked about the rumors of witchcraft on Brightrock, but now Mark knew the truth. Austin may have been the first clue he had seen, but he was far from the only. The devils were careful, but they weren't good enough to escape Mark. He could see. He was smarter than them. Names repeated through the years. Images caught shots of people who should have been long dead. The history of the first arrival mentioned a few deaths first, but then a few others, most of whom, when he looked, had been people who never existed. No records of any kind except for birth and death. All of natural causes.

The cemetery on the eastern part of the island was an obvious sham, with maybe a dozen headstones, all from original founders. With the maps, he had been able to search the entire town from above, spying on the devils whose wealth made him sick.

Even now, sitting in the ferry, white rage clouded his vision and fisted his clawed hands as he had seen the cars, houses, yachts, and beauty of the island. All of it created and held by evil, unnatural things that tried to shroud themselves away from the world, hiding behind their money. For too long, their greed kept others, like himself, down.

But he was too smart. Mark had found images and then college and military records that all repeated themselves too.

Reading about the government told him what he needed to do. Thanks to the Commonwealth of Massachusetts, the monthly Town Hall meeting times had been posted and, surprise, surprise, the bastards didn't leave them open to non-residents.

Once the plan had come to him after another sermon, Mark saw himself again bathed in fire, strong and rightfully feared like he had once been in his youth. The screams in his nightmares now echoed in his head. All of it had been preparing him for this moment when he would become God's messenger.

As the ferry lifted with a swell and launched toward the horizon, Mark clutched the handle of his army duffle bag, the tools of death inside calming him, and prayed. Though he should have been scared, for the first time since he had returned to the ungrateful country he had fought to protect, Mark smiled with excitement.

CHAPTER 43

The next day, every time Caitlyn looked at a student or colleague, Austin's confession haunted her. She hadn't slept at all. The pictures of Austin, or someone he had said was him, kept her awake. The chances of the name, birthmark, and the same face all matching were unreal.

What shook her down to her core were the smiles. Both the vintage photograph and the Austin she knew had broad, happy, slightly lopsided grins. They were identical. Thinking of it reminded her of seeing Austin in her apartment. He had given her the same puppy dog smile then.

The fear had burned off and had given way to rational thought. All of her feelings for him remained despite how she wanted to feel about him now. Even after last night, his energy drew her to him. Caitlyn smiled to herself at the memory of him bursting into the classroom with a chessboard. All of the stories and jokes they had shared over the past months had been real. A genuine connection existed between them. At least it had until last night.

Caitlyn dug her fingers into her hair before closing her

eyes and pulling her hands down over her face. Whether or not she thought Austin was out of his mind no longer mattered in the grand scheme of things. What mattered was how many boxes Caitlyn could gather from the cafeteria to box up the few personal items she had acquired while here. Caitlyn drummed a pen on the desk calendar she hadn't changed since September and drew a little doodle in the corner where there was still space from all of her earlier scribbles.

She didn't want to run into anyone else. Caitlyn hated small talk at the best of times. Though what Austin told her last night made her normal social anxiety look like spilling water in the bayou. It wasn't going to matter, and there were much bigger things to worry about in the water.

After she drew another heart and traced over a star she had sketched earlier, Caitlyn tossed the pen down onto the desk and shoved up out of the chair. The hell with it, she thought. It wasn't like the people here had talked to her much anyway regardless of the reason, she added to herself when Austin's words started to float back to her. All she needed to do was to pack and get ready for her big move to the Cape.

Fed up with hiding, Caitlyn strode out of the room as she had for months now. She intended to march all the way down to the cafeteria and come right back, but what she saw in the hallway stopped her.

Connie stood in the hallway with another teacher named Glen. She played with her bangle bracelets, looking worried. Glen had a grim expression on his face and stood there with his arms crossed, his eyes on the floor while he listened to Connie speak.

"Have you heard about Austin?" Connie asked, seeing Caitlyn.

Caitlyn wondered how old each of the people in front of

her was and then chided herself for even entertaining the crazy notion.

"I haven't talked to him today," she said, reaching up for her necklace.

Glen sucked in a long breath. "Well, he resigned this morning. Shocked the staff."

Caitlyn stood there stunned for a second. "What?"

Connie frowned and furrowed her brows. "Yeah. I'm surprised he didn't tell you."

The heat in Caitlyn's cheeks told her pure annoyance flooded her face. "Where is he?"

"Uh, probably in his office?" said Glen, who now had a frown on his face too.

Caitlyn didn't even respond. She just started marching in that direction. If he resigned with intentions to follow her, he needed to knock that shit off right now. They were done. After last night's little bomb, Caitlyn had about had it with the whole island. Moving to the Cape would be for the best. As she passed the library, Caitlyn could see other staff members talking in little huddles with looks that ranged from mild surprise to flat-out stunned.

She hustled by the trophy case fueled by a pissed off feeling. Austin had been at this school for years. To just up and resign, midyear no less, in any other district would have burned a bridge so bad that teacher would never be hired again.

Caitlyn rounded the corner and stopped in the doorway to his cramped office, not because she ran out of steam, but because a pile of boxes blocked her way. Beyond them, she could hear rummaging and the telltale sounds of packing tape.

She should've turned around and walked away, but against her better judgment she said, "What the hell is wrong with you?"

The rummaging stopped. Caitlyn heard swearing, and the boxes started to move away from the door.

"I didn't think I'd see you today," Austin said with a shrug. "After last night and all." His normally ramrod straight back now had a defeated slump. A sail without wind. "I'm just packing a few things. Let me move these." Austin kept stacking the boxes elsewhere until he carved a small path into the cramped office, revealing total chaos beyond.

"What the hell do you think you're doing?" Caitlyn said, marching inside. She folded her arms in front of her chest and lowered her lids at him.

"What?" Austin said.

"Don't give me that," she snapped, causing him to wince. "Why the hell are you resigning?"

"I'm leaving Brightrock."

Caitlyn glared at Austin. If he was trying to guilt her into something, it wasn't going to work.

"What do you mean 'leaving Brightrock'? Where are you going to go?"

Austin eased back behind a towering stack of empty boxes. "I don't know. Anywhere, I guess."

"Aren't you forgetting something?"

Austin turned around and frowned at her. "What would that be?"

Caitlyn stared him down before waving her arms around. "You know—the whole immortal thing you dropped on me last night? Assuming you were telling the truth, which of course you weren't."

"Hey, keep your voice down! The kids don't know. They won't find out until after they graduate."

Caitlyn crossed her arms again and leaned a shoulder into the wall. "Oh, I should keep it down, huh?"

"Besides," Austin said. "I've gotten bored. Figured now's a good time to start aging properly."

Caitlyn studied him and debated walking right back out of the room. If he wanted to turn to dust or whatever, that wasn't her problem. "Wouldn't you come back like your brother?"

Austin faced a bookcase and resumed lowering stacks of books into an old frozen French fry box. "Ah…no, I don't think so. In my situation, it's more of a one-time deal. Ethan's not attached and has to check in with the elders about his situation all the time to make sure he isn't getting too close to anyone. He's worked that angle for a while now. I'll have to sign an NDA."

"Bullshit. You were in the navy."

Austin shook his head and grabbed the tape to close up the box of books. "Yeah, there's a whole procedure for deployments. Fake IDs and council of elders give permission. It's a thing." He sighed and started on the next box of books. "Moving away and cutting ties is different. I don't want to have to get approval for every single move I make, so…" He shrugged. "They cut ties. Safer that way, and besides," he added turning around to face her, "I'd rather be with you. That is, if you'd still have me." Austin raised his lashes to meet her stare with hopeful, blue eyes. "I mean, I know you don't want that after last night, and I don't blame you, but I was hoping you and I could be in the same town and have coffee or lunch. Just friends."

"What if I don't want that?" Caitlyn asked, trying to sound as if her stomach wasn't floating outside her body over what he'd just said. He liked her. Enough that he was leaving to follow her.

"Well, then I have the time to convince you."

Caitlyn let her arms fall and slap against her legs. "Austin, this is crazy."

"Not really," he said, packing again.

"What if I go back to Louisiana?" Caitlyn knew it was a

bluff, but she didn't care. None of this was based in reality anyway.

Austin froze and looked up, lids low and suspicious. "To be with Caleb?"

"No, just to go back to where I'm from."

Austin shrugged. "I love spicy food."

"What are you going to do? Stalk me for the rest of my life?" Caitlyn threw her hands up in disbelief at what her life had devolved into over the past twenty-four hours.

"That escalated quickly, but unless you insist on me not being around, then yeah. Maybe."

"I can't let you do this. If what you say is true, and that's a big-ass if, then this would mean—"

"Yep, and it's not your choice. It's mine. Would you hand me that box?"

Caitlyn stood there, stunned.

"It's okay. I'll get it," Austin said, reaching over and packing as if he were just transferring to a new school. Routine. Boring. All systems normal and ready for takeoff.

"Listen," he said, pausing after a few moments of silence. "I got a lot to do here, so if you want to talk, we should probably meet up later. The council of elders is going to want me gone like yesterday, so I need to pack kinda quick."

CHAPTER 44

Caitlyn pulled the packing tape across the top of the last box in her classroom. The loud ripping sound, which grated on her ears, making her reconsider even packing everything up again.

She swiped the hair out of her face and knelt down to lift the box onto the hand truck she had borrowed from the custodian. Even though the weather outside the school called for snow, Caitlyn had worked up a sweat packing the room. Most of it would stay behind, but in the short time at this school, she had inherited a staggering amount that would be making the trip to the Cape with her.

Looking down at the small heap of boxes, Caitlyn knew if they all fell overboard on the ferry, she wouldn't care all that much. Back when she had first started teaching, she guarded her supplies like a sniper, but now, after everything that had happened, she could just walk away. Because she had already done that once, hadn't she?

Waiting for the familiar anger to come racing back in, Caitlyn stood surprised when nothing happened. She rubbed her chest and propped her hands on her hips, still waiting.

Unsure and hesitant, Caitlyn closed her eyes and tentatively pictured herself not in a classroom, but far away in her parents' old shotgun house that smelled of Tide and perfume. She retraced her steps in her mind, remembering the house as it had been.

Caitlyn waited for the anger and sorrow to peel back the curtain, shut down the memory, and send her racing back to the present, but it didn't. In her mind, the living room had everything back in its place, the kitchen complete with a box of doughnuts on the stove and dishes drying on the counter. The smell of fresh coffee hit her senses in her mind, and everything seemed right, but still, where anger and pain had lived for months, only a warm familiarity lingered.

Caitlyn opened her eyes to look at the boxes on the desks again before she drew in a breath and, for the first time since her passing, remembered her mom sitting in the recliner chatting on the phone in a mix of English and French. Her feet were up, no doubt after cooking. In her memory, Caitlyn's dad sat there in his coveralls in another recliner, watching her mom talk with an intrigued smile on his face.

Caitlyn smiled as she drank in the image of the pair, sitting there as they always had been and always should be. Before she could pull away from the memory, she could see her mom's eyes. The memory of the face she had loved so much lit with a full smile as she recognized Caitlyn before her as if she saw her and waved her down to take a seat with them. Caitlyn let the warmth wrap around her in comfort. Everything about it seemed right.

Caitlyn blinked a few times and did a quick swipe under her eyes, looking around at the pile of boxes she'd loaded onto the hand truck without even realizing it.

Shutting every memory out of her mind had been the easy solution, but while she knew there would always be a dull ache—a hole—maybe this is what everyone had meant when they talked about the power of time.

After a quick glance around the room, she grabbed the handle, ready to tow it to her car—well, the car she was borrowing. She'd need to buy one on the Cape. A door slammed in the hallway, and through the glass window, she watched Connie leave, walking down the hall, her heels making a fast tapping noise before she pushed into the stairwell.

So much for goodbye, Caitlyn thought with a snort. She angled her head out into the hall and saw the same scene repeat itself as Glen shut his door and made a beeline for the exit.

A chill washed over her, prickling the skin on her elbows. She reached up to play with her necklace, letting the chain thread through her fingertips as she chewed on her lower lip. Glancing behind her, Caitlyn strode past the cart of boxes, grabbed her keys, and hustled down to the parking lot.

The only cars left were backing out now in succession. Caitlyn followed suit, not making eye contact with anyone. What weirded her out was the fact that usually people would go out of their way to avoid her, but now everyone was so distracted, they had forgotten about her completely.

Pulling out of the spot, Caitlyn drove the little Escape behind Glen's truck but made sure to leave enough distance so he wouldn't notice. Sure enough, Connie's car was ahead of his, along with a string of cars she had seen in the faculty parking lot.

All of them were heading in the same direction. Caitlyn followed suit on the winding road that Austin had given her a tour of back in September. Houses faded away as they approached the refuge.

Glen slowed, the red brake lights glowing in the

retreating sun. Caitlyn slowed too and watched as the truck turned into the refuge.

Frowning, Caitlyn did the same, turning off the pavement and onto a bumpy gravel road through a rusty old gate, sitting in the open position despite the sign that read "no trespassing." Judging by the deep ruts in the path, the kind only a bunch of cars could make, plenty of people came here often.

She lurched along in the car over the bumpy path, climbing a hill through the dense forest. With her hands tight on the wheel, Caitlyn looked in every direction, wondering what she would do whenever she got to where she was going. Austin's story from earlier lingered in her mind alongside the consequences of an outsider penetrating their sacred and secret world. She didn't know what to believe anymore. How much she did believe made her feel like turning around, boarding the ferry first thing in the morning, and getting the hell out.

The driveway opened into a clearing on top of a crest. Rows of cars sat parked like they were at a county fair, and people, most of whom she recognized, all headed into what looked like an old church. Caitlyn parked near the tree line and watched, waiting to see what would happen.

The sun hadn't quite set, and in the fading glow, the white church looked ominous. A large oak tree sat to one side with a smattering of slate headstones that looked to be hundreds of years old. On the other side, a small building stood alone, whitewashed like the two-story church in front of her. The shape of it reminded her of the mausoleums down in New Orleans, but what had caught her eye was the old iron gate blocking the entrance. It was too far to get a good look at, but she could almost make out something like a series of locks on one side.

With rocks jutting out, the whole landscape seemed eerie

and unnatural. Caitlyn studied everyone that drove in, parked, and ambled toward the entrance, all the while wondering how old each of them was. If Austin had served in World War II and looked thirty, then his great aunt who had just shown up must be...

She shook her head, rejecting the impossible.

Austin's aunts had ridden with his parents, none of whom looked happy to be together. They moved as fast as possible with the older women, both looking grim and quiet. Austin's mom had a pained expression on her face, and his dad looked deeply concerned.

Caitlyn kept scanning and watching, until the number of cars entering the parking lot dwindled. Studying the cars, she told herself she wasn't looking for anything in particular, but her body immediately reacted when she saw the old Ford Ranger pulling in. Through the windshield, she could see that Austin was still dressed from work but had his sleeves rolled up and tie slack. He parked on the far side of the lot, straightened the tie, and headed in alone. Caitlyn reached for the car door but stopped herself. Judging by all of the cars here and the secret creepy church, this was not exactly a place she wanted to hang out.

Caitlyn watched him weave through the cars to the entrance where he opened the door and let himself inside.

Whether or not she believed what Austin had told her didn't matter. She needed to get in there before he did something stupid like leave his home. Unlike her, he belonged here with his family. She'd kill to have the chance to live near her parents again. He didn't know what he was wasting, the bastard.

Emotion swelled in her chest, and as she watched him disappear into the darkness beyond, Caitlyn wanted to scream. It was all her fault. He was doing this for her, to stay with her, and God, she wanted him, but she couldn't let him ruin his future. If what he had told her last night was true, what Austin was about to give up couldn't be allowed.

Caitlyn started to shake as the revelation hit home. She believed him. God help her if it made her crazy as a loon, but she believed him. Shoving the repercussions of that thought aside, Caitlyn stepped out of the car into the dusk. She believed him, and she loved him too much to let him destroy himself, no matter what happened. She couldn't stand by and let that happen.

Movement caught her eye. Caitlyn snapped back behind the door, watching to see who else might be coming. At the edge of the woods, a shadow shifted. Caitlyn waited and watched, but he didn't go in like everyone else.

The hairs on her neck rose as she watched him limp out of the shadows toward the back of the building, avoiding the windows. He carried large pots under each arm.

Caitlyn crept closer through the line of cars, using them and the fading light to her advantage. When she reached the first row of cars, she crouched and watched.

The man had bent down and messed with one of the pots against the wall of the church. When he stood, Caitlyn sucked in a curse and held it.

She had seen him before.

The man who had asked her about her ticket on the ferry stood and lifted the other pot around the side of the building. Caitlyn watched and waited, trying to figure out what he was doing.

When he didn't come back after a minute, Caitlyn hustled across the lawn to get a closer look at what he'd left. She crouched behind a headstone and leaned out. She needed to get inside and talk to Austin.

Ice filled her veins. Her heart pounded.

Tucked against the wall in the dark, Caitlyn could see the outline of a pressure cooker. Panic gripped her, forcing her breaths to come in quick succession as she clung to the headstone.

The man limped back around the corner. Her heart thundered in her ears. She wondered if it would give her away and tried to hold her shaky breath.

Caitlyn watched him stumble back toward the woods and come back with a gas can. He worked quickly, pouring the thin stream around the back wall. Caitlyn heard something and realized she was praying while judging the distance from the headstone to the closed door where Austin and everyone else sat unaware. She waited, holding her breath, hoping he would give her a shot. One chance to act.

With another gas can in hand from the woods, the man walked around the building. Caitlyn tore off toward the entrance pounding over the grass. She climbed the slate steps and ripped open the old oak doors.

The scene in front of her reminded her of a movie. Yellow candles gave the space a soft glow. Austin stood in the front, facing what looked to be like some sort of panel on a small stage. Hearing the door, everyone turned toward her, expressions sliding from concern to shock, one by one.

Time stilled into fractions of seconds.

All at once, Austin turned around and met her eyes, his surprise getting blacked out by panic. He turned on his heel and sprinted toward her, yelling something. A man stood up and started to reach for her arm. Other voices rose around her. A man in a vest at the front stood up and bellowed in the chaos, but Caitlyn couldn't hear anything over her own screaming.

CHAPTER 45

E than walked into his office after what had been a solid two-and-a-half-hour meeting. He kicked off his shoes and tossed his suit jacket onto the coat rack. The expansive view of the New York City skyline that could be seen out his corner window always calmed him, especially on late nights. Seeing the twinkling lights of apartments, cleaning crews, and other night owls made him feel less alone.

Brightrock smothered him with family. When it came time for him to go to school, Ethan leaped at the chance, but unlike others, he'd never entirely come back. Sure, he returned for the seasonal renewal. One sip from the well to prevent wrinkles, a quick bite at his parents' house, and then —boom—back to the city. Most people on the island had no idea how he did it. The risk of exposure scared all of them into settling for a life with the same people they'd known all their lives.

Being outside that tiny speck on the map meant he could live life the way he wanted to, but of course he had to take care not to get too close to anyone.

Ethan flopped down into the ergonomic leather chair his assistant had bought for him and flicked his hand across the trackpad to wake up the new screens on the sleek new desk. More substantial than his apartment, the office had been a big move for him and caused jealousy among some of the other fund managers. Because he looked so young, more than one had alluded to the fact that he had a bright future ahead of him. Some even added a back slap and referred to him as kid or son on a regular basis. Little did they know he could draw Social Security checks if he needed to. Not that money was going to be a problem for him anytime soon, even considering his life expectancy. His accounts had more than enough for several lifetimes of luxury.

He scanned the screen, checking afternoon emails. Finding nothing needing urgent attention, he stood and crossed to the seating area. The plush carpet under his cashmere socks was a far cry from the basic straw mats in the lobby and cubicles. Passing through a sleek sitting area, he headed for the wet bar. Dark cabinets and stainless steel lined one wall, containing coffees, teas, artisanal waters, and a snack for every kind of allergy and special diet known to man, though most of the time, clients preferred to meet out of the office.

Ethan set the coffee pot to brew and propped a hip on the countertop. He liked the space and enjoyed the work. It was really too bad he was going to have to disappear again so soon.

The smell of coffee mixed with the clean, fresh carpet and the scent of window cleaner. Somewhere far on the other side of the office, a vacuum cleaner fired up.

Feeling restless, Ethan grabbed the TV remote and flicked on the screen. Breaking News bled across the screen.

"...on a small New England Island. The bomber is reportedly in custody. We have obtained video from a local..."

Ethan watched in horror as images he knew all his adult life flashed across the screen. Towering flames blocked out most of the view of the well as the old meetinghouse burned.

"Fire crews have been deployed but were unable to save the original structure. We are awaiting reports on the conditions of the people inside during a town hall meeting."

Sheer terror gripped him. He bolted over to his jacket and ripped out his private phone, jabbing his fingers into the buttons before holding it up to his ear.

He stood frozen in shock, helpless as he watched the cherished and carefully preserved building collapse on itself. The ringing continued.

"Hi, you've reached Fred. I can't come to the phone right now—"

"Goddammit, pick up!"

Frantic, Ethan jabbed at the buttons again. He clutched the phone to his ear. Waiting, hoping, praying.

He could have been in there. All of them could have been in there. Mom, Dad, Austin. Was Lizzy still in Virginia? His breath came in short spurts. His face was damp, but he didn't care why or how. The newsreel looped the same footage sent in from an iPhone, but he couldn't make out the name who had shared it. The building collapsed again as the word 'terrorism' flashed across the screen.

His mom's bright voice came on the line. "Hey, this is Katie. I'm not available—"

"Come on!" he yelled at the phone.

"Mr. Brooks? Is everything okay?" The night cleaning lady stood in the doorway, her face full of concern as she clutched a rag and spray bottle.

Ethan could only shake his head as he hit more numbers on his phone. He pulled a hand over his face, covering his mouth. He was powerless to do anything. Standing there in absolute horror, he could do nothing but watch his home succumb to what the report was calling an attack.

Why were they even there? They had all just had the renewal a few weeks ago. There was no reason for them to report unless something had gone wrong.

Maybe if he chartered a plane he could get there in a few hours, but still. He couldn't bring himself to face what could be. He knew if there were injuries the best place would be Hyannis. Maybe a helicopter—

"Ethan?" Austin's voice broke the dam. Sirens sounded from behind him. Ethan clawed at the phone as tears streamed down his face. He crouched over the cellphone and plastered it to his face.

"Oh, thank God! I just saw the news. Where is everyone? Where's Mom and Dad?"

"They're safe. We're all safe." Ethan slumped onto the modern leather chair he had never used. His bones clattered with their actual age, and all of the tension seeped out of his body while relief flowed in to fill the void. The cleaning lady smiled at him, full of hope. He flashed her a thumbs-up, and she thankfully left to go finish vacuuming.

"What the fuck happened?" he asked, still transfixed by the footage. "I'm seeing the fire now."

"Yeah, dude, we gotta catch up. You've missed a lot."

As Austin filled him in on everything that had gone down with Caitlyn, Ethan watched the TV on mute. Whether Austin was still going for exile seemed to be tabled for the moment, and Tim Chappell could be an asshat, but after what Caitlyn had just done, it seemed logical that she should get some sort of pass or something. Ethan listened as Austin walked him through everything before handing the phone to their mom and dad. Relief crashed through his body, bringing tears to his eyes. Ending the call with a promise to talk to them again tomorrow, Ethan stood in his office and felt decades older than he had only minutes before.

The TV report still cycled on the screen behind him. Restless, he paced in the office that he had worked so hard to get and had wanted for so long. Stopping to stand in front of the large floor-to-ceiling windows, Ethan looked out at the buildings around him. A few lights remained on, their offices mostly populated by cleaning crews but a few workers as well. The icy cold night had cleared most of the sidewalks, leaving only the dumb and the brave to huddle against the wind in a race to get home. Most of the homeless had even moved into shelters this time of year.

Ethan uncrossed his arms, spun on his heel, and shut off the TV. Going home to his apartment seemed like the right thing to do, but he didn't know why. The only thing that was all that different was the style of furniture his assistant had ordered. Just in case he had to leave quickly, there wasn't anything personal there beyond a few leftover fortune cookies—not that he had anything in particular to keep anyway. His life outside Brightrock needed to be as sterile as possible to avoid suspicion.

In the beginning, the thrill of business and making money with money had brought enough appeal, but tonight had rattled his calm. Almost losing everything and everyone he had known and loved shook him deeply, throwing him off balance. Ethan didn't want to be alone, but the only thing waiting for him at home was a hot shower and some Scotch.

Deciding that was better than nothing, Ethan headed over to his bespoke overcoat and pulled on the dark wool before shoving his feet into his shoes and heading out into the night.

CHAPTER 46

Caitlyn ran a hand up over Austin's inner arm as they lay on the soft bed on the *Bombshell*, rocking with the gentle waves. Bolts of morning sun streaked through the windows overlooking the sea, bathing everything in a soft glow. Dark lashes rested on her cheeks as she looked down at his skin. Her cheeks still glowed, but her breathing had resumed its normal pace after what had been an encore performance. It had been their first chance to get away from everyone on the island, and Austin had been dying for some privacy.

First they had talked about everything, laying out all of the baggage right there in his cramped living room. Austin had held her while she cried over her parents and student, Amber. Caitlyn had done the same when Austin had told her about the ship going down in the navy and the funerals of his fellow sailors. Through the grief, they clung to each other, drawing strength from the other, and made love more times than he could count in a celebration of life that only a near-death experience could inspire.

She was so damn beautiful. Austin could've watched her

forever. The pale curve of her shoulder poked out of the fluffy duvet. Though he had seen every inch of her last night, he still craved more. His hand itched to nudge the fabric lower so he could take in her beauty again. Austin didn't think he would ever see enough of her.

After she had burst through the doors right when he had started the process of exile, he thought she had totally lost it. Her hair had been floating around her head, creating a halo like an angel. When someone had grabbed her, all of his instincts had gone into overdrive. Sprinting toward her hadn't even been a conscious thought, but a natural reaction to her being in danger. On an average town council meeting night, she could've been killed. No one had ever found out about them before, and the stakes were too high to let even one person get away with their secret.

Even now, he shuddered to think of it.

"Does this spot hurt?" she asked. Her voice had a husky richness that made him want to kiss her deeply all over again. It took him a minute to figure out what she was asking about.

"What spot—oh, that?" He looked down at the port wine stain on his inner arm. It had been a while since he had looked at it. He watched her thumb lazily stroke the area, which felt no different than the surrounding skin around the maroon blotch.

"No," he answered, studying it again for the first time in recent memory. The blotch had been a deeper red the last time he had noticed it, but maybe it was just the light. People had mentioned that over time they faded, but it remained as it had since he was eighteen.

"I've seen a few of these, but never anyone I knew well enough to be nosey." Caitlyn shifted on her side toward him. The duvet eased down her arm, revealing more perfect skin. "It's a birthmark, right?"

Austin paused. Did other people on the mainland have them at birth? He couldn't remember. Had she seen anyone else's? The Islanders didn't even fully understand why it happened, but it seemed benign enough, so no one put much effort into the matter.

"Once we drink the water, people often get a mark somewhere, like this one. We call them firemarks."

"Oh, that's neat. You think I'll get one?"

"Maybe, we'll have to see."

Caitlyn studied the ugly, unremarkable blotch, running her hand up and down over the darkened port wine stain on his skin.

"It looks like a duck," Caitlyn added after a minute. Her eyes studied the ugly blotch that scarred his arm. The dark lashes lining her eyes fanned out against her cheeks which were flush with lovemaking. Austin angled his head to try to get a better look at her eyes.

"Yeah...wait, a duck? You think this looks like a duck?" Austin shifted his arm around and brought it to his face. He frowned. "I don't see it."

Caitlyn propped herself up on one elbow. "Here, look. Do you see the beak?" She pointed toward a small area that jutted out to one side.

He frowned and sat back to look at his arm again. The only time he had thought about it this much was in the navy, back when he had considered adding a tattoo to the blotch.

"I've always thought it looked like Antarctica," Austin said, turning his head to try and see the duck. Sure enough, now that he was looking for it, he saw the beak.

"Well then, I guess Antarctica looks like a duck," Caitlyn said, leaning back into the pillow before shifting onto her side to face him. "I love it."

"I love you."

Caitlyn smiled and kissed him fully. "I love you. I'm sorry

I didn't believe you. I wasn't sure I was ready to love until I faced losing someone again." She ran her finger over his skin. "You're so precious to me. You've helped me find my way when everything else had fallen apart. I thought I was running away, and in a way I guess I was. I didn't want to be close to anyone. Couldn't bear to share my pain and shame with someone else. I didn't want to even deal with it myself. With you, though, all of that changed. I can't thank you enough."

"Caitlyn, I love you. I think I have from when I first gave you your keys."

"I highly doubt that."

"Okay, yeah, maybe not then. Definitely the coffee spill."

Caitlyn sucked her teeth. "Stain never did come out."

"I'll buy you a new dress. You deserve it." He wrapped his arms around her and breathed in her smell, bathing in it and letting it sink down into his core.

The bomb had scared the shit out of him and everyone else. If Caitlyn hadn't followed him—hadn't loved him enough to believe and not run away—she wouldn't have been there screaming for all of them to run for the exits. Once Caitlyn screamed the word bomb, Austin had charged forward toward her, tackling her and dragging her body to his own before racing outside across the cold grass. Screams had filled the air while the other men grabbed their families and shoved them out the doors. Aunt Tee, Aunt Mary, and Timothy Chappell had escaped, moving faster than Austin had ever seen them, each carrying something sacred, like the roster of old names.

Everyone had screamed and dove onto the cold, hard, rocky ground when the bombs went off, blowing the side off the old meetinghouse, sending shards of wood into the air before the flames leapt into a towering blaze, eagerly devouring the old wooden structure. A thundering wave of heat rushed over Austin's neck after the second blast. The blaze formed an eerie glow as it lit the darkening sky. The last ones out had been Glen pulling Connie by the elbow, both of them coughing with smoke. A few men then took off with a few others to chase down whoever might be responsible.

They found him trying to hide in the woods, dead from a self-inflicted bullet wound to the head. An old 9mm was next to him in the cold dirt.

Because Caitlyn had saved them all, a unanimous vote had passed immediately to allow Caitlyn to stay if she wished and, of course, agreed to Timothy Chappell's laundry list of terms and conditions.

She hadn't accepted yet, and the town council had been more than willing to give her time. Besides, they had enough of a news frenzy to deal with on their own. No one had learned anything about the bomber other than that he worked on the ferry. Austin figured he had found out about them somehow, and the thought chilled him to the bone. He had been racking his brain but came up empty every time on the hows and the whys of it all.

Still looking into Caitlyn's eyes, he let out a deep, peaceful exhalation. She again looked at him with tender love in her eyes that made living for hundreds of years too short instead of too long as he had initially thought.

With her, an eternity would never be enough.

"Want to get married?"

Caitlyn sucked in a gasp of breath and looked at him. "Is that a proposal?"

"Yes." He had never been more sure of anything in his life.

"Call me old-fashioned, but I don't see a ring here."

"I'll buy you one the size of Boston Harbor if you want."

"I don't need anything that fancy."

Austin let the slow smile spread across his face. "Fine by me, as long as I can look at you. I should thank you too. I didn't want to trust anyone. I didn't think I could trust anyone with the knowledge of what happened to the ship, to me. I didn't believe anyone would understand or want to be around me if they knew what really happened."

"I'll always love you, and you're always going to be a hero to me."

"You're the one who saved everyone. I owe you my life. I'll have to work to please you for the next three hundred years just to make it even."

A sly smile grew across Caitlyn's face to match his own. "I'll take that deal."

CHAPTER 47

Caleb sat on a bench as he had been doing for the past month and watched the waves come in on Easterly Bay as he waited for the ferry. The cold air ran off the water and plowed into him like a linebacker from LSU. Caleb couldn't say he was used to the frigid temps or that he would miss the windburn, but he had sat here almost every day for the past few weeks and hadn't hated it.

The last few days had been the most different. After an explosion had blown up some old building in the reserve, reporters had worked the ferry into overtime trying to get the story as they threw the word "terrorism" around every which way.

If anything good came out of it, Sal and Alex had been doing a hell of a lot of business. As the only inn in town, they were now staying with friends, electing to rent their back house to Caleb to make room for the reporters. They hadn't wanted to inconvenience him, but after a month of being their only guest, he had gotten to know the pair pretty well, fixing a few things here and there in the old building. He had always liked taking things apart and solving problems with his hands.

They had seemed sad to see him go, and the feeling had been mutual. Unlike all of the reporters that came for the story and left to chase another, Caleb had a fresh loaf of banana bread wrapped with care to travel back home with. They had even asked for him to call when he landed, just to make sure he was okay.

He crossed his arms, hearing the rustle from the new coat he had ordered a few minutes after he had arrived. The cold was one thing, a New England island in the winter was a whole different ball game. Still, he had liked it. At least it had been different.

He watched the horizon as the ferry came into view, making the turn into the bay. Time to go.

Caleb reached down and grabbed his little overnight bag. He had a house, but since he was only there half the year, everything that mattered fit into the small, worn carry-on bag.

Smiling to himself, he cracked his knuckles and thought about the giant bags Elizabeth had carried. She called herself Lizzy, but Caleb thought she looked too refined for that name. All elegance and regal beauty, Elizabeth was far more fitting for the dark-haired knockout he'd helped a few weeks ago.

She'd knocked him on his ass the second he saw her. Everything about her looked classy and expensive. Elizabeth also knew how to talk. Even though they hadn't known each other for more than a minute, her blue eyes had pierced into his as she dominated the conversation, wanting to know everything about him.

Meanwhile, Caleb had been so stunned, he could barely string two words together. No wonder he hadn't seen her since.

Every day he had walked the island and sat on this bench, just in case he might run into her again.

The ferry approached closer now, and he could see men scurrying about on deck, getting ready to load up their single passenger from the look of things.

Christ, it was enough for a guy to feel bad that they had to make the extra trip just for him, but he hadn't found another way to get back to the mainland. Sure, there had been an airport, but when he had inquired about it at the inn, Sal and Alex had just told him it was for private planes.

"Hey! I'm glad I caught you," a voice said from behind him. Caitlyn jogged up toward the bench in a fleece. "Are you leaving today?" she asked, out of breath, with an eye on the bag at his feet.

Caleb stood up and glanced behind him. "Yeah, guess that's what it looks like."

"You should've told me. I would've come to say goodbye."

Caleb shrugged. Now didn't seem like a good time to bring up the last time one of them left, they hadn't bothered to tell the other one.

"It's okay. I know you got stuff to do and…" Caleb stalled out and popped a knuckle out of nervousness. He wished like hell he had the gift of words.

"I'm going to hug you now," Caitlyn said before coming in and wrapping herself around him.

Hugging her now felt different. While before, Caitlyn seemed to sag under a weight of despair, she looked bright and more vibrant now.

Caleb searched for feelings on his end and found only the sadness that came with leaving a good friend behind in a beautiful place.

As if on cue, Austin came down from the Two Scoops ice cream parlor. He sauntered toward them, looking Caleb dead in the eye.

Yeah, don't worry, buddy, Caleb thought. You won't need to worry about me anymore.

"Are you going back to Louisiana?" Caitlyn asked, stepping back.

Caleb glanced behind him. The gangway wasn't ready yet.

"Yeah, it'll be good to see Parrain and everyone. Check in on things."

"It's almost Christmas."

"Yeah, my family will all get together at Barbara's house."

"Tell them I said hi."

Austin had reached them now and wrapped one arm around Caitlyn's shoulders. Message received, thought Caleb, but when he met the guy's eyes, just kindness and mild curiosity met him.

"Yep, I'll do that. Definitely will." Caleb popped his knuckles and hated the silence. It would've been better if she hadn't seen him. He sucked at this goodbye shit.

"Caleb—"

"Listen—"

Caitlyn and Austin both spoke at the same time and smiled at each other, the warmth and love between them making Caleb analyze the concrete sidewalk. For no reason in particular, he noticed little white shells throughout the cement. Dear God, he needed to get on the ferry and get away from here.

Austin coughed, and Caleb looked up. "We were hoping you'd be able to come back for the wedding?"

A square diamond glinted back at Caleb. "Hey, what do you know? Congratulations," he said, hoping it sounded sincere.

"Thanks," Caitlyn said, glancing from him to Austin and back again. Hope shone in her eyes. "So, you'll try and come back?"

She really did look happy, and he was glad for her, but once again he was always on the outside. Friend zones were a bitch.

"It'll depend on my schedule, but yeah, I'll try to come." He popped a knuckle, debating whether to drop his news, but didn't want to ruin the moment.

"You're always welcome," Austin said with his hand still around Caitlyn. "Anytime you want to visit, just give us a ring."

Funny choice of words, Caleb thought, grabbing the outstretched hand and giving it a firm pump.

He wasn't sure what to do with Caitlyn, but she launched herself against him, squeezing him tight. "I hope you come," she said over his shoulder.

"I'll try. I really will."

She pulled back and looked at him. "I know how working on the oil rigs can be."

"Yeah," he said, thinking it wasn't really going to be a rig schedule problem anymore, but didn't share that thought. They didn't need to worry about where he was actually going.

CHAPTER 48

Lieutenant Nora St. Clair pushed into the small piece-of-shit house in the part of Hyannis that hadn't been bought out yet and was hit with the rank smell of human despair. She knew the smell too well for someone in her thirties.

But then she had wanted to be a cop for as long as she could remember.

It had been almost ten years since she got her wish.

Now with her boots planted in the small house that looked like it should've been condemned around the time she had been born, the smell of old carpet, sweat, and mold filled her nostrils. Nora wrinkled her nose in response. Turning her head to take it all in, she scanned the piles of crap covered with paper like an alien landscape, like it was a cancer over the original furniture.

"Damn sad if you ask me," Jorge said to her left. "Poor bastard has enough overdue notices to wallpaper my mother-in-law's dining room."

Lieutenant Jorge Manillo stood next to her with his

hands on his hips, his face snarled into a mask of disgust and pity.

"Let me see those," Nora said, taking one from the pile. Shit, he wasn't kidding around. Everything from oil bills to credit cards—several of them by the looks of it.

"I'm going to check things out upstairs," Manillo said before disappearing into the kitchen.

When she flipped over the statement, almost all of the lines were for either gas stations or the liquor store. Nora pulled her mouth into a thin line.

The newest division of the Massachusetts State Police, the fifth division, had been tasked to confront acts of terrorism as well as fighting the war against opiates. When Mark Schmidt turned Brightrock's historic meetinghouse full of people into a fireball, her department picked up the case.

Schmidt had offed himself right after things got toasty, falling right next to the detonator, so the question wasn't who, but why and were there others? In reality, since no one had died, just a couple of scrapes and burns, the media had already moved on, and Nora knew her time with Mark Schmidt's legacy wouldn't be that long before another case came around.

She and Manillo had already checked for next of kin and came up empty with two deceased parents and no other ties. The next best thing had been coworkers. When she and Manillo had paid the ferry a visit, one kid named Scott had seemed pretty shaken up over the idea he could've stopped Mark since he'd seen him last.

Nora had given the kid her card with a few names of good people to talk to about that, but the kid would probably take that weight to his grave. Looking at this house, she could have told him for a fact there wasn't anything he could've done to help on that day. Whatever had happened to Mark Schmidt, it hadn't happened overnight.

Nora walked over to the one empty chair facing the TV. A towel covered the seat where the orange plaid upholstery had worn away. Papers were strewn all around. Crouching down, she picked up a few. Overhead shots of Brightrock covered the top of the pile, which wasn't really a surprise.

According to interviews in the town, no one had paid Mark any attention when he had arrived. He hadn't spoken to anyone, just arrived on the ferry at 5:42 and presumably walked to the meetinghouse like he knew where he was going.

Because he did.

"You'd been studying, hadn't you?" Nora said to the papers in her hand.

The printouts all had time stamps on them at the bottom. The one in her hand had been printed three days prior.

"Manillo, you find a computer?"

A rustling upstairs and then the heavy footsteps of her partner clomped above her.

"Nada. Looks like these rooms haven't been touched in years. You should see the john. Nightmares. I'm totally going to have nightmares."

"You're really big into home improvement these days." Nora raised her voice to reach him, but didn't stop shuffling through the papers. A Bible was cracked open next to one of those free DVDs people got in the mail of some sermon from a televangelist.

"Yeah, well, the only way I'll ever retire is getting my damn equity."

"I don't even understand that word."

"That's a shame," he called back down to her.

"I've got a lot of printouts. Like, just about a shit ton."

Manillo came down the stairs and stood behind her.

"He was obsessed or something."

"Yeah, but I wonder what caused it," Nora said, sorting the images by content. With the initial few out of the way, the rest were all focused on one guy. Some of the printouts were of the same picture zoomed in really close on his face and arms.

"Looks like he had a crush."

"Yeah, I think we need to talk to him," Nora said, reading the name.

Austin Brooks.

"Obviously he knows something about this. Let's get these together and take them with."

"Yo, here's some more—Jesus, they're way old."

Nora frowned at the image Manillo flashed her from across the room. A little metal box sat open, full of pictures of sailors in the navy. "Weird. Well, grab them too."

She turned back to her picture as she placed them in an evidence bag, studying the handsome face looking back up at her. "Time for a visit, buddy."

CHAPTER 49

Caleb played with the change in the pockets of the suit that felt too tight. He loosened his tie again and wondered, not for the first time, what in the hell he was doing here. Seeing his ex-girlfriend get married was a special kind of self-inflicted punishment reserved for idiots who didn't know how to say no.

It had been a beautiful wedding on a beautiful June day in New England. The white church glowed in the sun, and the sea breeze danced with the flowers that lined the landscape on the church grounds. The wedding had been perfect, and both the bride and groom had looked stunning and over-joyed. Afterward, the reception went off without a hitch in the churchyard overlooking the same bay he had watched so much during his stay back in November. Servers passed around food and drink. The happy couple cut the cake. Everyone seemed delighted and charmed. Everyone except for Caleb.

Sure, guests had come up to him and greeted Caitlyn's friend from back home in an attempt to make him feel

welcome. Caitlyn squeezed him before and after the cere-
mony with tears in her eyes, showing her sincere gratitude.
All it did was make him want to throw himself into the
Atlantic.

Sal and Alex had come and said hello, and because they
were the only people he really knew well, aside from the
bride, he chatted with them for a good, long while before
they got pulled into the crowd of family and friends.

Still, sometimes it sucked being a nice, quiet friend. That
was the only reason he still was standing outside the church
on bright green grass, holding a tumbler containing some
sort of punch which, in his opinion, could've been stronger,
while everyone else chatted in groups. He shook hands with
most of them and exchanged polite pleasantries. He didn't
remember anyone's names and doubted he would ever see
them again. He checked his phone. Only four more hours
until his ferry ride to the plane that would carry him home.

It couldn't come fast enough.

If Caleb didn't see Brightrock ever again that was a-okay
with him. Coming here the first time had been all about
Caitlyn. Now she was married, but not to Caleb, so that plan
had backfired. Even then, he had stayed to represent her old
friends that couldn't make the trip to the island on such short
notice. That was him. Mr. Nice Guy. Mr. Reliable.

Caleb rolled his shoulders and watched as a few kids
darted in and out of the white tables, their tablecloths
billowing in the wind. Caitlyn looked incredibly happy. She
and Austin were attached at the hip, laughing and visiting
with his family and friends. They took every chance they
could to glance at each other with a knowing smile that
made Caleb's stomach somersault.

Caleb took another drink. The bushes around him looked
expensive, but they smelled like cat piss. Again his eyes
scanned the reception, hoping for a chance glance at the one

person he might miss. He had lost track in the exodus from the church.

"Looking for someone?" a coy voice said behind him. He smiled to himself before he even turned to see who it was.

"Maybe." He turned to face Lizzy, the woman he had met briefly back in December and hadn't been able to stop thinking about. In his opinion, she was Elizabeth, with her regal and fearless attitude. Of course, she'd never know he felt about her that way.

Her dark hair offset perfect blue eyes and a porcelain complexion. Bright red flowers covered the bottom of her black dress, which flowed around her in the wind.

"I didn't know you stayed for the reception." Caleb had been trying not to stare at her during the ceremony, with little success.

"Me? Austin and I go way back, so yeah, I had to come. Heading out soon though."

That got his attention. "I thought people didn't leave this island much."

Perfect red lips parted into a bright smile, revealing bright white teeth. "You got that right, but a few of us manage to escape. I haven't had a good cup of coffee in a while." She flicked her thumb out like a hitchhiker. "Time to head out."

"You've been here since December?"

She tossed her hair again. Caleb caught the smell with the wind and wanted to press his face against her neck so he could inhale some more of her scent, but instead nodded while she talked, trying to catch up to what she had been saying.

"...so my program director said I should just finish my research here until summer, but school's out now, so yeah." She tilted her drink to him. "Back I go."

Caleb smiled and looked at his drink. He wanted to say

something to her. Caleb was crap with conversation, especially when it came to women. Since he had first seen Elizabeth when she arrived on Brightrock, she had held his attention like an old hunting dog. Though she probably didn't know it, she could've ordered him around, and he would've followed to a tee. He wished like hell he had the confidence to say something. She had spoken last, and he knew he needed to come up with something, but he didn't want to sound stupid. His mind had gone blank.

Elizabeth tossed back her head again, scattering her dark curls into the wind. "So, when do you head out?"

Caleb could've sagged with relief at the broken silence. "Four hours and counting."

"You seem excited."

"Been a while since I've been home. Got to check on things. See my family."

"So, you miss the coffee then too? Oh wait, you're from Louisiana—you probably miss the food. Am I right?'

Caleb let out a laugh. "Yeah, I guess I do."

A cheer and cries of laughter erupted behind them. Caleb turned to look and catch the tail end of what must have been a great story from the bridegroom himself. Seeing everyone laughing and happy reminded Caleb that his suit felt too tight, and on instinct, he rolled his shoulders trying to get free.

Elizabeth pierced him with one of her stares and raised an eyebrow as if she were sizing him up to eat. "You don't say a whole lot, do you?"

Not that he would mind one bit.

Caleb felt his skin shrink a little. "Uh…I don't know. What would you like me to say?" He wished he didn't suck at small talk. He had no idea what it must be like to be the life of the party instead of on the sidelines, practically hiding in the bushes. Now, one of the best women here wanted to talk to him of all people, and he was totally blowing it. Major, epic fail. Maybe he should just jump right in the ocean.

She cracked a smile. "Well, you had better get talking because we're on the same ferry out and I think it's just us."

ACKNOWLEDGMENTS

There are so many people to thank for inspiring me, encouraging me, and helping me to get this book into your hands.

I appreciate everyone in the Virginia Romance Writers and all of the beta readers and critique partners who helped answer my questions, gave me feedback, cheered me on, and empowered me with the knowledge that I needed to forge ahead and make my dream a reality.

I am deeply grateful to my editor, Kate Studer who took my story into her expert hands and helped shape it into what it is today. Her guidance and feedback allowed me to create a stronger, more complete story.

I owe many thanks to Caroline Johnson, who created the most magnificent cover, capturing not only Austin and Caitlyn but precisely what Brightrock Island looked like in my mind.

I am grateful to all of the teachers who saw something in my writing when I was young. I have never forgotten their encouragement.

Thank you to my biggest fans, my friends and family. I appreciate all of you more than words can ever say.

I would like to thank my dearest friend Jennifer Gosselin, who taught me that life is like bringing in the groceries, you have to get it all in one trip. Her constant praise, encouragement, and faith in me is a gift I can never repay.

To my husband, thank you for inspiring me to chase my dreams. You have been there through it all, encouraging me to step out of my comfort zone, invest in myself, and thrive. Thank you for all that you do to make this happen. This book would not exist without you pushing me to go to that first conference in New York, where on the train ride home we talked about the idea for this story.

Lastly, thank you to my cats for always being there in the quiet, late nights when I write. I appreciate your company.

ABOUT THE AUTHOR

Kathryn K. Murphy writes action-packed, small-town romance novels bursting with emotion.

If you want to know when Kathryn's next book will come out, please visit her website at www.kathrynkmurphy.com, where you can sign up to receive email updates.